CLOSE QUARTERS

A Selection of Recent Titles by Adrian Magson

The Marc Portman Thrillers

THE WATCHMAN *

The Harry Tate Thrillers

RED STATION *
TRACERS *
DECEPTION *
RETRIBUTION *
EXECUTION *

The Riley Gavin and Frank Palmer Series

NO PEACE FOR THE WICKED
NO HELP FOR THE DYING
NO SLEEP FOR THE DEAD
NO TEARS FOR THE LOST
NO KISS FOR THE DEVIL

* *available from Severn House*

CLOSE QUARTERS

A Marc Portman Thriller

Adrian Magson

severn
House

This first world edition published 2015
in Great Britain and the USA by
SEVERN HOUSE PUBLISHERS LTD of
19 Cedar Road, Sutton, Surrey, England, SM2 5DA.
Trade paperback edition first published 2015
in Great Britain and the USA by
SEVERN HOUSE PUBLISHERS LTD.

British Library Cataloguing in Publication Data

Magson, Adrian author.
  Close quarters
  1. Ukraine–Foreign relations–Russia (Federation)–
  Fiction. 2. Russia (Federation)–Foreign relations–
  Ukraine–Fiction. 3. Central Illustration Agency–
  Fiction. 4. Spy stories.
  I. Title
  823.9'2-dc23

ISBN-13: 978-0-7278-8504-3 (cased)
ISBN-13: 978-1-84751-606-0 (trade paper)
ISBN-13: 978-1-78010-657-1 (e-book)

All Severn House titles are printed on acid-free paper.

Severn House Publishers support the Forest Stewardship Council™ [FSC™],
the leading international forest certification organisation. All our titles that
are printed on FSC certified paper carry the FSC logo.

Typeset by Palimpsest Book Production Ltd.,
Falkirk, Stirlingshire, Scotland.
Printed and bound in Great Britain by
TJ International, Padstow, Cornwall.

With unfailing love and gratitude, as always, to Ann, who puts up with my absences, even when I'm there.

AUTHOR'S NOTE

This book very nearly didn't happen. I was halfway through completion of the manuscript when the news broke about the shooting down over eastern Ukraine of Malaysian Airlines Flight MH17 en route from Amsterdam to Kuala Lumpur on July 17, 2014.

I tend to use a flavour of current events where I can, and had chosen the Ukraine in 2013 when I began writing because it offered a plausible backdrop on which to hang the story. What I hadn't reckoned on was this terrible tragedy taking place in the same location, and for several days I felt reluctant to continue with it.

However, the timeline of *Close Quarters* was set several months earlier than July, so in the end I decided to continue with the project, since there would be no reference to it in the book, nor would I have had to deliberately ignore it, which would have been unjust for the 298 victims.

At the time of writing, the perpetrators of this act remain unproven.

ONE

The man I knew as Arash Bagheri was walking into a trap. And there was nothing I could do to stop it.

It's hard watching that kind of thing happen while knowing you've got to get the man out. It's three parts telling yourself you should have seen it coming and one part knowing it's your job to do something and it has to be right. Recriminations can come later.

Bagheri was approaching a street named Kandhar, not far from Tehran's central fruit and vegetable bazaar in the south of the city. A local CIA asset, he was there to conduct an exchange meeting with a man named Farshad Kasimi, an old friend who worked as a laboratory technician for the nearby Iranian Centre for Fuel and Technology Research Laboratories. Or, as the site is more accurately known among those who watch these things, the workshop where they build deadly weapons with which to kill people they don't like.

I had no idea what precisely Bagheri was here to exchange with his friend, only that it had to involve money going in and information or technology coming out. That's usually the way of these operations. My role was to make sure he came away without getting burned.

And right now that was beginning to look unlikely.

I'd scouted the area the previous evening, which was close by the ring road known as the Azadegan Expressway, noting the street layout, the exits and escape routes, and I'd left a vehicle parked in the shadow of a small park down the block just in case. Forward planning is a major element of getting this stuff right and staying out of trouble.

I hadn't seen anything about the surroundings to ring alarm bells, unless you call being stuck in a traffic jam on the expressway alongside a parked fuel tanker while the driver had a smoke and a chat with a friend, as normal. But what I had seen of Farshad Kasimi the technician, who I'd followed for a while, told me he wasn't the full deal. If you're going to put your faith in someone while spying for a foreign country, notably the USA, you should choose a man who isn't loud and gregarious and seems to like spending money freely. For a lowly technician in a state-run industry, that felt all wrong to me.

With these reservations in mind, I'd got here nearly an hour ago and found a position atop a deserted three-storey warehouse. The rooftop gave me a view of the streets near the bazaar and of the expressway running past in an east–west direction, and at least three exits if I needed them.

It was seven a.m. and the morning was heating up rapidly. I already had a coating of motor fumes, smoke and dust tasting gritty on my tongue, which sipping water from a plastic bottle did nothing to shake. And the tarpaulin I'd rigged up in the shadow of an air-conditioning unit wasn't doing much to keep the heat or the flies off me. But I knew I wouldn't have long to wait before we could be on our way out of here; the moment I saw Bagheri appear and do his thing, I'd be ready to pick him up and scoot.

The traffic in the area was a mix of private cars, buses, cabs and pickup trucks of every kind, all being buzzed by motorbikes like flies around rotten fruit. Everybody seemed eager to get their business over and done with as soon as possible before the heat of the day really set in, which meant a lot of pushing and shoving and blowing of horns.

Impatient people, the Iranians.

As I checked Kandhar Street through binoculars, I saw a familiar figure appear on the next block. From the photo I'd been shown I knew it was Bagheri. He was slim and of medium height, with receding hair down the middle and a heavy moustache. He was walking slowly and carrying a bag of fruit, and looked relaxed. He was even chewing on an apple to add a touch of casual colour, as he'd been trained to do.

Not standing out; that was essential for this business, but easier said than done when your life is on the line and you feel – *know* – that you're being watched because you're in a society where everybody is a suspect, even the innocent.

I ran another check of the streets around Kandhar, but there was no sign of Kasimi. He was either suffering the pains of a hangover or he'd been delayed by traffic, which is easy enough in a frenetic, crowded city like Tehran, where time is a fluid concept and apologies are always effusive and well-meant.

Then I discovered I was wrong and the day was about to get blown apart.

A black sedan had appeared on the expressway. It was surrounded by other vehicles, yet somehow stood out within its own space, as if in a bubble. I knew instinctively why: it was too big, too new and too unlike anything a private citizen here would want to drive. Black sedans absorb heat but they also give off bad historic vibes. It had to be a car from the Iranian Ministry of Intelligence and National Security, known as MOIS, the successor to the dreaded SAVAK of the old regime, some said with many of the same senior personnel in place with the same nasty habits.

I thought it might be on its way elsewhere at first, that being here in this section of the city was just a lousy coincidence of timing and circumstance. But when it signalled and slipped on to the nearby exit ramp which led to the area around the bazaar, I felt hope take wings and fly.

I focussed on the car, which was full of men. Not unusual for ministry heavies; they like to travel in packs. But the screw in the coffin, as it disappeared from sight behind a scrum of traffic, was seeing a familiar face staring out of the rear window, which had been dropped to let in some air. It was Farshad Kasimi, his hair and shirt collar moving in the breeze. He was laughing at something that had been said by the man next to him, before taking a luxurious drag of a cigarette and tossing the end out of the window.

I ducked out from under my cover and crossed the flat roof for a better view, dodging the array of television aerials and satellite dishes, and bending low before I got to the parapet. For a second I thought I'd been wrong. No sedan in sight. Then it appeared from behind some buildings and began to weave through the streets, jinking occasionally left then right, but from up on my perch, ultimately heading in one direction.

It was in no hurry – there was still a good fifteen minutes before Bagheri's scheduled meeting – but from up here I could see it was somehow too focussed on a single destination, like watching a shark closing in on its kill.

I dialled Bagheri's number. He had to get out of there now. He'd been blown by his supposed friend and he was now a target. It rang several times. No answer. Damn. Hell of a time to have it stuck at the bottom of his shopping bag. I stood up and ran downstairs, surprising a building superintendent, an old man in a long shift who popped his head out from a room and shouted. It was too late to get the car and intercept Bagheri before the sedan reached him, but

I had one chance of getting him out: I knew precisely where the sedan would go once they'd picked him up.

MOIS has a number of facilities in regular use around Tehran, mostly because of the logistics of operating in such a crowded city, where traffic in the narrow streets is a constant hazard. The nearest base to this quarter was less than a mile away, and that was where I headed once I hit the street.

The interior of the car, an old Fiat, was already like a pizza oven. I dropped the windows and switched on the fan, but it moved the air with the sluggish speed of stirring toffee. I drove as fast as I dared, hand on the horn, the little car skidding neatly between delivery trucks, cars and the ever-present motorcycles, some loaded with unidentifiable mountains of baggage. Three minutes later I was at the end of a boulevard in a mostly quiet commercial quarter where MOIS has its local security compound. It has a high wall topped by wire, and impressive double gates with a permanent armed guard, and it looked exactly what it was: the last place any sane person would want to be taken.

I left the car two hundred yards away close to a pedestrian crossing and figured I had maybe three minutes before the sedan appeared. Three minutes in which to arrange an accident.

Three minutes before I poked a hornets' nest with whatever stick I could find.

I checked out the buildings nearby. Two half-completed but deserted warehouse units stood on one side of the road, the bare walls un-rendered and grey, now covered with graffiti; and a row of empty stores on the other, gutted shells blackened by fire and long abandoned by their owners. Rubbish from the buildings had been piled nearby and was spilling out across the sidewalk; blocks of broken concrete, scaffold poles, lengths of burned timber and the ruined detritus from a dress shop.

It was going to have to be a MacGyver moment.

First, though, I leaned over and peeled back the carpet on the passenger side and lifted a section of the flooring. It revealed a box recess welded to the underneath of the car. Inside was a cloth-covered bundle. I removed the cloth and was left holding a 9mm Browning High Power and a fat tube suppressor, or silencer. The gun showed signs of being well-used, but the suppressor was new. Both looked ready to go.

It was hardly anybody's idea of an arsenal but it would have to do.

TWO

Arash Bagheri had the taste of blood on his lip and a swelling on his cheek where he'd been hit before being bundled into the black sedan. It was just one of many bruises he'd sustained and he knew there were many more to come.

He also knew that he would never see freedom again.

He had known within a split second of seeing the car waiting at the far end of Kandhar Street that he had made a grave error; that somehow he'd been betrayed. The vehicle was shiny black with tinted windows, and hung low on its suspension, a sure-fire sign of reinforced bodywork and bulletproof glass. Only one agency used such cars and he didn't even like to think of its name for fear he might utter it aloud. Secret police were the same no matter what they called themselves, and this lot were as feared as their cars were sinister looking, and with good reason.

He had stopped walking, his legs turning to liquid. The car was stationary, a large black bug. Maybe he was wrong and they had come here for somebody else. But who? The street was empty. Then he saw a puff of exhaust smoke and the car began rolling along the street towards him, a flash of sunshine bouncing off the windshield as if to greet him. A touch of irony, he decided, on a bad day.

He turned to run back the way he had come, to lose himself in the maze of narrow streets where people would provide the best cover and where he could duck into a doorway, God willing. But he realized his legs wouldn't carry him far enough or fast enough; there was no escape and nowhere he could go that would be safe.

He made a noise deep in his chest and wondered about his friend, Farshad, the man he had come to meet. Farshad had suggested they meet today at this very place, telling Arash that he had vital information to give him of new weapons being created in the 'laboratory', including small explosive devices that could be concealed in very restricted spaces such as hand luggage. Arash had expressed doubts about the location, preferring somewhere else. But Farshad had been insistent. He was certain he was being watched, he said, by security officers in the government laboratory where he worked, and was expecting to be questioned any day now. Somebody, he feared, must have noticed his interest in weapons development and had reported him.

Keen to secure the information, Arash had convinced himself that he would be safe among the crush of people and traders and traffic that clustered around the bazaar in great numbers. And in exchange for the information there would be money waiting that would be Farshad's safeguard to a better life.

In any case, they were old friends meeting up for a chat. What was wrong with that?

It struck him now that he had been stupidly naïve.

The sedan had stopped alongside him, the motor humming with suppressed power. The front seat passenger had stepped out and slammed him against the wall before punching him with vicious force in the stomach. Arash dropped the bag of fruit and curled away from his attacker, a heavy man in plain clothes, feeling a rain of blows descending on his head and back, and a heavy blow from another man hitting him in the kidneys. He felt his knee split on a piece of stone as he fell to the ground, and wondered if this was to end here.

'What are you doing? Why are you? What—?' He tried to protest, even though he knew it was useless. Protests of innocence were all he had left, but they never worked with such people, who only knew everybody as guilty, if not in deed then by intent. The men continued their beating without saying a word, their breathing growing heavier as they spent their energy in the growing heat of the sun, punching and kicking him with almost casual detachment as if he were no more than a punch bag in a gymnasium.

Then he was grabbed by his arm and spun around to face the car. He immediately saw the face of his friend Farshad staring out at him from the back seat. For just a second Arash felt a flood of relief. At least Farshad wasn't hurt; there were no signs of violence, no bruising or bloodshed, no face like death. That was good, surely . . .

Then he realized that Farshad was smiling. And he knew he was finished.

The two men dragged him across the sidewalk and threw him into the back alongside Farshad. But he couldn't even look at the man he'd once valued; the friend who had espoused the same anti-government beliefs as himself and talked often of how he wanted to get out of the country to America, where he could begin a new and exciting life.

For Arash the betrayal was too much to bear and he tried to shrink away until one of the men jumped in after him and elbowed him aside.

There were three men in the car apart from himself and Farshad: the two who had attacked him and the driver. None of them spoke, although the one sitting next to him kept using his elbow, striking him viciously in the side of the head for no reason other than that it seemed to be something to do.

It was the silence that scared him most. If they had raged at him, spat on him, accused him of being a traitor and a criminal, threatened him with certain death, it would have been easier to take. But this wordless violence was the most frightening of all, in that it carried no message.

As the car pulled away and accelerated, he caught a last blurred glimpse of the outside world, his bag of fruit spilled across the sidewalk and already of interest to one of the many dogs roaming the neighbourhood. He assumed the driver was heading towards the expressway, no doubt on their way to MOIS headquarters where he would disappear, like so many others had done before him. He sank down in the seat, trying to control his bladder and wondering what would happen to his sister and brother, now his only living family who had a house far to the south of Tehran. Would they also be dragged in, bruised and beaten, victims of his desire to make a difference in the country, later to disappear? Or would they simply never hear from him again and be left forever wondering at his fate?

The driver and the front seat passenger were talking quietly and smoking, the air heavy with harsh tobacco fumes and adding to the stale smell of perspiration and unwashed clothing. Farshad and the man alongside him were silent, each looking out at the passing scenery.

The journey was surprisingly brief. Arash looked up. They were nowhere near the MOIS headquarters, but turning into a wide street in a quiet commercial district not far from where he had been picked up.

He looked around and felt his stomach flip. He knew of this place; he'd seen and read of people being taken here into a compound located at the far end of this street, never to emerge.

It was a place of death.

He moaned softly, earning another sharp elbow dig from the guard. The passenger in the front seat turned his head to say something, but was interrupted by the driver, who cursed and slowed sharply.

A couple had made to step into the road maybe thirty metres ahead. The man was nondescript, dressed in a dark jacket and tan pants. Alongside him was a slim figure in a long dress and a scarf covering her head, being supported by the man's arm.

'Drive on!' the passenger snapped. 'Let them wait. We don't have time.'

The driver shrugged and hit the horn, and the heavy car surged forward, visibly possessing its space on the road as a warning. As it did so, the man on the sidewalk stepped back a pace and watched it approach.

Just before the car drew level, the man hurled the woman into the road.

Someone inside the vehicle screamed like a girl, and Arash wondered if it had been himself. There was a loud bang as the woman's body surged over the radiator grill and bounced off the windshield, shutting out the sunlight for a brief moment. Then she was gone, leaving her scarf snagged on the radio aerial and snapping in the wind like a pennant.

The passenger cursed. A single finger was trapped behind one of the wiper arms and pointing accusingly at them all.

The driver swore repeatedly and stamped hard on the brakes, throwing them all forward and ignoring the other man's orders to drive on regardless. Alongside Arash, Farshad had doubled over, striking his head on the back of the front seat and was now throwing up in the footwell. The guard on his other side was swearing and reaching for the gun at his waist.

Then the rear passenger door was flung open and a figure appeared. It was the man in the dark jacket. He was holding a pistol with a large bulbous shape over the end of the barrel, and Arash noticed that the ground around his feet was scattered with fragments of pale plastic; an arm, a foot and part of a leg. And rolling into the gutter was a head with the empty, sightless eyes of a mannequin.

The man shot the armed guard once in the head, then pulled Arash out of the car, before turning to fire with absolute calm three more times into the interior.

The engine died and was silent.

'Come,' the man said urgently, and hustled Arash away to a small car parked back down the street. They climbed in and the man drove away, steering into a maze of streets until they were lost to any possible pursuit. As they drove up a ramp on to the expressway and joined a mass of other traffic, Arash finally found his voice.

'I don't understand,' he said weakly. 'Who are you? Where are we going?'

'I was sent by Langley,' the man said, and smiled. He reached into his jacket pocket and took out a passport and a driver's licence, which he handed to Arash. 'Remember that name; it's yours until we get out of this country.'

THREE

'm a close protection specialist. I run security, evaluate risks in hostile situations and, where needed, provide hard cover. To do my job I have to look ahead of where a principal is going to be at any time, checking details, terrain, routes in and out – most especially out – and providing the best possible solution for a happy outcome. If it works the principal won't even know I'm there and will go home happy. If it doesn't, I get involved.

Which is where the hard cover comes in; it means I fight back. Like in Tehran.

Traditional security pros – the kind who wear suits and ties and have those little squiggly wires tucked behind their ears, work up close and personal in teams several operators strong. They cluster tightly around the VIP in a physical screen, their function to display a visible deterrent to a would-be assailant. If attacked, they provide a rapid evacuation exercise and get their VIP out of harm's way. Mostly it works fine.

The main problem is if the threat comes from outside the obvious security cordon. And the larger the perimeter, the longer it takes to shut down. By the time the team reacts and mounts a search, especially if the target area is surrounded by tall buildings or raised elevations from where a sniper can calmly take his shot, the VIP is down and the shooter is long gone.

Staying back, I get to see more of what's going on in the surrounding area. If the principal suddenly becomes a target and I've done my job right, I can take preventative action. That might mean snatching him or her up by force if necessary and moving them on. Mostly it comes down to neutralising the threat before they can attack. No fuss, no mess. Well, maybe a little mess.

Overall, I like to be ahead of the game to see what's coming. Like in Tehran.

I pick up most jobs by recommendation. Others I hear about through a loose network of former military personnel, spooks and private security contractors trading information on intelligence or security assignments around the world. I vet as many as I can before making a judgement, but you can't always be too selective. And I like to work alone.

The Tehran job had come through a contact in the US intelligence world, a man who'd steered jobs my way on previous occasions. He followed it up pretty quickly with another call a few days after I got back.

'You're in demand,' he'd said, when I responded to a message on my voicemail. 'A certain government agency not a million miles from Washington wants you to ride shotgun on an operation. Level urgent and critical. You interested?'

He could have been talking about any one of a dozen agencies, all gathered around the seat of government like vultures on road-kill. But I was guessing CIA, since that was the one Arash Bagheri had worked for. Urgent and critical was how they usually operated, and they use private contractors like me. 'Where to?'

'That hasn't been specified but if I'm reading the news right, it's probably somewhere in Europe.'

Russia. It had to be – or over that way. Where else in the world right now was the focus but on Ukraine and the surrounding states? Where else might the CIA be running an operation requiring an unassigned operative like me?

By unassigned, read deniable. It's what they call it when they want to keep their hands clean and their teeth pearly white. If the operator gets caught or blown, he's on his own. It's part of the risk in this business.

I'd worked in central and Eastern Europe before and knew my way around. And I had contacts from previous operations, although how much use they'd be depended on the precise location. Going in cold looking to buy resources is hard work – and risky.

But, as I was going to find out, using known resources also has its problems.

Twenty-four hours later I met up with a Clandestine Service Officer named Brian Callahan in a CIA front-office in New York. Urgent and critical was about right. This was fast work and I wondered what had got them in such a spin.

Callahan was tall and lean and had Langley written all over him. He had cropped grey hair and the eyes of one who'd spent a lot of his time peering around corners and not liking what he saw, but was capable of dealing with it. He seemed relaxed, but I could tell he was wound up tight. A man under pressure.

'That was good work you did in Tehran,' he'd started out, after we'd been served coffee from a Starbucks down the street and got over assessing each other. 'Getting Bagheri out of there in one piece was a hell of a feat.'

'You were in on it?'

'I was an observer. It was an important mission. Pity it didn't get us the information we needed, but at least we – you – saved an important man and got him out alive.' He looked squarely at me as if trying to get in my head. People in his position do that a lot, I find. 'You're a hard man to pin down.'

I didn't respond to that. I don't advertise my services, and few people know where to find me. But those that do are connected and word soon gets down the line. It's not exactly the Better Business Bureau method but it works well enough for me.

'Have you been watching the news?' he asked.

'Some. I take it you don't mean the showbiz segment.'

The smile didn't quite work, but he tried. 'I wish. We'd all make more money and sleep better at night.' He tapped the desk. 'I think this is your kind of job. I hope so, anyway. You can pull out of this anytime during the initial briefing – but only up to the point of names, places and times.'

'Which is when?'

'I think you'll know soon enough. Can we proceed?'

'Go ahead.'

His brief was simple. A foreign policy statement by Secretary of State John Kerry had made it clear that the US would stand by Ukraine during its problems involving pro-Russian separatists and a growing show of non-cooperation from Moscow in spite of talks in Geneva in April 2014 to rectify the situation between them. To that end, the White House had decided that there was a need to talk to the increasingly beleaguered Ukrainians as a show of support. But there were problems with that. In the same way as in Syria, Iran and Egypt during and after the Arab Spring, there were different factions involved, each with their own agenda. It was a nightmare of tactics, diplomacy and judgement, and someone, somewhere was going to end up unhappy.

In this instance the talks had to be low-level, which meant without any media presence, flexible in nature and ready to ship out at a moment's notice and run for home if things got hot. Moscow was keeping a close eye on US and European Union involvement so it wasn't going to be easy.

'It was supposed to be a one-man operation,' Callahan explained, 'in and out with the minimum of noise. What the State Department calls "exploratory in nature and designed to move talks forward with various parties to find out who controls who". What that means is finding a way of leveraging a safe outcome without getting us all involved in a messy civil war – or worse. Once Moscow goes in with all guns blazing, nobody will be able to predict the outcome.'

'What's the likelihood of that?' I could guess, I suppose, but it's always useful hearing an insider spook's take on world events.

Callahan played it cute. He prevaricated. 'Who knows? Our best analysts are still working on it. Putin played hardball with Georgia over South Ossetia, but scaled things back quickly. He might do the same again long enough to gain control elsewhere, but the scenario is not the same. Ukraine is a mix, some pro-Moscow, some against. The country is already divided, and the best outcome is seen by some as a split. It wouldn't be easy but if it avoids open warfare it would be better than tanks rolling down Main Street, Kiev anytime soon.'

Good luck with that, I thought. But their intentions were good – on the surface. If the State Department wanted to help cool things down, and they had a man ready and willing to go do this, it was difficult to fault their commitment. How it would turn out was anybody's guess. Which prompted a question.

'You said this was supposed to be a one-man operation. What did you mean?'

He hesitated and I got a sudden sense of where the stress was coming from. This wasn't a plan in the making, something they were sketching out on a mission board; it was a done deal. The train had already left the station. Callahan confirmed it.

'Our man's already in place, but under house arrest and imminent threat. I need you to go in and pull him out.'

FOUR

I did a tour of the room for a couple of minutes while he sat and waited. It was pretty much a dance routine; we both knew we'd reached that point where I either went to the door and walked away, or stayed and listened to a full briefing of names, details, dates and other data. After that I'd be committed.

What Callahan was describing was not an escort job, but a rescue operation.

I sat down again.

The person they'd sent in was a State Department officer with some field experience and a brief career in the military. It was a wise choice – as far as it went. Long-time desk-jockey staffers don't usually have much of a handle on field action, which can be good and bad. Good means the caution factor keeps them from taking risks; the bad comes when they have a little knowledge or experience and think they can talk their way out of anything.

My own opinion was that while this negotiator wasn't expected to get physical, some experience of moving around in hostile areas wouldn't do him any harm. The simple truth was, they'd sent a man to a region where he could be picked up and locked away without warning if he stuck his head down the wrong rabbit hole.

And by the sounds of it, he'd done just that.

'Where are we talking about?'

'I'll come to that.' Callahan took a folder out of a drawer and slid it across the desk. It held a colour photo of a man named Edwin Travis. The career summary told me he was forty-five years old, married with two kids and lived outside Washington D.C. It was almost nothing in real terms, but since we weren't exactly going to meet up and be best buddies, I didn't need to know more. Too much unnecessary information would merely cloud the issue and not help me watch over him. All I needed to do was recognize him when I saw him.

The photo showed a man in apparently good physical condition, with fair hair going thin and close cut at the sides. He had the confident, stern-jawed look of a man who had been out there and done stuff. But photographs lie. I could tell instinctively that he was no action figure, unless it was on the sports field with his kids. My instinctive impression was that it would have been better if he'd looked a little more average. Average is bland; average gets you by almost anywhere in the world and gets overlooked. It's the confident or brash that gets pulled out of a line-up.

Callahan must have read my thoughts. 'We put him through an intensive course in how not to stick his head in a noose, but that was as far as the State Department wanted us to go.' He gave a cynical smile. 'I guess they didn't want him exposed too much to the dark arts, in case he turned rogue on them.'

'What happened?'

'He got through the first round of meetings in Ukraine, gradually working his way around the various groups and their decision-makers, up to the potential leaders of tomorrow. Then two days ago he was a guest at a late-night meeting in the city of Donetsk, in the east. As he was leaving, a bunch of armed men lifted him off the street and took him back to his hotel. They were described as militia – local men in uniforms stolen from a nearby barracks. They didn't explain why, but told Travis not to leave the building or he'd be shot on sight. He's been held there ever since.'

'Did he tell you this?'

'He got a brief message out but the signals in the area are being interrupted, my guess is by Moscow. Putting pressure on the groups opposed to separation includes blocking telecommunications and internet traffic to disrupt appeals to the outside world. Nobody's heard from him since he was lifted, but a Swedish diplomat saw him thirty-six hours ago. He said he looked OK but seemed to be having a rough time.'

'So he has to come out.'

'That's our advice. The situation is deteriorating and there's a risk he'll simply disappear. Foreign media personnel are being given a hard time entering the country and some road trips are restricted by troop movements. The problem is our hands are tied; we've been instructed that sending in a team to lift him out would amount to a declaration of force.'

A team. In CIA parlance that meant a group of their own specialists with expertise in escape and evasion.

'So what's the plan?'

'Our best chance – his best chance – is to simply walk out of the hotel. The level of security seems pretty haphazard and the people holding him won't be expecting him to move. The problem is he has nowhere to go. But with low-profile help he could be clear and away before they can organize themselves.'

It wasn't a bad plan; if Travis wasn't under lock and key, and guarded by guys who weren't professionals, the only thing keeping him inside was the threat of being shot. So walking out was probably the last thing they'd expect him to do.

'You have somebody local?'

'Yes. If we can get him to walk, the plan is for you to pick up his trail and shadow him to safety through a series of cut-outs across the border to Moldova. It's no good trying to fly him out of Ukraine – they'd be on the lookout for him.' He shrugged as if he was short on choices. 'It's a long way but Moldova is really the best bet.'

Cut-outs are a means of passing information or material from one 'cell' to another, often in isolation so that one cut-out won't know – and therefore can't blow – the identity of another. 'Who are these people?'

'Local assets we've used for some time, on and off. They're reliable but non-operational. Civilians. The most we can expect of them is transportation and guidance, not heroics.'

In my opinion such people – assets as they're known in the business – are heroic enough, living a double life. It doesn't make them all traitors or spies, depending on which side of the fence you're on. Some do what they do out of political or religious conviction; some because they enjoy the buzz. Others do it for money.

'Will Travis know I'm there?'

'Not if we don't tell him. If he did he might take risks and go places he shouldn't. We don't want that; we're not looking for a hero's return. We want him out of the hotel and on his way home. That's it.'

'Why not get the embassy involved?'

'It's too risky. Our personnel there have been under observation ever since the whole Crimea and Ukraine thing blew up. If any one of them was seen heading east, we'd be accused of fomenting trouble and internal unrest, even though they undoubtedly know Travis is already there and why. The situation for them is getting worse as world attention focusses on the unrest. One way or another Moscow is steering this and waiting to use any situation it can to divert attention away from their own increasing involvement. We want you to get Travis away before that happens.'

'Who else is in on this?' I like to know if an operation is general knowledge. If it is, I'm out.

He looked slightly conflicted at that and I could guess why: bringing in an outsider doesn't always go down well among some CIA die-hards, who regard their own people as the only solution to a problem. The fact is, Langley uses sub-contractors all the time where they need bodies on the ground to intimidate or deter, or where the government insists on the deniability option in case things go bad. But a single individual with specialized skills causes internal doubt, as if it's a sneaky move, somehow, or an insult to their own special brand of integrity. 'There's a restricted list of people in the know on this operation and I want to keep it that way. It includes a couple of people in the State Department, of course, along with my operational support team and senior people. But that's pretty much it.'

'I report to you?'

'When you can, when it's safe. But you're accustomed to operating in the dark, right?'

'Yes.' In the dark, at long distance and often beyond reach. It sounds insane but it's the way I like it.

'Good. Your primary support contact twenty-four-seven will be drafted in from our trainee program. He or she will be your voice and ears during this assignment, with minimal interruption. You need anything, you tell them and they'll see it gets done.'

'A trainee?'

'Don't worry – they will be selected from the top three per cent. We're a little short on the ground at the present time, but they will already have some operational experience and will be embedded throughout your time in the field, so you won't have to deal with any informational gaps.'

Informational gaps. That was a term I hadn't heard before. But I knew what it meant; whoever my contact was, they wouldn't leave the building – presumably a darkened room somewhere in the bowels of Langley – until this job was done.

I hoped whoever they selected had balls of steel and didn't need a lot of sleep.

FIVE

L indsay Citera was nervous. After being pulled out of a training session on firearms and tactics and told to report to an office on the second floor, she was wondering what she could have done wrong. She'd felt the eyes of her course colleagues following her out of the room and knew what was going through their minds: that she had somehow screwed up and was being dropped . . . or she'd struck lucky and was being given an early assignment.

Sympathy and envy; they went hand-in-hand where competition for success was intense and positions were eagerly sought. And nobody wanted to be a trainee for ever.

She hoped it was an assignment. She'd been pulling high marks in pretty much every module on the training program so there was little chance that she'd messed up unless it was something she hadn't been prepared for. Like her age. Or her family.

At thirty-four she was older than most of her intake colleagues. She had a law degree but no previous law enforcement or military experience, and had wondered if the lack of experience would count against her, especially after being comprehensively whipped on the brutal physical exercises by people ten years her junior. She hadn't actually come in last, though; that honour had gone to a guy who'd tried to take a stockade-style fence in one go and missed. But neither had she broken any finishing tapes on the endurance runs.

Her biggest concern was her family background. She'd answered all the questions about family honestly, aware that applying to join the CIA would open them all to an intensive round of vetting. She doubted her parents separating would count against her, but having a brother, Tommy, currently in a military garrison accused of bringing in drugs from a tour in Afghanistan might limit her scope for advancement, as could a younger sister, Karen, deeply in debt and running with a crowd of delinquents that had already seen her pick up some DUI misdemeanours and a couple of warnings.

While waiting in what looked like an unused second-floor office, she'd checked herself over for presentation. Smart but not too stand-out, clean and tidy with no obvious marks from the pistol range, although a faint smell of burned powder residue hung around her shoulders; hair short and neat, nails just the right side of acceptably long. Make-up light.

The door opened and she jumped to her feet. A tall, slim man entered and sat down across from her. He was carrying a plain folder. When he flipped back the cover, she saw her name printed on the inside flap.

'Brian Callahan,' he said by way of introduction, and motioned for her to sit. 'Lindsay Citera. Soft "C", right?'

'Yes, sir. Like the guy from Chicago. The rock group, not the musical.' She clamped her mouth shut and felt herself colour up. Jesus, where did that come from? Hell of a way to start an interview.

Callahan gave a ghost of a smile. 'I know who you mean. It says here that you're single, with no current attachments or dependants, that you live alone. Is that still correct?'

'That's correct, sir.'

'Good.' He sat back. 'I could go through your file and tell you what you already know – that you're top of your grades on all fronts where it matters. But that would be wasting both our time and we don't have a lot to spare. I'm a staff operations officer; you know what that means?'

'Yes, sir, I do.' She felt a buzz of real excitement and remembered to close her mouth. He hadn't mentioned family background, which was surely good, wasn't it? Callahan's tone was urgent, and she wondered if that was how it always was around here. SOOs, as they were known, were the main links with intelligence gathering and operations personnel. They were the mostly unseen officers who refined and translated proposals and planning into action, and guided the people at the sharp end: the men and women in the field. The spies, although nobody referred to them that way. Spies worked for the other side.

'Good. Saves me having to explain. I need a comms support officer, Lindsay, who won't mind ducking out of the light for a while. I don't know how long, but it shouldn't be more than a week, ten days. You interested?'

'Absolutely, sir. When do I start?'

'You already have. You've been signed off all ongoing training schedules until further notice, but any summary I write of your work will count towards your overall training program assessment. You OK with that?'

'Yes, sir.'

'No animals to worry about? No family members or significant others on the horizon to distract you?' He looked at her without blinking and she wondered if he was waiting for her to mention Tommy or Karen. They were distractions sure enough, she being the big sister, but only when it suited them. She hadn't spoken to Tommy in a couple of months and Karen only called when she was in need of money and desperate enough to play the emotional blackmail card. Well, she'd have to suck it up and do without for a while. Big sister was dropping off the radar.

She opened her mouth to reply, but found her throat had gone dry. My God, she wondered, does he mean I'm going undercover? 'Yes, sir. I mean, no, sir. I'm fine with that. No animals, no family or anything to worry about.' Certainly no boyfriend, she thought; not since she'd joined the program. There had been a few cautious approaches from colleagues, and a couple of the more obvious chat-up lines from guys in the administration area. But she'd steered clear of all of them. It was no secret that romantic entanglements, while not forbidden, could prove a serious hindrance on the trainee program. Not that she'd sworn herself into holy orders or anything like that; but she wanted to succeed in the job she'd always wanted to do since she was in high school and wasn't going to stuff it up for a quick roll in the hay.

'Good. You'll stay in the operations centre for as long as it takes. I'll arrange for meals to be brought to you from the cafeteria, and if you need a break we can assign one of the other trainees on assignment down here to take over. But keep it short. If we have to, we can stand you down for a few hours but you should regard this as a twenty-four-seven assignment until further notice.'

'Doing what, sir?'

He nodded at the folder. 'It's all in there. Read it now and leave it here when you go. The short version is you've been assigned to support an operative in the field in Eastern Europe. He's not one of ours but he is to be given the same degree of focus and attention that you would give a full-time serving CIA officer. Understood?'

'Yes, sir.'

Callahan leaned forward. 'I know this is stuff you'll have been told but hear me out – it's important. Over the course of the next few days, you will learn things that never leave this facility. The operative's code name is Watchman. He's highly experienced and you could go many hours, even whole days when you don't hear from him. But when you do, you go into overdrive and give him every second of your attention because he will need it. Doesn't matter what time of day or night it is; to Watchman, just like any other clandestine officer, you're there to make sure he has whatever backup he asks for. That could be anything from map coordinates to travel schedules, down to the route to the nearest hospital or the name of a friendly doctor. Get me?'

'Yes, sir.' She reached across and picked up the folder. It felt as if she was making a momentous move, like she'd just taken a major step forward in her career.

Callahan's face softened as if he understood. 'I don't mean it to sound harder than it is, and I'll be here to guide you. But it's vitally important you understand how critical your role is to Watchman. This is going to require all of your focus, understood?'

'Understood, sir. Am I allowed to ask why he's from outside?'

'You might have heard talk about the differences between Langley personnel and outsiders – what are often called private contractors. Don't listen to it. This man's job is to keep another person alive in the field, and to get him out in one piece. It's what he's good at and is why he was selected. The fact that he's not CIA is not an issue to me; it's what he can do that matters. That makes him vitally important to us and the country. It makes you an important part of it, too. I know it's a huge thing we're asking of you this early in your career, but I wouldn't be speaking to you now if I hadn't been assured that you were more than capable of doing this.'

'Thank you, sir.' Lindsay's throat was dry with nerves. 'Will I be talking to this other person?'

'No. He has a limited line of reporting. If he runs into trouble, it's up to Watchman to get him out. Watchman is your focus.'

'I understand. I won't let you down.'

Callahan smiled, for the first time without apparent reservation. 'I know that, Lindsay. Just make sure Watchman knows it, too. Yours could be the only friendly voice he hears over the next few days, remember that.'

*   *   *

As soon as Callahan had gone, Lindsay opened the folder and read the briefing notes three times, a habit ingrained into her by her dad, a pharmacist. Read three times, he'd always told her, and you'll know it forever. It had worked pretty well so far and got her through law school, so she wasn't complaining.

Ukraine. It had been all over the news for a long time now, yet she knew ridiculously little about it. Maybe now was the time to update her education.

As part of her training she had already sat in on selected 'live' operations, listening to real-time and recorded audio feed from officers in the field and watching visuals via drones over Afghanistan, Iraq and other hot zones. Sitting in a darkened bubble with a bunch of other trainees, however, had made some of it seem a little unreal, and she and others had suspected they were simulations to help weed out the romantics, fantasists and the uncommitted.

But this was different; this was about a man she was shortly going to be joined to more closely than to most of her friends. She could put down the phone on them, and they her, and they'd still be friends in the morning, hangovers and fights notwithstanding. But not the man code-named Watchman. And that made everything seem frighteningly real.

His very life might depend on everything she heard, did or said.

SIX

'Help is on the way. Travis will move as soon as he receives the green light.'

Brian Callahan suppressed a shiver as he sat down after making the announcement. He was in an annexe to the Operations Suite in the Central Intelligence Agency's Langley HQ. The air was clean and pure, with the slight chill and dead feel peculiar to sub-level rooms, where the walls were bombproof and the fabric sowed with auditory disruption networks. But it wasn't the atmosphere that made him nervous; he was used to that.

It was the presence of one of the three men already seated at the boardroom-style table.

'Remind us of the situation for the benefit of Senator Benson, will you?' The first speaker was senior CIA Assistant Director, Jason Sewell. He had the genial smile and manner of a happy golfer, but the watch-fulness in his eyes was a dead giveaway; here was a man experienced in the field of espionage and high-risk operations who knew what was involved. Like Callahan, he also knew the risks of not having all his ducks in a row for the man sitting at the far end of the table.

'That would be very useful.' Senator Howard J. Benson was prob-ably the most influential – and potentially dangerous – man the CIA could have ever admitted through its blast-proof doors. A former politician from Virginia, he was a long-time fixture around Washington, and a member of the ultra-powerful Intelligence Community, an umbrella organization for all US intelligence agencies set up to coordinate and support, among other things, special activities connected with US foreign policy objectives overseas. But what made him a person for Sewell and Callahan to be wary of was his Congressional oversight role regarding CIA operations and activities. Outwardly a supporter of the Agency, it was generally known that Benson was a CIA sceptic and would not hesitate to drag it kicking and screaming before an investigative committee if given half a chance.

'Senator. As you may know the State Department recently sent a negotiator named Edwin Travis to Ukraine tasked with holding fact-finding talks with the various groups involved in the troubles

over there; that's both separatist pro-Moscow, and Ukrainian nation-
alists opposed to the split. Sending a government representative
openly would have caused problems with Moscow, so we advised
them to place him on a ticket from the Centre for International
Coordination and Collaboration, based in Geneva. CICC for short.
They would still know who he worked for, but would give them a
face saver if it got out.'

'Let's hope you're right.' The next man was seated sideways on,
looking at nobody in particular, his mouth pursed tight. His name
was Marcus Kempner, and he was the State Department's representative. He had good reason to look uncomfortable; this was his first
time in the rarefied atmosphere of the CIA Operations Suite and he
was carrying a lot of the responsibility for what was currently
unfolding with Edwin Travis. He wore a slightly patrician air that
many found irritating, and liked to talk of his interest in arts and
culture to hide a lack of social ease.

'Pardon me?' Callahan looked surprised by the comment.

'This was a high-risk but extremely worthy venture – but we had
to try. We can't have anything coming out of the woodwork that
might suggest that it was actually some sort of CIA spying mission.
There's more than just one man's safety at risk here.'

'The Geneva end is not a problem, sir. We've used it before. They
have a genuine plate on an office along the Rue du Hesse and are
absolutely secure. I hope I can say the same about other aspects of
this "mission".'

'What are you trying to suggest, Mr Callahan?' Kempner blinked
rapidly. He wasn't accustomed to being confronted by lowly
members of the espionage community, who usually kept their heads
down and left it to senior people to do the infighting.

'With respect, sir,' Callahan continued calmly, 'you specifically
allowed us little to do with Travis's mission logistics other than
providing some background information and suggesting he use the
CICC cover. That has stood up as we believed it would.'

'Gentlemen.' Jason Sewell raised a placatory hand. 'Please. We
don't have time.' He glanced at Kempner and added, 'I'm sorry,
Marcus, but Callahan's right; your people put this thing together
with minimum input from us. Travis was up and off before we could
fully evaluate the situation. Now you want our help to get him out
of a jam, which we're happy to provide, of course.'

Kempner looked as if he were about to protest at this quiet

reproof, but changed his mind and sat back in his chair. Making enemies with senior CIA personnel wasn't a good idea, especially when asking for their help.

Howard Benson cleared his throat, bringing further discussion to a halt. Dressed in a conservative suit and college tie, he looked exactly what he was: old money and old family. But behind the façade lay the sharp teeth and ambition of a modern-day bureaucrat and political in-fighter. 'How many people are involved in getting to Travis?' Benson asked softly.

'One man, sir. As soon as he's in place we'll get things moving.'

'One? That's a hell of a task, even for your Specialized Skills Officers. I'd have thought you'd commit a team, at least.'

Callahan hesitated. In spite of his elevated clearance level, Benson was pushing into territory that was not his. The SSOs were paramilitary members of the Agency, recruited mostly from former special forces personnel such as Delta and Seal Team 6, and were responsible for security operations in hazardous areas. They were considered the best of the best at what they did. 'Sir, the situation on the ground is unpredictable. The entire region is falling apart and is under close scrutiny from the media and local intelligence and security agencies. I decided a contractor would be our best and safest option in case of any fall-out.'

Benson frowned. 'You're using an outsider?' The words were icy in tone, reminding everyone of the senator's oft-quoted opposition to private military contractors and security groups. He had shown no hesitation for several years now in condemning their use, especially in connection with 'black flight' exercises, or rendition, as it was popularly known, and the rumoured torture of insurgents and suspected terrorists.

Callahan took a breath and glanced at Assistant Director Sewell, who merely nodded to show he would support Callahan's response. He'd known this was going to happen. The CIA used sub-contractors all the time and always had. But there was still an innate knee-jerk reaction against them, as if it were a criticism of CIA ability. And for a sceptic like Benson, any stick with which to beat the Agency would do.

'I considered it prudent, sir. We needed a clean pair of hands so that there are no links back to us. However, the main reason I chose him was because he has an unparalleled record and this work is what he does best.'

'What's his name?'

'His code name is Watchman.'

'His real name.'

'That's something I'd prefer not to go into.' He felt the air crackle with tension the moment the words came out. He'd just as good as told a man with the highest degree of security clearance possible to mind his own business. 'Don't misunderstand me, I don't mean to be impertinent.'

'I'll take that as read. So why bring him on board?'

'Because from what Mr Kempner's State Department colleagues outlined in the briefing for this mission, and knowing what we now know about Travis's situation, I believe there's a real and credible risk to him and the outcome of this venture. I have to do whatever I can to protect both.'

'He's right.' Kempner stirred reluctantly. 'This mission is not some half-hearted fool's errand hoping to get lucky. We went into it knowing the risks. What's going on in Eastern Europe right now is not a whole lot different to the Arab Spring of a few years ago. It's about power and influence and we can't sit idly by and hope for the best. But getting the embassy involved is not an option.'

'I agree. But don't you have a "friend" in the new president? Couldn't he help?'

'That rumour is without foundation, Senator. President Poroshenko has never been an agent of the State Department, whatever WikiLeaks might say to the contrary. In any case, we wanted to engage with all parties. If Putin continues on what we believe is his intended course, he's going to destabilize more and more of the previously Soviet states and grab more control in the region. If we can make contact with those independents early and keep them on-side, we might make his work a little harder.' He winced. 'That appears to have gone a little sour. But getting Travis out and back in one piece will go a long way to showing we won't be messed with.'

It was an uncommonly long speech for anyone in this room, where orders were issued, information relayed and results passed on in usually quiet, measured tones that rarely lasted longer than a few words. But it was a measure of the speaker's status that nobody ventured to disagree or haul him in.

'It's a mess, alright,' said Assistant Director Sewell. He was studying a large map of central Europe and the Middle East on one wall.

'To be honest, it's a little late for Ukraine.' Kempner followed his look. 'That scenario was becoming divided before we were aware of it. We're hoping not to have the same thing happen with the others, which is why we decided to engage with them.'

Sewell looked at him, and it was clear he was trying to identify if there was any subtle criticism in the statement. 'We assessed the situation in Ukraine as best we could but the picture was clouded.' His jaw was tense and he looked ready for a fight.

'We know that, Jason.' This time it was Benson's turn to smooth ruffled feathers. 'Nobody's disputing it. As I understand it, the point of this exercise with Travis was to get inside the region and make contacts, yes?' He looked at Kempner, who nodded. 'Then it's a lesson learned for future exercises, I think we all agree.' He shifted in his chair and looked at Callahan. 'How does this man of yours get in touch with Travis?'

'He doesn't, not directly. If things go right Travis exits the hotel where he's being held and he'll be picked up and passed along a line of cut-outs until he's home and clear. He won't even know about Watchman's involvement. That's Watchman's specialty; he works at a distance and clears the way. If any danger arises he deals with it.'

'He's done this kind of work before, you say?' There was a slight hesitation on the word 'work', as if Benson had difficulty getting it out without spitting.

'Correct.'

'Who for?'

'For us, the DEA, the Defence Intelligence Agency, and the UK's MI6. I can't go into details but he was also responsible for pulling an important CIA asset out of Tehran just a few days ago. He did that from right under the noses of their Ministry of Intelligence and National Security. The asset had gone in to secure details of new weapons development by the Iranians.'

'And how did that go?'

'It didn't,' Sewell replied. 'The asset was blown by a friend. But at least we got him out alive.'

'What's this Watchman's background? How much money are we throwing at him?'

'I can't go into that, sir. Sorry.'

Benson threw Sewell a look loaded with meaning. 'You see, that's what I don't like about these operations. But we'll discuss that later.

When does Watchma— Who the hell thinks of these names?' He
puffed his lips with a tinge of exasperation. 'When does he report in?'

'When he's ready and it's safe to do so,' Callahan replied. 'It's
the way he works.'

'So that's it? We sit and wait on the convenience of a hired gun?'

'We have to. Where he's going there won't be one-hundred per
cent reliable cell coverage due to extensive electronic disruption.
In between that, outgoing signals are easy to pick up by Russian
monitoring stations. He will call.'

'Let's hope he does.' Benson glanced at Sewell before getting to
his feet. 'I have to say, I don't like the sound of this operation. But
since it's already up and running, there's not much I can do about
it. As soon as the ball is rolling I'd like a tour of the facility to see
the nuts and bolts of how you're going to work with this man.' He
didn't wait for assent, but looked hard at Callahan. 'It had better
be good, because if your contractor gets picked up and blown,
believe me, your career path will follow very close behind.'

If it was meant as a joke, nobody was laughing.

SEVEN

Entering a potentially hostile country can be accomplished in a number of ways. You can go in under the badge of an official or accredited body, such as government, trade mission, approved NGO – a non-governmental organization – or, if allowed, a member of the media. Or you can use whatever independent routes or means might be available that require a visa and a business plan. Since Callahan had told me an official badge was out of the question, and media personnel were already getting the run-around because of the deteriorating political situation, I was having to be inventive.

I'd flown in to Ukraine's Sergey Prokofiev International Airport at Donetsk late in the afternoon on papers supplied by Callahan. I was of mixed Polish/German parentage from a small German town near Cottbus on the border, and was looking for building work and possibly setting up a small business. Although I wasn't planning on going to any meetings, I'd had Callahan's people make a couple of appointments beforehand with the local department of trade and chamber of commerce. With everything else going on in the country, I figured they would soon forget all about me, and by the time someone realized I hadn't shown up, I fully expected to be on my way out of the country.

The atmosphere in the airport terminal was tense, with a heavy presence of soldiers and cops around, all heavily armed and looking jumpy. There was a variety of uniforms, some complete and reasonably smart, others with men wearing a combination of combat jackets, jeans and trainers. Anywhere else and they could have been special forces, but these guys had the rumpled look of militia rather than highly trained specialists.

Given the situation, I wasn't the only optimistic business traveller entering the country. There was a mix of German and French convention delegates, with a sprinkling of Koreans, and their numbers gave me useful cover until I was certain I hadn't attracted any official attention. As soon as I could, I broke off and headed for an anonymous hotel close to the airport where I'd made a reservation. I was already dressed for the part, in a dark leather jacket, pants and heavy shoes. I'd sourced them from a German chain store specializing in work casuals, and looked about as invisible as it was possible to get in this part of the world. Just another working stiff edging his way through life.

Ed Travis was being held at a large hotel half a mile away, within the airport boundary. I'd tried to get a room there, but had been told there were no vacancies 'for the foreseeable future'. It sounded as if whoever was preventing him leaving had taken over the whole building. Travis was waiting to receive the 'go' message as soon as I got myself organized and called in to Langley. At that point the local asset would be given the nod and the rabbit would begin to run.

I didn't have much time to spare. I needed to get on the ground and busy, ready to locate and check Travis's surroundings and follow his progress. With all the military activity in the area, that wasn't going to be easy. I'd have to run the risk of roadblocks and random stops by militia, but I figured I could talk my way through.

The first priority was to pick up some wheels. I'd automatically ruled out any of the usual rental agencies. If they weren't already closed through lack of customers and the risk of not getting their cars back, they soon would be. But that wasn't my only reason for avoiding them. I didn't want to risk leaving an electronic trail; hiring a car requires a credit card and a passport or driver's licence, neither of which I wanted to show unless absolutely forced to. The passport I'd used was good, but I didn't want to risk placing it under intensive scrutiny. Any experienced immigration officer giving it a thorough scan would eventually find holes in it. The fact was, I was now off the grid and that was the way I wanted to stay.

I'd picked up the name of a supplier in Donetsk through a contact in Berlin. Max Hengendorff was a go-between for resources; if you needed a weapon, a car or a couple of enforcers, he was your go-to guy. He had connections with certain people among the criminal elite across Europe and knew everybody worth knowing. 'Ivkanoy in Donetsk,' he'd said, when I told him where I was headed. 'He will get you what you need. He's rough around the edges but I hear good things about him. I'll give him a call and let you know when and where.'

'Fine,' I'd replied. 'Usual rules apply.'

He'd laughed. 'Of course. Don't they always.' Usual rules meant no names, no questions and no dud deals.

I'd heard back within the hour, which was why I was now preparing for a meeting in a bar not far from the main railway station.

I checked my appearance in the room mirror, used some product to muss my hair, then placed a few things in a folding overnight bag and slipped out the rear of the hotel.

It was getting dark now, and the glow of lights over the city was throwing shadows across the station buildings and surrounding streets. The traffic was light and I was able to move without attracting attention, keeping to the inside of the sidewalk, just another worker on the way home.

The Dynamo Bar was a medium-sized place with a mix of manual workers and men in shirts and ties, most of them talking about the football, which was being played out on a large screen behind the bar. If the customers had any opinions about the unrest threatening to tear their country apart, they were staying off the subject and focussing on the game.

I ordered a beer and looked around for the man named Ivkanoy. Max had described him for me in unflattering terms, and I soon spotted him. He was sitting alone at a corner table, a fat man in a rumpled, greasy suit and tie, with a battered briefcase at his feet and a cell phone clamped to one ear. In what was a pretty crowded room he had managed to retain a wide space around him, which told me something about his reputation locally. He looked me over when I signalled that I'd like to sit down, and finished his phone conversation before nodding at a seat. I noticed a few looks coming my way from other men in the bar, and figured this man was well-known but not exactly popular.

'Ivkanoy?'

He didn't say anything. I figured he was playing mean and moody because it suited his self-image and he wanted to keep up a front for the others in the bar. So I mentioned Max in Berlin and reminded him that I'd come for a car.

He gave me another cautious look, eyes flicking over the cheap clothes, my bag and day-old stubble. I'd been speaking in German-accented Russian and was hoping he didn't have anything against the old enemy.

'Max? I don't know a Max. And I've never been to Berlin.' He looked back down at his phone, his whole bearing uninterested. 'And if you want a car, try the airport. They have lots of them.'

'I prefer to go private,' I told him. I was puzzled by his attitude and wondered if there was some kind of needle thing going on between him and Max. Or maybe he was suspicious of a set-up and thought I was an undercover cop trying a sting operation. 'Look, do you want to do business or not? If not, tell me and I'll go to somebody who does.'

The straight talking got to him. He adjusted his tie, which looked as if he'd used it to strangle somebody, and waved his cell phone. 'Hey, calm down. It's no problem. I need to make a call,' he said and glanced at his watch. 'You asked for an "extra". You know how much, right?'

The 'extra' was a weapon, a semi-automatic. I was going into some dangerous territory with all kinds of militias and unofficial armed groups roaming the streets, and I didn't feel much like putting myself at a disadvantage from the get-go. A gun was a last resort, but it might just be necessary to get me and Travis back home again in one piece. 'Max told me how much.'

I saw the glint of speculation in his eyes. Now I was here the agreed figure wasn't going to be enough. He knew what he wanted and was going to hold out for it, figuring I would pay up since I didn't have time to play games. I added thirty per cent to the figure and he nodded, pleased with his bargaining skills. 'You wait here and I'll be back.' He grabbed his briefcase and ambled away towards the front door, a path clearing for him as if by magic. By the time he hit the street, he was on his cell phone.

EIGHT

Twenty minutes later, as I was beginning to think I'd been duped, Ivkanoy appeared in the doorway. He was still carrying his briefcase. He didn't come all the way in, but clicked his fingers in the air and signalled at me to follow. The way you do things when you want everyone in the place to know you're the boss.

What a pro.

He was moving with a lot more energy now, hustling ahead of me like his feet were on wings. We passed a row of shops, mostly closed for the night or maybe out of business, their owners unable or unwilling to operate in the current climate, and rounded a couple of corners, all without seeing anybody. If the authorities wanted to impose a curfew here, they weren't exactly going to have their work cut out. Most of the locals were off the streets already.

We ended up in a narrow, ill-lit street with a dead-end formed by the embankment of a railway line. There was a single vehicle in sight, a Toyota Land Cruiser parked beneath a tree. It looked oddly out of place, and I checked all around me, seeing nothing but darkened windows and deserted doorways. It reminded me of some of the fake city lots I'd been on for close quarters combat training in the military, although if anybody was going to jump out at me, they wouldn't be cardboard silhouettes. And if any cops were watching, they were staying well back.

Something didn't feel right, but maybe it was mission nerves.

Ivkanoy saw me looking and smirked. 'No need to worry about police,' he said, and rubbed his fingers together. Whether it was a nervous reaction or meant he'd paid them off, I wasn't sure, but I took it to be a good sign – with reservations.

I walked round the Toyota, checking out the shadows as I went. The vehicle was well-used and looked a dirty red under the poor light. Its life story was easy to read in the tracer-work of dents and scrapes on the body panels and fenders, and a multitude of scratches on the windshield. But it looked ready to go with good tyres and wipers. So far so good.

'What about the extra?'

'In the glove box with a spare clip. Add another fifty per cent, cash,' Ivkanoy suggested heavily, 'and I won't ask you to bring them back.' He chuckled as he said this and jiggled a key on a plastic fob.

It was an odd thing to say. A deal was a deal. I looked at him, wondering if he was a joker or just plain greedy. 'Is the car clean?' The last thing I needed, travelling with a gun, was for the car to be on a stolen vehicle checklist.

He shrugged in a take it or leave it kind of way. 'Why should you care?'

Then I got it. There was no deal; it was a set-up.

I heard a shuffle of movement in the shadows to my right. I turned just as a man in a leather jacket stepped out from a narrow gate in a wall a couple of yards away. Even in the shadows I could see he was big and carrying what looked like a sawn-off pool cue in one large fist, and was grinning like he would enjoy using it.

I heard a click and Ivkanoy had his briefcase open and was taking out a nasty-looking blackjack. I was surprised; it's pretty old-school as a weapon, and most gang-bangers in the US would laugh at it. It's basically a leather sack full of lead or sand, but its main advantage is that it's silent.

'You're kidding,' I said, just to keep him off-guard. A talking mark is one who might just give up the game without resisting.

Ivkanoy dropped the briefcase to one side and held out his empty hand. He wasn't listening and suddenly he didn't look quite so tired or rumpled.

He'd done this before. No doubt the local situation was giving him ample opportunity to screw anyone he could with no come-back guaranteed. With everything else on their plates, the local cops would be too busy to investigate minor crime, and he knew damn well I wasn't going to make a complaint, anyway. It was win-win for him.

'The money,' he said. 'Also your wallet and passport. All of it. You want to go home in one piece, yes?'

I really didn't want to get into this. I made a mental note to have a word with Max, maybe pay him a visit when I next got to Berlin. Knowingly or not, he'd served me a dud deal. 'OK,' I said, showing my open hand. 'There's no need for violence. We can sort this out.' I was talking to stop them attacking, knowing they would want to do this without having to work too hard. But I was also playing for time and advantage. I took a fold of notes out of my pocket and held them out to him, letting my fingers shake as I did so.

Ivkanoy saw the movement and grinned. He understood fear; it was part of what he traded in, what made his world go round. I was a mark and he'd got me where he wanted me. Easy money – and he'd probably only need to give me half a beating before letting me go.

Just as he reached out to grab the notes I dropped them on the ground.

It caught him flat-footed. He hesitated and looked down. Dumb move – this wasn't the way it was supposed to play out. Before he could react, I stepped in and slapped him hard enough to spin him like a top and drop him to the ground, the sound of the impact echoing along the street. The blackjack rolled out of his hand and the sound of his head hitting the sidewalk told me he was out of the fight.

His wingman hadn't been prepared for this development, either. But he tried. He made a noise deep in his chest and ran at me, the cue raised above his head and no doubt hoping his size would be enough to intimidate me. I gave it half a second then threw my bag in his face, turned away from him and delivered a mule kick. The advantage of such a kick, which is delivered backwards, is that your own danger area – your head – is furthest away from the attacker, and if timed right the extended foot makes contact first – and hard.

It took him just below the gut, sinking in deep. He squealed once and fell to his knees, eyes wide and mouth open in shock. Surprisingly, he started to get straight back up, whooping for air and clutching his groin, but ready to go. He was clearly made of tougher stuff than his friend and still had hold of the cue. So I scooped up the blackjack and while he was trying to get his other leg to work, tapped him once under the ear. He fell over to one side and I gave him another tap just to make sure. This time he didn't move.

I checked his jacket pockets and was surprised to find he'd come weighed down by something heavier than a pool cue. It was a small submachine gun clipped to a chest strap and tucked under his jacket. It looked like an Uzi, but I was betting on a local copy. It was a typical gangster's scary badge of courage, and I wondered if he'd ever used it or whether it was just for show.

I unclipped it, along with a spare magazine in a strap, thankful that he'd come out wielding the pool cue and not the gun, otherwise it might have ended differently. Then I went over to Ivkanoy and checked his hand. He was still holding the car key and groaning in pain. As I took the key he looked up at me and made a wild grab at my face.

I took hold of his hand and knelt on his chest, making the air go out of him like a punctured cushion. Then I grabbed his middle finger, bending it back until I had his full and undivided attention. He stopped moving.

'We had an arrangement,' I reminded him. 'You were to supply a car and a weapon and I was to pay you some money. That was a simple enough transaction, right?'

He didn't say anything but hawked and tried to spit in my face. Tough guy. So I broke his finger and left him screaming like a girl.

I climbed in and started the Toyota, then checked the glove box. Empty save for a bunch of sweet wrappers. No extra. But no surprise there; I hadn't been expected to get this far. I drove away, flicking on the lights and testing the heater and wipers. Overload a car like this right away and any faults in the electrical circuit should show up before going too far. If I was driving a glammed-up wreck I'd need to find an alternative pretty quickly. But it ran sweet enough, so I stopped near a small car park shielded by a line of scrappy bushes and went walk-about. I spotted a small Datsun pretty much the same age as the Toyota and got to work, switching the plates and caking the ones I was leaving on the Datsun with a liberal amount of dirt. With luck the driver wouldn't notice the switch for some time and I'd have some leeway before I needed to trade the ones I'd taken for a new set.

Next I needed to hide the submachine gun, which turned out to be a Croatian Ero model. If I ran into a problem, having it out in the open would be inviting trouble. The simplest solution would have been to drop it down a convenient sewer. But that would be like going naked. If Ivkanoy was the kind of man I figured he was, he'd be sorely pissed at having been dumped on his ass with a busted finger, and the chances of meeting up with him or his friends was too high; he'd be on the look-out and I'd need some heavy backup for that eventuality somewhere down the line.

I also needed to have the gun within easy reach, which left out anywhere on the outside of the vehicle. So I sliced open one of the rear seats and made sure it was tucked away out of sight, then took a drive back out to the airport for a look-see.

Game on.

NINE

A low murmur of voices reached Lindsay Citera over the discreet swish of the air-conditioning in her room deep in the Langley Operations Centre, and she turned away from the notes she'd been making while waiting to hear from Watchman. She automatically checked her desk was clear of unnecessary paperwork. Clutter, she had soon learned, was anathema to the Agency and to be avoided at all costs. And mission notes were the most sacrosanct of material and to be closely guarded at all times.

She recognized Assistant Director Sewell's easy tones floating along the corridor. He'd given a welcome speech to her intake on her second day at Langley, and like her new colleagues, she'd been impressed by his easy-going air of authority. She didn't recognize the other voice, however, which was harsher and more commanding in tone, as if the man was on a public platform rather than in the bowels of the Agency. She heard the word 'Congress', and he appeared to be making a point about pushing forward recommendations for the next round of budget talks by the Senate Select Committee on Intelligence.

She switched off the monitors displaying maps of Ukraine and Moldova, along with a bank of local data she was putting together that might be of use to Watchman, such as military movements, trouble spots, secondary roads and local weather updates. Although she had been given a secure unit inside the ops 'bubble', surrounded by other similar rooms and personnel, Callahan had warned her that few of her colleagues would resist the temptation to see what she was working on, and that employees of the Agency were as prone to gossip as anyone on the outside. Being responsible for an information leak through canteen chit-chat wouldn't go down well on only her second day.

She resisted the temptation to push the door shut. She felt certain A.D. Sewell wouldn't be bringing anyone who hadn't got the highest level of security clearance down here. In any case she'd already left it too late; slamming the door now would make her look guilty.

The footsteps were close to the door when a soft voice came

over the public address system. 'Assistant Director Sewell, please. Assistant Director Sewell.'

'I'm sorry, Senator – I have to take this. Can you wait here? I'll be two minutes.'

'Of course. Go ahead.'

Sewell's footsteps receded and Lindsay waited for the inevitable. She heard the soft brush of clothing fabric and turned her head.

The man standing in the doorway was impressively dressed with the groomed air of a senior politician. He was heavily built with greying hair carefully styled and brushed, and his skin bore the tan of the outdoors, as if he had spent time on the water. Probably in a fast yacht off Cape Cod, Lindsay decided.

'Sir?' she said, and waited. She couldn't exactly tell him to go away, since Sewell had left him alone down here and that must mean he had the appropriate level of clearance. But actually inviting him in seemed instinctively wrong. She stood up to present a physical barrier just in case.

'At ease, miss,' the man said, and waved a manicured hand. 'I haven't come to steal any secrets. I'm Senator Howard Benson; I'm with the Intelligence Community and sit on more top secret committees than I care to think about.'

The name was familiar to Lindsay, and she relaxed. Senator Benson was a regular on CNN. 'Sorry, sir. I didn't know.'

'No need to apologize, young lady. Should I call you agent or officer? I never know what terminology people around here like to use these days.' He smiled, showing a line of perfectly white teeth, and she had the feeling he probably knew exactly what people round here were called. 'Maybe a first name would be better.'

'It's Lindsay, sir.'

'Well, Lindsay, it seems we were destined to meet, in any case. Assistant Director Sewell was telling me earlier about you and your current task.' He looked over her shoulder at the monitors. 'This is a first for you, I understand?'

Lindsay blushed under his steady gaze and the knowledge that she had been the subject of conversation between two such high-powered men.

'That's correct, sir. I'm honoured.'

Benson moved through the doorway and into the room, his bulk and authority making it impossible for her to stand her ground. She stepped back a pace, checking that there was nothing for him to see.

He caught her glance and said, 'Don't worry, Lindsay, I know what you're doing here: you're looking after Watchman. That's a big responsibility for one so young . . . and inexperienced.'

'Yes, sir. Thank you, sir.' She told herself not to read too much into the comment or, worse, in the way he was standing so close and smiling at her, and said, 'I'll do my best, sir.'

Benson turned to a world map on the wall and studied it for a moment, nodding. 'I've been over there myself – Eastern Europe. Interesting part of the world. You ever been?'

'No, sir, I haven't.'

'Of course. Too busy building a career, I suppose. I've read your training program assessments. Most impressive, by the way.' He turned and gave her another warm smile. 'So how are you getting on with all the terminology and code names? Watchman, for example; heck of a label to work with, don't you think, when talking to a live human being? What's his real name?'

Lindsay shook her head. 'I don't know it, sir. I haven't spoken to him yet. And I guess it would be against regulations to ask. Sorry.'

'Really?' Benson looked doubtful, and something dark flickered deep in his eyes. 'I find that hard to believe. It's pretty unusual for people working together, one relying on the other, especially in such stressful circumstances, not to ask a simple question.'

She hesitated for a moment, then decided the truth was best, even if expressing an opinion. 'I guess if he asked, I'd tell him. My first name, anyway.'

'Of course. But wouldn't that also be against regulations?'

She shrugged. 'He's a colleague, sir. It might be the right thing to do, depending on circumstances.' She swallowed hard as she realized that this could count against her when Benson got back upstairs. She sensed an instinctive distrust of this man, influential though he undoubtedly was, and felt a burning desire to get him out of this room as quickly as possible. She couldn't tell why she felt this way, only that she knew he was trying to intimidate her into talking about what she was doing.

'But he's not really one of us, is he?' Benson rocked back and forth on his heels, eyes on the far wall, his tone almost disinterested. 'He's a contractor – although I suppose you knew that.'

'No, sir. I didn't.' Lindsay decided to play dumb. She wondered why he was talking like this and asking these questions. Was it some kind of internal test, to see if she would talk about what she was doing within seconds of meeting a complete stranger? If so, it seemed a very high-powered way of going about it.

'Really? Well, I guess not. He must have an interesting background, to be doing this job, don't you think?'

'I . . . I don't know, sir. I haven't seen his profile. You would have to ask Staff Operations Officer Callahan about that, sir.'

'Callahan.' His voice turned cool and soft, and she felt sure the temperature in the room dropped a little. 'Yes, of course. We've met. I'm sure he'll tell me.'

'Yes, sir. I mean . . . I don't mean to be obstructive, sir. It's outside my pay grade.'

'Of course it is.' He smiled and leaned towards her, his aftershave suddenly close and pungent, followed by a scent of warm peppermint on his breath. 'But not mine.' The expression in his eyes and the sudden change of mood was almost malevolent, and Lindsay forced herself not to place her hands on his chest and push him away. 'Understand me?'

Lindsay said nothing. Her throat was dry and she was suddenly too aware of the threat this man was making, with absolutely no fear of her objecting or arguing back.

'I carry a lot of influence around here, Lindsay,' Benson continued, his voice almost a whisper. 'I've been in on more secrets than most people could even dream of knowing and I have friends in the highest places, even and especially the large white building down the street. You know the one?'

'Yes, sir. That's . . . impressive, sir.'

'Influence usually is. Believe me, in the right hands it has its uses.' He waved a hand at the room they were in. 'For example, I could have this facility and everyone in it closed down by noon tomorrow if I chose; I have that much influence. All I need to do is make a single phone call and I could have you – where do you hail from, Lindsay?'

'North Carolina, sir.'

'I could have you back in North Carolina checking licence plates for the rest of your days. But I'm sure you wouldn't want that, would you?'

'No, sir.' She heard footsteps approaching and prayed that it was Sewell, or better still, Brian Callahan. She was finding it hard to breath under this sudden assault on her senses and was closer to panic than she'd ever thought she could be.

'Good. So, no need to mention our little chat, then.' With that he turned and walked out just as Brian Callahan appeared, looking puzzled.

'Is there a problem?' he queried, before Lindsay could turn away. 'What was he doing here?'

'No problem, sir.' She hesitated, aware that he must have noticed something in her face. She felt sickened at the realization that she had just been bullied and threatened by a US senator, and wasn't sure what to do or say. 'Sorry – his cologne . . . it was a little too much in this room and made me feel queasy.'

'Oh. OK. If that's all.' He looked at the darkened monitors. 'He shouldn't have been here alone, anyway. Looks like you switched everything off, though, so well done.'

'Thank you. He was . . . he was asking about Watchman.'

Callahan lifted an eyebrow and looked mildly annoyed. He was silent for a moment, then said, 'I bet he was. Any news from our man?'

'Not yet, sir.'

TEN

Senator Benson waited until he was well away from the encompassing aura of Langley before checking the courtesy window between himself and the driver was closed and dialling a number from memory. It rang three times before being answered in a clipped voice.

'Two-One. Go ahead.'

'I want a trace on a CIA Staff Ops Officer named Brian Callahan. Get me his movements over the past three weeks. Where he went, who he saw – everything.'

'Will do. Anything specific I should look for?'

'Yes. Sometime over the past few days he met with a non-agency asset – a freelance gun. Callahan's Langley-based, so he must have travelled outside to find him. This wouldn't have been done on the phone. I want anything you can get on the people he met.'

'Sure. Shouldn't take too long.' The man sounded assured and relaxed. Professional. 'Anything else?'

'Yes.' Benson was thinking about the young woman trainee assigned to be Watchman's comms support. She might prove a weak link he could exploit if necessary. He had no hesitation about ruining a promising career if the situation demanded, and if she complained, it would be her word against his, no contest. 'Build me a file on a Lindsay Citera. That's C-I-T-E-R-A. She's on the trainee program at Langley and comes from North Carolina. If there's dirt, I want it.'

He disconnected and made another brief call. This time he left a voicemail message on a multi-user subscriber number which initiated an automatic alert to everyone on the group list. 'The State Department has asked Langley to mount a rescue operation on their man Travis. I believe this could be a situation we can use. We need to meet right away.'

He switched off his cellphone and told his driver where to go, and sat back to think about what to do next. Howard J. Benson had two interests in his life. The first was to be seen to grow and protect the involvement and budgets of the US intelligence agencies in the ever-increasing threats to the country from terrorism and the twin evils of Moscow and Beijing. That interest did not necessarily include the CIA, for which he harboured a deep loathing for its cavalier and blatant disregard of conventions. To his mind they were a bunch of modern-day pirates who had done whatever the hell they liked in the name of America for far too long. News of this latest jaunt to recruit a freelancer to rescue a man in the field did nothing to change that viewpoint and he was already mentally composing his next report which would be severely critical of the Agency's actions.

However, his reason for calling this latest meeting via the subscriber service was entirely different and served his other main interest, which was neither benign nor patriotic. It was to ensure that he and a small group of friends prospered from whatever was about to blow up in Eastern Europe.

All he had to figure out was the best way to go about accomplishing both aims.

ELEVEN

Callahan's briefing update just before I left for Donetsk had told me that Travis had been moved out of a hotel in the city centre to one at the airport. He had no information on why, but the general guesswork was that it was for his safety while the group holding him figured out what to do with him. His new location had a history of being used as a transit hub for officials and military officers coming in and out of the region, but was now thought to have few if any genuine paying guests.

I arrived back at the airport and located the building. It was situated a few minutes from the main visitor and transit areas, along a side road linked to the main approach road. It easily fitted the picture of being government-run, as it lacked the glitz and glitter of most commercial hotels and wore a slightly tired air. It hadn't been painted anytime recently, and a large chain looped across the entrance to the car park made it clear that the place was not open for business. Most of the rooms were in darkness, so I figured Callahan's information had been correct.

The roads in the area were busy, with a heavy presence of uniforms and military vehicles. But if there was any coordination of movement going on, it didn't look obvious. Every man was armed and looked alert and it didn't take much imagination to see that they were a hair trigger away from going on the offensive if they saw something they didn't like.

I left the Toyota in a nearby cargo lot and walked back to the hotel where Travis was being held. I had my bag in my hand as cover; if I got stopped and searched, I was looking for somewhere to put my head down before heading into the city.

I saw the first of the guards as I walked past the entrance. He was standing beneath a large wooden panel bearing a schematic of the hotel's facilities and topped by a line of weather-worn international flags. He was dressed in a combat jacket and jeans and had an AK-74 assault rifle looped over one shoulder. He looked bored and cold, and I kept my head down and avoided eye contact. Even in the reflected light from the street lamps I was close enough to

see that the rifle looked clean and well cared-for. I spotted another
man fifty yards further on, similarly dressed and tucked into a line
of bushes by the side of the building. He was holding a Bison-2
submachine gun and, like his colleague, although not dressed in full
uniform, had the air of a more professional soldier than some of
the others I'd seen.

I circled the block and counted four other guards. They were in
a variety of pseudo combat uniforms, but all were holding clean
weapons and looked ready for war. A UAZ Russian military jeep
was in the rear car park, a clear signal to anyone who cared to look
that this situation was far from ordinary and casual visitors would
not be welcome.

I left them to it. There was nothing I could do now until I got
word to Callahan and the ball was set in motion for Travis to take
a walk. Once that happened I wasn't going to get much sleep. I
retrieved the Toyota and drove away from the airport, threading my
way carefully through a choke-point of military vehicles and troops,
all waiting for something to break out.

I was mentally composing my call to Langley when I saw a line
of lights ahead and several vehicles surrounded by armed men.

Roadblock.

It was too late to turn back and there were no side turnings I could
use. On each side of this stretch of blacktop was open land dotted
with clumps of darkness which I took to be trees. Beyond that –
way beyond it – I could see the flicker of lights from streets and
buildings. If all else failed I could abandon the car and hope none
of the troops felt like chasing after me in the dark. But I had no
way of telling if the space in between would give me a clear run
or I'd find my way blocked by a river, canal or rail line.

I decided I'd have to bluff it out. I knew the submachine gun
was safe unless the car was given a serious going-over, so I slowed
down and joined the short queue of other vehicles.

If the soldiers manning the roadblock had any point to the exercise, they weren't making it obvious. In the lights from the vehicles,
the ones at the side of the road looked sullen and bored, smoking
cigarettes and flicking the butts into the air, while the ones doing
the checking were taking their sweet time, scanning papers and
asking lots of questions.

One man in particular seemed to be enjoying playing the role of a heavy, waving an AK in the air and walking around the cars and staring intimidatingly at the occupants. He looked unsteady on his feet and it was easy to see he'd been drinking.

I inched forward until it was my turn, keeping one eye on the drunk and hoping the safety on his rifle was in the 'on' position. None of these guys looked like Ukrainian regulars, and I wondered which faction they were from. All I knew for sure was, they had to be pro-Russian and pro-breakaway.

'Papers,' said the drunk, stepping forward and planting the end of his gun barrel on the edge of the car window. He had a tag with the name 'Rambo' stitched above his breast pocket, and close up I could smell a combination of alcohol, body odour and stale fried food. He wore a combat jacket like his colleagues, but the T-shirt underneath had a non-military logo across the front.

I kept my cool and handed over my papers.

He thumbed through them although I don't think he took much in until he noticed where I was from.

'You're a German? Christ, I hate Germans. What the fuck are you doing here in our city, Heinrich? You're a long way from home, you know that?' He lifted the gun barrel and placed the tip against my cheekbone and grinned, showing a line of bad teeth. 'This is a war zone, Heinrich. Although you Germans are used to war zones, aren't you?' He blinked suddenly as a thought occurred to him. 'Hey – are you a spy sent to see what's going on here – is that it, huh?' He prodded my cheek with the gun barrel. 'A filthy German spy come to shoot us in the back?'

Heinrich wasn't the name on the papers, so I figured it was what he called all Germans.

'I'm a maintenance worker,' I told him, and looked past him for his colleagues, but they were all standing in a group a few yards away, letting him get on with it. A glance in the wing mirror showed me that I was the only vehicle left. For a moment I debated hitting reverse and getting out of here, but there was enough fire-power right here to stop me before I'd gone fifty yards.

'Perhaps I should shoot you now and be done with it,' Rambo muttered. 'I mean, save a lot of trouble later, wouldn't it? And who the fuck would miss you, eh? You got a wife and kids, Heinrich? Or do you play the other side of the fence?'

I didn't say anything. It was obvious what he was doing: he was ramping himself up right in front of me, just looking for an excuse to use his gun. It was nothing personal in spite of the 'Heinrich' digs; I'd simply happened along at the wrong moment and had become the focus of whatever was bugging him. I'd seen the same kind of behaviour at roadblocks in trouble spots around the world, and it was always the same: a hyped-up man with a gun and an attitude looking for someone to push around. It gets a lot of people killed for no good reason. All it would take was a wrong word and he'd lose it completely.

'Get out.'

'Sorry?'

'I said, get out.' He yanked the door open and put the rifle back in my face. 'Get out right now or I'll blow your miserable German head off.'

I did as he said, moving very carefully. The last thing I wanted was to give him an excuse to start blazing away with the AK. As I stood up, I was close enough to him to have taken his rifle away and shot him; but his colleagues were too close and there were too many of them.

'Pick them up,' he said, and threw my papers on the ground. 'Fucking littering – that's an offence in our country.'

I bent down to do as he said, and risked a call to his colleagues. 'Hey – you want to help me, here? I haven't done anything wrong – I'm just here looking for wo—'

'Did I say you could talk?' Rambo shouted, and kneed me in the ribs. 'Keep your mouth shut, you hear me? Now, empty your car.'

'What do you want him to do that for?' one of the other men called to him. 'Come on, let's go eat. Let the poor bastard go.'

But Rambo was beyond listening. His breathing rate had increased and in the reflected light from the car I could see he was sweating profusely. Whatever he'd been drinking had finally tipped him over the edge. He waved the others away. 'Piss off you lot. I haven't finished talking to this pig-sticker. I'll catch you up when I've dealt with him.'

I watched as my last hope of intervention shuffled away and climbed into a small truck, and drove off with a few backwards shouts to their colleague. If they had any idea what he was about to do, it didn't seem to worry them as much as getting some food inside them.

He watched them go, then reached into his combat jacket and took out a bottle. 'Hey – tell you what, since we're such good friends, how about a drink? Well, I'll drink and you stand and watch. That's fair, isn't it? We're just getting to be good friends, aren't we, you liverwurst-eating scum?' He shook the bottle to see how much was left, adding, 'After that we'll see what you've got hidden in your car, shall we?'

I looked around. We were almost in darkness, other than the lights from inside the car, and as far as I could see we were not overlooked. But Rambo had developed a drunk's heightened sense of caution and was staying beyond my reach, the rifle pointed at my chest.

He took the lid off his bottle and tilted it up for a long drink. I waited for him to finish, wondering what I could do to get him thinking about something he could gain from me rather than simply shooting me. Whatever it was, it had to be something he'd want badly enough.

'It's in the back,' I said.

'What?' He blinked and wiped his mouth on his sleeve, spilling some of the booze. 'What is?'

'I have a box in the back. It's where I keep my stuff.'

'What kind of stuff?'

'A couple of bottles of vodka and some cash. Let me go and you can have it all.'

He looked at me and shook his head. 'Are you trying to trick me? You think I'm stupid, is that it? Why didn't you tell me this before?'

'Because I didn't think you'd want to share it with your mates.' I waved down the road after them. 'I mean, they've gone off and left you. What kind of friends are they?'

He looked into the darkness and considered that for a moment, rocking slightly on his heels. 'Hey – good point. Cheap bastards, the lot of them.' Then he pointed to the back of the car. 'Right. Get it. Get the money and the vodka. But don't try anything, you understand?'

I stepped round to the back holding my hands out to the side and opened the rear door. I had no idea what was in the back, only that I had to draw him in closer than he was now standing. The interior light came on, showing me a spare tyre and a square of filthy plastic. The rest of the space was as empty as Rambo's brain. Damn. Where's a handy tyre iron when you need one?

'It's here – look.' I lifted the plastic sheet. 'Under here.'

He stepped closer, breathing alcohol over me and dropping the tip of the rifle barrel so he could lean in and peer down at the floor.

I flicked the plastic sheet in his face. To a drunk, it was enough to confuse him for a split second. Then I reached up and grabbed the front of his jacket and pulled him past me as hard as I could. His head met the rim of the Toyota's roof with a sharp bang and he grunted, but it didn't seem to have much of an effect. He didn't even drop the bottle. So I did it again, this time following it up with a hard punch to his belly and a kick to the side of his knee.

He yelled in agony as the bones gave way, and fell sideways, the bottle skidding out of his hand. He tried to bring the gun round, so I tore it off him and threw it into the bushes at the side of the road. Gunshots right now would carry too far, and there was too much risk of his colleagues coming back to investigate.

I picked up the bottle and found it was still half full. So I tugged Rambo cussing and swearing to the verge and lay him down, then stuck the bottle into his mouth and made him swallow. He didn't like it at first, but after a few seconds his instincts took over and he gurgled away like a baby as the spirit poured down his throat.

By the time I stepped away from him, he was almost unconscious.

I got back in the car and drove away. With a bit of luck his friends would find him and figure he'd overdone the drink after letting me go.

TWELVE

I drove out into the suburbs until I found a small hotel that accepted cash and asked no questions. I'd given up on the other place, and I doubted they'd miss me until morning. Once I'd tucked the car away out of sight at the rear and was in my room, I made my first call to Langley.

The woman who answered had a soft voice, professionally calm and clear, and I got the impression of someone youngish, brown-haired and serious. I tend to paint pictures of people I can't see. Every once in a while I get it right.

I told her my call-sign and she said to go ahead. No surprise, no questions about timing or asking for a repeat. Businesslike.

I kept it short. 'I'm in place and mobile. Tell Callahan the area's too hot with military to be able to keep a constant eyeball on the location, so I'm having to stay back until I get the word to go.'

'Understood, Watchman. I'm sending you a list of encrypted addresses. Callahan says you'll know what they are, am I correct?'

'Yes.' They were the addresses for the cut-outs handling Travis's journey out of the country. It must have taken some persuasive arguments to allow that kind of sensitive information out of the building, but I guess Callahan knew I'd need to check the areas out before Travis reached them.

'Good luck. We'll be in touch.'

I signed off and dialled another number. This one was to an unlisted Berlin phone.

It took twelve rings before Max picked up. He sounded cautious, but I wasn't surprised; the kind of people he dealt with, he had to be sure he wasn't being set up in a sting by the cops looking to find evidence of dealing in stolen goods and illegal arms. But this sounded ultra-careful, even for him.

I told him my name and heard an intake of breath. Then the words came out in a rush. 'Mr Portman, what can I do for you? The exchange was good, I hope?' He was trying to sound breezy but it didn't work.

'You know damn well it wasn't, Max. What's the deal with Ivkanoy?'

'What do you mean, Mr Portman?' He was trying to sound normal but his voice slipped off the scale and I knew something was wrong. For a Berlin wheeler-dealer, Max could lie about as well as I play the harpsichord. I was sometimes amazed he managed to stay in business, but maybe everybody knew he only ever told the truth.

'You're a lousy kidder, Max. If you don't tell me about Ivkanoy, I'm going to come right over there and rip your tongue out.'

Over-dramatic, sure. But with some people it's the only method that works. And Max hates the idea of violence.

'Seriously, Mr Portman, I am saying the truth. It was not a thing I knew.' He was babbling, and when he babbles, his English goes to shit. Same when he lies.

'It was a simple enough transaction, Max. A car and an extra, for cash. We've done it before, you and I, and you've arranged other deals like this in your sleep.'

'Yes, I know—'

'Only Ivkanoy wasn't ready to play. He tried to rip me off. Why was that?'

'Please, Mr Portman. I can only apologize. I was not to know this.' He was rattled, the words tumbling out of his mouth in their haste to escape. 'I was given his name as a reliable supplier of . . . services. The kind you, as you have said, are asking me to arrange before. But this man, this Ivkanoy, he is not what I believed. He is . . .' He hesitated, gasping for air and a decent explanation that would get him off the hook.

'He's what?'

'He is a cousin of a man in Volgograd. A leading businessman. I swear on my mother's life I did not know Ivkanoy would do this to you.'

A businessman. In Volgograd. What Max really meant was Ivkanoy's cousin was a member of the Russian mob, which by association, family ties and plain criminality in their blood, made Ivkanoy one, too.

I should have guessed. Volgograd, formerly called Stalingrad, lies across the border in southern Russia, and the connections with eastern Ukraine run deep and deadly. And the Russian mob has never been good on borders.

I took a deep breath. Max should have known, if he'd done his homework properly. The people I deal with, the suppliers of the kind of material I use from time to time, like Max, are always freelancers.

There are two reasons for this: a supplier with ordinary gang affiliations is too restricted, even unimaginative and unlikely to venture far from the home nest. It means they'll take the easiest route, the cheapest and least reliable. They also don't care about repeat business so they rarely stick to an agreement. If anybody complains, they can always call in a favour for a couple of heavies to provide backup.

But tie that supplier to the Ukrainian or Russian mob and that's a whole different level of no-go in my book. I was surprised Max hadn't worked it out; or maybe he'd got caught into trying to cut deals using the mob to further some other business interest he had on the go.

It explained a lot about Ivkanoy's attitude. To him I was just a mark passing through his territory, to be fleeced and disposed of, my travel documents and anything else he could use to be sold on in the city. He'd have known that anyone wanting to hire an untraceable vehicle and a weapon, cash down with no questions, would be in no position to complain to the authorities if they didn't get the deal they expected. And in the worsening atmosphere that had taken over the region, with more guns and guys keen to use them per square mile than anywhere outside of the Middle East, he'd reasoned that there was no chance of anything coming back on him if I simply disappeared.

'How bad is this, Max? What's the likely fall-out?'

'Huh?'

'Don't play dumb. You're already scared, I can hear it in your voice. How deep in with them are you?'

He coughed. 'Scared, yes. Of course I'm scared. You know me, Mr Portman. I do not get into bed with such extreme people normally. Never. But I was made an offer I could not refuse . . . as also were others in the same business here in Berlin and Munich.'

'So it's a takeover.'

'I believe, yes. Two who refused have gone, disappeared. Now since I hear what you have done to him, I am hearing that Ivkanoy is blaming me! He says I must pay restitution for the damage and the car. I have tried to refuse but two times now I am having telephone calls with nobody speaking. Just breathing.'

I felt almost sorry for him. He was in a low-end business where most of his suppliers were crooks, gang-bangers and thieves, not hard-core mafia. On the outgoing side he had clients like me who

were selective about their sources of supply. It was a difficult place
to be. And now the Russian mob were muscling in and dictating
how and with whom he did business, and threatening to break legs
or worse if he didn't play ball.

'What else have you heard, Max?'

'That you have hurt him . . . that you have harmed his reputation.
That you stole a car and you make him look foolish.'

'He tried to screw me, Max. It was a set-up. He was ready to
beat my brains out.'

'I am sorry. Really.' He hesitated, then added, 'I believe he will
come for me soon. For this reason I am leaving town. It is too
dangerous to stay, even here.'

He was right to worry. The Russian mob's reach wasn't confined
to within its borders, but worldwide. And Berlin was right on their
doorstep. Getting someone to pay Max a visit would take a simple
phone call. I was surprised the heavy breathing hadn't escalated to
something more deliberate already.

'I am sorry, Mr Portman. This Ivkanoy will not stop. Others of
his kind will know what happened, and he will follow you until his
honour is satisfied. Until you are dead.'

THIRTEEN

I woke early the following morning and ran a visual check of the outside of the hotel in case Rambo and his friends or Ivkanoy had got lucky and found the car. But the area looked quiet and deserted, and if either of them had been around, I doubted they would have waited for me to show myself; they'd have come in hard and fast and gone on the attack.

Sleep had been elusive but I was rested and ready to go as soon as I got the call from Langley. Anyone experienced in action knows that sleep is a luxury rarely enjoyed to the full; there's too much tension, too much adrenalin and sometimes too much of everything but peace and quiet. But occasionally there's silence, which is worse. It leaves you wondering about what's going to happen, with nothing to focus on but your innermost thoughts and fears, until sleep finally claims you.

Every person deals with it in his or her own way. I rely on breathing exercises to reduce my heart rate. It sounds more mystical than it is, but was a technique I picked up in West Africa from a Vietnamese Foreign Legion corporal. It's cheaper than drugs, easier than drink and healthier than both.

While I waited in my room I checked out the list of addresses the Langley comms support officer had messaged to me. There were five in all, in various cities across the country, including Kiev. The nearest was here in Donetsk. I was hoping I wouldn't have to use them, but that might not be my choice to make. Given the choice I would have Travis in the car and be driving west as fast as I could.

Thinking about the car, I went outside and checked the Toyota was in one piece. In the cold light of day the red colour was an eyesore. But at least the dark last night would have made the colour less likely to be remembered by Rambo and his pals. In any case, there wasn't much I could do about it right now. Hopefully if everything went to plan I wouldn't be in the Donetsk area for long, anyway.

News reports on the television showed the political situation locally was deteriorating further, with uniformed militia sympathetic to Moscow openly parading their numbers and armaments on the streets, and several clashes around the city outskirts with Ukrainian army units. Further east a helicopter had been shot down and a number of pro-Russian separatists had been killed, but the figures were unverified. As usual, it was the claim and counter-claim culture of all armed conflicts, where mind-games aimed at the world's media were almost as vital as ground gained or lost in combat.

I decided to take a trip back out to the airport. If anything kicked off, I might have very little time to get close enough to Travis to watch his back.

The roads were uneasily quiet and traffic-free, save for the usual military vehicles, and when I got close I found the area around the hotel was a mess, with trucks and APCs parked up wherever there was room and troops standing around in bunches, smoking and watching a couple of planes taxiing out ready for take-off. More worryingly, as I cruised along the perimeter road, I noticed four trucks with blanked-out markings parked in a deserted lot in front of a hanger. About a dozen men were standing close together and on the alert, overseen by an officer.

I recognized the type as soon as I saw them: they were Spetsnaz, Russian special forces often attached to the FSB (Federal Security Service) or the GRU (Military Intelligence).

The air close to the hotel was choked with diesel fumes, with a thick layer of sooty-grey exhaust smoke hanging close to the ground. Aside from the trucks, it was strangely quiet for an international airport, and I wondered how much longer it could continue to operate with the current unrest before the authorities decided to close it down altogether.

I was circling the airport and trying to keep a low profile when my cell phone buzzed. It was Callahan.

'The situation's changed,' he said. 'Our local cut-out in Donetsk has gone silent. Without him we can't get a message to Travis and Travis isn't answering his phone. We may have to delay things. How's it looking on the ground?'

'Forget it,' I told him. 'If you want your man out, it has to be now.' I described the build-up of troops and militia, which added to what he knew already from satellite over-flights and news reports. But what satellites can't do is to give a sense of the tension around a conflict zone, that electricity that crackles in the air during the build-up to something momentous happening. And right now I was feeling that electricity like a live force. 'This place feels like it's going to blow any minute. And Travis is stuck right in the middle.'

'If that's your assessment, I understand. Do you know who's holding him?'

'Not yet. But he's not in the hands of the good guys, I'm pretty sure of that. The longer he stays here, the more likely he is to get sent further east.' Even though Travis was here under a cover name, Callahan had said it was highly likely people knew he was connected to the US, British or European governments. If it came out that he was from the US State Department his situation would be even more delicate than it already was. In fact I was surprised it hadn't already been made public by one side or the other for propaganda purposes.

Callahan agreed. It was a definite problem. Then came the kicker.

'Can you get to him?'

It was a moot point. From what I'd seen of the guards, there was no way into the building without running a gauntlet of security checks and questions. In a normal busy hotel, I would have simply walked in and booked a room. But so far I hadn't seen anyone enter or leave, so normal was out of the question.

'I'll try.' It was the best I could say. It was as risky as hell, but it was what I was there for – to take risks.

'Good man. Did you get the cut-out addresses? You might need to check the first one yourself and see what the situation is there.'

I signed off and thought it through. If I got to Travis, I'd have to hope I could get him out of the building and away without being stopped. After that I would be playing it by ear and relying on speed and luck. I'd already decided that we'd have to head west, away from the trouble spots where we could be stopped at any time by random vehicle checks. That included not going anywhere near Kiev, the capital. But that left a lot of territory in between here and the border with Moldova. My best bet was to plug Travis into the cut-out line as quickly as possible. At least they could move him with far more detailed knowledge of the terrain than I had, and I'd be able to focus on watching over them to make sure he stayed out of trouble.

I approached the airport again and found even more trucks had arrived, choking off the roads by parking wherever they pleased. Staying with the car was too risky, so I left it near some old main-tenance sheds and made my way on foot towards the hotel. I left my bag in the car and trusted to luck in openness and innocence; if anyone stopped me, they'd see that I wasn't a threat.

I reached the front entrance and saw one of the four blanked-out trucks I'd spotted earlier was now in front of the main doors, with at least a dozen fully armed soldiers in the back. The guards I'd seen earlier were watching them, but they looked nervous and didn't seem as if they wanted to tell them to go park somewhere else.

I veered off and walked round to a yard at the rear of the building, where there was a loading bay with a closed roller shutter and a clutch of rubbish skips. The sound of splashing was echoing around the yard, and I looked up to see a stream of water spewing from a broken pipe on the fourth floor.

A uniformed guard with an AK-74 slung across his chest stepped out from beneath a tree and told me to get lost, that the building was off-limits. He was big and unshaven and I guessed he'd been here all night and was feeling hostile.

'I'm looking for work,' I told him. 'This is a hotel. I've worked in lots of hotels.'

'Big deal.' He nodded back towards the front of the building and the road beyond. 'Leave, now.'

Just then a picket gate to one side of the loading bay clanged open and a chubby man in a creased shirt and tie emerged and stood staring up at the overflow, which was gradually turning his loading bay into a swimming pool. He swore loudly and glared at the guard as if it were his fault. Which, as it turned out, by association, it was.

'How can I operate when my staff can't get to work?' he yelled in frustration. I guessed he was the manager and was clearly too mad to be intimidated by the sight of the gun, and happy to vent his anger on the only military representative he could see close by. 'I need my maintenance engineer here right now.'

'Not my decision,' the soldier replied. 'Ring those in charge.'

He might as well have told him to ring someone who cared. The manager looked ready to have a fit. 'Huh? Who do I ring, smart-arse? You think there's a directory I can pick up and find out who's responsible for stopping public transport? Is there a person I can shout at for bringing this entire city to a standstill?' He waved a hand which told the soldier what he thought of the whole shooting match and turned to go back inside.

'I could fix it,' I said.

He turned back. 'Who the hell are you?'

The soldier decided to help calm the situation and get the manager off his back. 'He's a hotel worker,' he said, 'looking for work.'

The manager hurried towards us and peered at me, checking my clothing and making an instant assessment. 'Is that so? What sort of work? Don't say waiter – I've got waiters coming out of my arse.'

'Maintenance, electrical, repairs – whatever,' I said. 'I don't have any tools, though. I wasn't allowed to bring them with me.'

'Of course you weren't; with all the military might standing around here, think of the damage you could do with a screwdriver and a wrench!' His angry sarcasm was wasted on the guard, who merely shrugged and picked at his teeth. 'We've got tools. Plenty of tools.' He looked at the guard. 'I'm allowing him in. You OK with that or do I have to ring Moscow and speak to the judo player?'

If the guard minded the reference to Putin, he didn't let on. 'Do whatever you want. I'm off duty shortly, anyway. Not my problem.'

The manager grabbed my arm. 'Have you eaten this morning? I bet you haven't. You fix that damned overflow and I'll send you to the kitchen and you can have a meal. At least we still have some food. How's that? Then we'll see what we can do about keeping you on for a few days to sort out some other problems.' He hustled away through the side door, beckoning me after him and slamming the door behind us.

I was in.

FOURTEEN

The manager's name was Yuriy and if he didn't slow down he was heading for a seizure. He didn't ask to see any papers but marched me down a flight of concrete stairs to the basement where there was the usual mishmash of equipment, stores and furniture awaiting repair. It smelled of damp and the drip-drip of water was echoing along the corridor.

'That bloody pipe's causing me serious problems,' he muttered, gesturing at a growing pool of water on the floor. It looked fresh, without any covering of dust, and I guessed it was finding its way through the fabric of the building from the outside. 'You need to stop it quickly. Can you do that?'

'Of course. I'll turn off the water supply and fix the pipe. It shouldn't take long. Where are the stopcocks?'

He waved me towards the far end of the corridor. 'I believe the controls are all down there. But you can't turn them all off.'

'Why not?'

'Because it would screw up the heating. There are important people staying here.' He made rabbits' ears at the word 'important' and pulled a face to show his disgust. 'They'll have my balls if they can't have their little luxuries. Try and find a way round it, can you? Isolate that damned water pipe.' He checked his watch. 'Look, I'll have to leave you to it. Just do what you can. The tools are in a room down the end.'

I watched him go and checked for security cameras. There were none that I could see, but I made a show of grabbing a toolbox from the workshop just in case and made my way up the back stairs towards the fourth floor where I'd seen the broken pipe.

The layout on each floor was the standard design of a hotel: stairs and elevator, lobby and fire doors leading to a corridor running the length of the building with rooms on either side, with emergency stairs down the back. I checked each level through the glass panel in the doors but couldn't see anyone. In spite of the manager's comment about VIPs staying here, the place looked and felt deserted. I chanced a stroll down the corridor on the second floor and found no sign of occupation save for a couple of locked doors near the elevators.

It was on the third floor where things were slightly different.

I peered through the panel and saw an armed guard on the other side, standing about five doors down. Another guard was at the far end of the corridor, blocking entry from the other stairs and the elevator. Both men looked bored but wide awake.

I ducked back and went up another flight. No guard and an empty feeling in the air. Now I knew where Travis was being held.

I got on with finding the broken pipe while mulling over tactics in my head. I was in luck; it was located in a washroom at the end of the building, and I tracked it back to a stopcock in an inspection panel and turned it off. In spite of what I'd told Yuriy, I had a barely rudimentary knowledge of water systems, and had no idea if the stopcock would interfere with the rest of the building's water supply or not. If it did, I had only a short time to locate Travis and get him moving before Yuriy and a bunch of angry VIPs came looking for my scalp.

I went down to the third floor and pushed through the door to the corridor. It got an instantaneous reaction from the nearest guard, who swivelled like he was on ball bearings and pointed his rifle at me.

'No entry!' he shouted. 'What are you doing here?'

'I'm the maintenance engineer,' I told him, and made a show of putting down the toolbox and raising my hands. Over his shoulder I saw the other guard unslinging his rifle and walking towards us. 'There's a bad leak on the floor above. I need to turn off all the taps on this floor so I can isolate it.'

'There's nobody on this floor,' he said, the gun dipping away slightly. 'Try the other levels.'

'I've already done that. Someone must have left a tap or shower running up here,' I insisted. 'I can tell by the flow of water. I'll have to check the rooms – it won't take a minute.'

The other guard had opened his mouth to add his two cents' worth when he stopped and turned his head. He made a gesture for us to stop talking. The hum of an elevator was coming from the far end of the corridor.

'You must leave,' the first guard ordered, while his companion legged it back to his station. 'Come back later.' He prodded my toolbox with his boot. 'And take that with you.'

As I turned to leave, the elevator pinged and the other guard hurried to pull the door open.

Four men walked past him without even looking at him. Three were dressed in combat uniforms and armed with assault rifles, while the man in the lead was in a grey suit, white shirt and tie.

'Who is that man?' Grey Suit called out, looking at me. 'Get him off this floor.'

'He's building maintenance, sir,' the guard replied. 'There's a water leak.'

'I don't care if he's Mother Theresa. Get rid of him.'

As I was hustled through the door at the end, I turned to look back. The four men had stopped at the door where the nearest guard had been standing. Grey Suit nodded at one of his companions, who stepped forward and opened the door with a passkey and disappeared inside. Grey Suit followed, leaving the other two outside.

This wasn't looking good. If Travis was in the room, I had a feeling he wasn't going to stay here much longer.

FIFTEEN

E d Travis swung round from the window as the door to his room opened. He was aware of several people in the corridor, and wondered what was going to happen now. He'd become accustomed to the heavy tread of the guard pacing up and down outside, with occasional pauses to talk with a colleague. But other than that the silence within the building was clear evidence that the rest of this floor, maybe even the entire block, was unoccupied. The thought didn't fill him with confidence. Hotels with vacant floors were not a comforting sign, and those with a predominantly military presence were even more disturbing.

Since being stopped by a group of armed men in the street and told to get back to his hotel in the city centre, he'd had a feeling that his situation was coming unglued. The region around Donetsk was clearly on the edge of chaos, with troops and militia constantly on the move as if dancing around each other in a slow, deadly waltz. He had over-heard reports of gunfire and exchanges further east, and had seen palls of smoke and heard the occasional rattle of small arms, and the thumps of heavier weaponry further off. The growing knowledge that there were different groups in the area, nominally with the same pro-Moscow sympathies yet all armed and with their own differing agendas, merely added to the confusion and his own sense of vulnerability.

When another group of men had taken him from his hotel and brought him to the airport, he'd assumed that he was being ordered to leave the country. But that hope had been dashed by the confisca-tion of his money, passport and cell phone, and the open hostility of his guards, who he guessed by their haphazard dress and the variety of weapons, were not regular forces but militia.

Travis had served in the military, but none of what he had experi-enced or seen had prepared him adequately for this. His had been a peace-time role, somehow avoiding the various conflicts going on around the world in which the USA had seen fit to get involved. Seeing the sounds and fury of conflict up close was somehow more unnerving than he had ever imagined.

The door swung back and an armed man in combat uniform

stepped into the room and stood smartly to one side. This one had the appearance of a professional soldier, something Travis recognized immediately. He was followed by a man in a grey suit. He might have been a bureaucrat, but he had about him the aura of something darker. Travis had met security police of various nations in his time, and this newcomer had the same aura. He was over six feet tall, with a thin face and cold eyes, and his expression, the suit and the air of authority confirmed the impression of somebody accustomed to instilling fear and obedience in everyone he met.

'Why are you holding me here?' Travis demanded, determined to show anger at being treated like this. 'This is outrageous and unacceptable.' His throat was dry and he tried to put some steel in his voice, but the motors wouldn't work. He'd been warned during his briefing sessions at Langley about the possibility of being questioned at any time. The country was in turmoil and strangers were naturally treated with suspicion. There were various types of security in operation, some official, others less so. And not all were organs of the state – or, at least, the Ukrainian state. On the other hand, this might be some kind of elaborate robbery or con trick. He'd been warned about that, too. But this notion was cast aside when he heard more movement in the corridor and noticed two more men in uniform outside the door.

'You will come with us.' The man in the grey suit spoke calmly, ignoring Travis's protest. There was no threat in the voice, no look of menace, but the implication was clear: you will do what I say.

'Why?' Travis worked his tongue around his mouth to loosen the word. His gums tasted stale and acid, not helped by the sparse breakfast of rolls and coarse cheese that he had been served. 'This is not right. I'm here on official business and you have no right to hold me like this.' He shut his mouth, aware that he was gabbling and that this man looked as though he didn't give a damn.

He was right. But what the man said next was even more worrying. 'You are not here on official business, Mr Travis. You came here under the guise of a foreign non-governmental body with the intention of seeking representations with people opposed to the rule of law. Under Ukraine law that makes you a criminal by association.' His accent was heavy but he spoke without hesitation, as if his English was regularly used. 'Or would you prefer it if I accused you of being a spy? Is that what you are – an American spy?'

Travis tried to think, but his brain was sludgy with stress and lack of sleep. Criminal? A spy? What the hell? 'No! That's rubbish. I must protest. I want to speak to the American Embassy.'

The man didn't look impressed. 'Not possible. You either come downstairs with us,' he said coolly, 'or we throw you out of the window.' He shrugged as if it really didn't matter to him, and added, 'Faster but more painful. Your choice.'

The shock of the words was enough to get Travis's survival instincts kicking in. His fatigue drained away, leaving him at once clear-headed but somehow resigned. There was no point fighting; if these were security police, they would have backup nearby and be quite capable of carrying out their threat if he tried to resist. And who was going to stop them? He'd repeatedly tried the room phone, but that didn't work, and for all he knew the rest of the building was occupied by men similar to these. Better to go with them and live, than put up a pointless resistance and die with a broken neck.

Yet he was puzzled. He'd seen plenty of regular soldiers and police while he was moving around before being picked up; but he'd seen even more militiamen of one faction or another, and thought he could have identified them on sight. But these men were different; they dressed and moved like well-trained regulars, but the threat had been pure aggression with no obvious point other than to show superiority.

'What is it you want from me?'

'No questions. You will find out soon enough.'

'Where am I going?'

The man walked to the door and made a signal to the soldier to bring Travis. 'Well, it's not home, I can assure you of that.' He gave a ghost of a smile and left the room, leaving the others to follow.

As the soldier took his arm, Travis felt panic setting in. He even eyed the window as if it might offer a solution. An escape. Somehow he had to get a message back home. But how? Without his phone he was beyond reach. In any case, who would he ring? It would be pointless calling the State Department; they'd simply go into a flap and talk a whole bunch before opting to go through official channels. He'd be better getting through to the CIA spook named Callahan, in Langley. This was the State Department's plan, but Callahan was effectively running the nuts and bolts of the mission and would know what to do without calling a meeting about it first. But what could he do?

For the first time in his life, Ed Travis knew what it felt like to be utterly alone. And helpless.

SIXTEEN

I watched through the door panel as Grey Suit left the room and walked away down the corridor. He was followed by Travis, who was being hustled along by one of the soldiers, with the others falling in behind. Travis looked pale and uncomfortable, and it was clear he was apprehensive about what was going to happen to him.

The last two to leave were the corridor guards. They exchanged a look of confusion and shrugged, before trailing along in the wake of the others, their presence no longer required.

I gave it a few seconds and went into one of the rooms overlooking the front of the hotel. I flicked back a corner of the curtain and waited.

The road outside was busy with traffic, most of it military of one sort or another. A group of militiamen dressed in ill-fitting combat tops and boots, heavily armed and openly confrontational, was standing out in front of the building, watching what was going on and looking as if they wanted to defend their right to be there. I could feel the tension in the air from up here, and wondered how long this could continue before somebody squeezed a trigger and it all blew to hell.

It wasn't long before the four men and Travis walked out of the entrance and across to a military UAZ jeep. The militiamen turned and watched, but made no move to stop them. As they did so, the blanked-out truck I'd seen earlier started up, belching grey smoke from its exhaust, and the troops standing at the rear jumped aboard.

I hurried downstairs. I had to get to the car and follow them.

I walked out of the front entrance just as Grey Suit was giving instructions to a junior officer in the passenger seat of the truck.

Obluskva Street, 24d. Kyiv'ski District. Five minutes drive. Wait at the end of the street and don't go in until given the order.

I'd heard that kind of instruction before. They were planning a raid.

Obluskva. The name was familiar but I couldn't immediately figure out why. Was that where I'd picked up the Toyota? No. It had been too dark to see street signs. I let it go. Wherever these guys were going, I had to be there too. I had no clear plan in mind, but somehow I had to get Travis out of their hands.

I walked away with a silent apology to Yuriy and his staff problems, and hurried back to the car, where I fed the name of Obluskva into my cell phone and started the engine.

There was a bleep and I looked at the screen. The word Obluskva had come up showing a hyperlink to a document contained in the cell phone's system. I tapped the screen.

It brought up a cross-reference to one of the addresses from Langley.

It was the local CIA cut-out.

SEVENTEEN

had one advantage over Grey Suit and his men, and that was where I'd left the Toyota. It was just outside the growing snarl-up of traffic that was already bringing the airport to a standstill. I reached the exit road without a problem, and spotted the jeep and the blanked-out truck caught up in a mess of military vehicles, with soldiers and militiamen arguing over who had the right of way. If I was correct about the identity of the soldiers in the truck, the militiamen were in for a rough time if they pushed too hard.

I silently wished them a long and enjoyable stay and called up Langley.

'Go ahead, Watchman.' The woman's voice answered.

I said, 'Tell Callahan there are troops on the way to the Obluskva Street address in Donetsk. They look like special forces. They've got Travis with them.'

'Wait one.' There was a click and Callahan came on.

'I hear you. Go again?' He sounded calm but I could sense his tension all the way down the wire.

I told him what I'd seen and asked, 'Does Travis have the cut-out list?'

'What? No. He was told to wait until he was contacted. Why do you ask?'

'Because they're heading for the first address on the list.'

'It's a coincidence. It has to be.' But he didn't sound convinced. 'That's crazy . . . there's no way—' He stopped dead, then said, 'Stay on the line.'

He was gone two minutes, while I continued to head as fast as I dared for the Kyiv'ski District. If I could get there ahead of the troops, I might be able to give whoever was at 24d a warning to get out. Cut-outs, although part of a carefully built network, usually worked in isolation, known only by their handler. It was a matter of basic security: the less they each knew about others in the network, the less likely they were to give them away if they got picked up and questioned. But sometimes it was inevitable that one would come to learn the identity or location of another, by accident or instinct. If the person at 24d Obluskva was in that category, it would be a potential disaster for others along the line if he or she got picked up and grilled.

Callahan came back on. He sounded royally pissed. 'The State Department gave Travis the first address. Worse, they sent it by SMS in plain text. They had no right but they did it anyway. Seems they didn't have complete faith in us to keep him safe and wanted some control over what happened.'

I let it go by. The question of inter-agency jealousies and mistrust wasn't my problem. But the fact that they'd given out the address unencrypted showed a serious lack of judgement and lousy security. Handing over such a delicate piece of information to an untrained civilian in the first place was about the most dangerous thing they could have done. They might as well have broadcast it over *24 TV*, the Ukraine news channel.

Unless the address had been leaked by Travis himself somehow, then it must have been picked up and read by the authorities, who would have been sifting the airwaves for all communications from separatists and outside parties interested in the unfolding calamity. It wouldn't have taken long for somebody to have asked why a Donetsk address should suddenly pop up in a text message from outside the country.

'If they have one could they have the others?'

'No. We made sure of that. Each one will be given a rendezvous point where Travis is to be delivered along with a contact code and time, but that's it. The next in line will receive a message with that same RV and contact code, and will take over from there.'

It sounded a little vague to me, but I knew it had worked in the past. But when it came to protecting a network, any way of isolating individual members while having them come in contact with each other for an exchange was fraught with danger. 'So who does the messaging?'

'We do. As soon as we know the handover is imminent, we set the message in motion. Where are you right now?'

I gave him my location and where I was headed, but not what I was planning to do. The simple truth was I hadn't yet decided on that myself. I clicked off and concentrated on driving. I had a germ of an idea but putting it in action would all depend on circumstances and opportunity.

*   *   *

Starting a shooting war in a city street is not to be recommended. The potential for collateral damage – that anodyne term used by the military, politicians and media to mean innocent bystanders – is huge and real. Add to that the opposition – in this case a truckload of special forces with itchy fingers – and anything could happen.

But you can't always control these things.

I checked what I had in the way of armaments. It wasn't great. I had a small submachine gun, courtesy of the big guy with the pool cue. Set against a truckload of armed soldiers, it was little more than a peashooter. But peashooters don't come with an extended magazine of thirty-two 9mm shells. Somehow that fact didn't surprise me. The bigger magazine is popular among gang-bangers because it looks both cool and scary; even a lousy shot with his head high on booze, mescaline or whatever, merely has to point and pull the trigger and the full load will discharge in a few-second 'squirt'. The shots will go all over the scenery but that's half the joy for anyone using it; you're guaranteed to hit something, even if it's only a cow in the next county.

In short, it wasn't the best weapon for what I had in mind, but at least this one had a selector for firing single shots.

Obluskva was towards the east of the city close to the rail yards and bordered by an area of old industrial warehouses and factories blackened by years of smoke and the processing of metal. In the rail yard itself, the usual jungle of tracks, overhead wires and poles, stacks of storage containers huddled together, back-dropped by lines of freight cars of every description, with fuel tankers, gravel silos and piles of lumber waiting for shipment.

Through a haze in the distance stood the spectral outlines of three high-rise buildings, and I prayed that Number 24d Obluskva wasn't one of them. Finding and getting to a specific person in tall buildings is not something you can accomplish quickly. It needs a team to cover all the levels, the elevators don't always work and the network of stairways, familiar only to residents, are death traps for the unwary.

And for a single intruder, once in, there's no easy way out.

I was in luck. Before I got to the high-rises I hit a highway cutting through the district from north to south, and beyond it found a rambling series of potholed streets and tracks dotted with small single-level houses surrounded by scrappy fencing and untamed vegetation.

The car bottomed out with a crash of the muffler as I hit a dip in the surface and I slowed down. Having the suspension fall apart on me now would be a disaster. I checked the house numbers, one eye on the rear-view mirror in case the troops had managed to force their way out of the airport and were close on my tail.

Ramshackle fences seemed the norm, surrounding ancient wooden sheds with corrugated roofs, patches of untended, weed-infested ground, cars on blocks and all the detritus of an area left to moulder and die. It was a stark contrast; everywhere else I'd seen made Donetsk seem like a modern city, landscaped and pleasant with parks, lakes, wide roads and boulevards. Yet here was like a forgotten zone, where life could have been unchanged from a hundred years ago.

Number 24 was different. It was part of a long, two-storey apartment block, its flaking walls painted a deep yellow, with small balconies and a high wall at each end around what I guessed were communal gardens. The building stood out in more ways than mere size; it was an island of a different style of living, perhaps forgotten from some previous city plan long overtaken by the nearby highrises across the highway. I pulled up outside and hit the ground running, and went through the front door, which was unlocked. Each of the apartments had a letter suffixed to the street number. I found a, b and c but no 24d.

I banged on 24c. It took a while but eventually opened to reveal an elderly lady with wrinkled skin and white hair, blinking gnomishly at me through a narrow gap.

'What do you want?' She had a voice like dry paper rustling and smelled of vinegar.

'Twenty-four d,' I said to her. 'I have a delivery.'

She shook her head and began to close the door, so I put my foot in the way. 'Please. It's important.'

She stared at me for a moment and I wondered what I would have to do to get a break. Then she stuck a gnarled finger through the gap and pointed down the corridor at a blank door with a small glass pane at head height. 'See Yaroslav,' she muttered. 'Yaroslav.' Then she slammed the door on my foot with surprising force until I withdrew it.

I hoofed along to the blank door and knocked with authority. Whoever the hell Yaroslav was, and I was guessing he was the building superintendent, I hoped he had better social skills than the old biddy. If not, I was probably going to have to beat it out of him.

The man who came to the door was as fat as he was tall, and wore a battered beret with a greasy rim. He didn't look happy to see me, but I guessed that was his default position for callers.

'Yes?'

'I'm looking for twenty-four d,' I told him. 'Delivery.'

He looked immediately wary and his eyes went walkabout. 'There is no twenty-four d.' He started to close the door and I pushed it against his substantial belly until he gave way. The smell coming out of his apartment was ripe and nasty, and I figured he must have been boiling live chickens in there.

'There is no twenty-four d,' he hissed. 'Go away.'

'There is and if you don't tell me, I'll report you to the city authorities.' For good measure I flicked back my jacket to show the butt of the submachine gun. His eyes went walkabout again and his chin began to quiver. 'I don't mean twenty-four d any harm,' I added. 'I just need to speak to him.'

He nodded and pointed towards the back of the building. 'There's a narrow door at the end of the passage. No number. He's in there.'

I left him to his chickens and went in search of the narrow door. It looked little more than a cleaner's cupboard, but I was no architect. I pounded on the door hard enough to make the frame rattle, and hoped the neighbours wouldn't care to investigate and the resident inside would be too shocked to hear that he was about to be picked up by security troops to protest.

The door eventually swung open and a skeletal, academic type in glasses stood looking at me. His face was parchment coloured and an aura of sickness hung around him like a cloak. He was dressed in a worn dressing gown and slippers, and holding a bright yellow handkerchief to his nose, the veins in his wrist standing out like snakes.

'I don't know your name,' I told him, 'but you should know that the security forces know about your connection to Travis. They're on the way here right now. You've got to leave.'

He looked about as shocked as a man could do, and his face lost even more colour. I figured he'd been expecting this for some time but it was still a shock. Like anybody who lives a double life, you never know when discovery will come knocking at your door. He'd probably figured I was from the security police. 'Who are you? Why do you tell me this? I don't know a man called Travis.' His voice was throaty with cold, but cultured and precise, and I wondered if, when he wasn't being a cut-out for the CIA, he was a schoolteacher.

'Did I say Travis was a man?'

He looked as if he could have bitten his tongue and was probably praying I wasn't a member of the security police who'd just caught him out.

'You were asked to escort Travis from Donetsk to an address in Pavlohrad.' I spoke softly but fast, keeping up the pressure. We didn't have time to stand here playing word games. 'Once there you were to hand him over and he would be taken to another address further on. That's all you were told. Now, do you want to stay here to be arrested or not?'

That got to him. He made up his mind and backed away into what was really little more than a large cupboard with a curtain across a small bed, a small camping gas stove and a corner wash-basin. No wonder Yaroslav was reluctant to admit to his presence; Number 24d was a sub-tenant, undoubtedly here against building regulations, but a welcome back-pocket source of income as long as nobody spoiled the game.

While 24d did what he had to, I went back out and checked the street. This area was isolated from the buzz of the larger city, and other than a few birds in the trees dotting the neighbourhood and the distant sound of a piano playing upstairs, the silence was a relief. If the black hats arrived, I'd hear them coming.

I got back to hear Number 24d banging around in the depths of his tiny room for a few seconds, then he appeared dressed in plain pants and a jacket and carrying a small bag. He had developed a high colour and was breathing heavily from his exertions, and I hoped he was ready for what lay ahead. From now on in, his entire life was about to change dramatically.

'Is that all you have?' I asked.

'It is all I need,' he replied with great dignity. 'My life is very simple.'

And about to get a hell of a lot more complicated, I wanted to add. Instead I asked if he had somewhere to go and hustled him towards the stairs.

He nodded. 'I have friends who will help me. I have nothing to keep me here so maybe it's for the best.' He tried to smile but it didn't quite gel. Not surprising when a complete stranger arrives on your doorstep unannounced and turns your life upside down. 'I lost my job at the university,' he explained, 'and the money paid by your CIA was not enough to live on. So, I live here in this small box.' He shrugged philosophically. 'But we do what we have to in life, do we not?'

'Yes, we do. Will Yaroslav talk?'

He nodded sadly. 'Of course he will. He's a fat, miserable turd who feeds off the misfortune and sadness of others. I have no doubt he will have another person in there to replace me before the day is done. But don't worry – the authorities will not find me. The way things are going in this country, somehow I don't think I will be at the top of their list of people to deal with.' He smiled sadly. 'Ironic, is it not? Most of us spend our lives working to leave some small footprint, some memory of our passing in the vain hope that we as individuals were not entirely irrelevant. Yet here am I hoping that my footprint will be non-existent.' He waggled a set of car keys. 'Thank you for coming to warn me. I have my car nearby. I will complete what I was paid to do, but that will be all.'

'But I don't have Travis yet. You should go. Get away from here.'

He considered it for a moment in silence, his breathing harsh. We arrived at the front door, where he turned to me. 'But you are here to rescue him, are you not?'

'That's my job, yes.'

'Then we both have something to finish. Come to Vokzal'na Square directly west from here. It is not far. I will wait for one hour. If you do not come, I will have to assume you have not been successful.' He shrugged. 'I'm sorry.'

He walked away without waiting for a reply, towards whatever future awaited him yet still prepared to do what he'd been paid for. I could only admire his quiet courage.

I went back to the car and drove along the street, hooking a left at the end of the block then left again. I was now in a deserted back run behind the apartment block. On the other side was a large patch of communal vegetable gardens surrounded by sagging wire fencing and dotted with tiny sheds like matchboxes stood on their ends. Most of it looked neglected and weed-strewn, adding to what was already a desolate and moody backdrop, as if inviting the bulldozers and graders to come and do their worst.

I walked to the end of the street and ducked behind a section of wooden fence around a deserted plot of weeds, and found a vantage point where I could keep an eye on the approach road. With luck I'd hear the sound of any vehicles coming before they got to me, which would give me time to come up with a plan to spring Travis.

The truck was the first to arrive, no doubt having used its weight and the complement of troops on board to bully its way through the crush of vehicles at the airport. It stopped a hundred yards away out of my line of sight near a single property surrounded by a chain-link fence, with a barn-type building backing on to the road. Through the sagging open double doors of the barn I got a glimpse of a bunch of chickens in a wire-framed pen. I focussed on the truck and over the clatter of the engine I heard a brief burst of a voice coming over a radio link. '*Stay put and wait. ETA five minutes.*'

The jeep with Travis. The clock was now ticking.

My priority was to get Travis away from the men in the jeep, but the troops in the truck was a problem I couldn't ignore. Somehow I had to immobilise them.

I moved out from behind the fence and found a gap in the chain-link surrounding the property. I was out of sight of the truck or anybody inside the house and had an easy route to the barn. I ducked inside and breathed the overheated, musty atmosphere of about a dozen chickens. They ignored me, focussing on their feed or their grooming. So far so good. I moved over to the front wall for a look-see. And heard a cough very close by.

I stopped dead and froze. A trickle of water sounded. Somebody was relieving himself just a couple of feet away on the other side of the barn wall. Through a slim gap in the planks I caught a glimpse of a uniform.

I held my breath and prayed the house owner wasn't about to come out and protest at this invasion of their property, or to collect some eggs.

The soldier finished and moved away, and I peered through a knot-hole in the rough planking. The truck was a dozen feet away, but inching slowly forward as the driver held the engine on the clutch, the heavy ribbed tyres squeaking as they rolled over a line of stones half-buried in the earth close to the barn wall.

I slid back and tried not to cough. The barn began to fill with noise and the acrid smell of diesel and heavy exhaust smoke, and the structure was vibrating with the proximity of the engine. The chickens were getting nervous, too, and abandoned their feeding, electing to go into a protective huddle in one corner of the pen.

I reckon I had a couple of minutes, if that, to do something before Grey Suit arrived and gave the order to move in.

If that happened, all bets for Travis were off.

EIGHTEEN

I checked the interior of the barn, which was full of the rubbish and discards found on any smallholding or farm anywhere in the western world. Long-forgotten and rusted machinery, coils of wire, battered feed trays, folded cardboard vegetable boxes going mouldy with damp, dented buckets, plastic sacks and a tall stack of cut logs ready for winter. I picked up a length of metal tubing as thick as my arm, an idea forming in my head. I'd seen this done once before, but never tried it myself.

I had to work fast. I grabbed some of the cardboard and wrapped it in layers around the tubing, tying it in place with some string hanging from the wall. Next I slid the end of the submachine gun barrel into the tube. It was a loose fit so I used a fold of plastic sacking to wedge it securely in place and pack around the gun barrel.

I now had a very rough and ready suppressor, or silencer. It was cumbersome, and I'd only find out how silent it was when I pulled the trigger. But if it served to deflect some of the sound, it would be good enough.

I found a gap close to the ground where a piece of planking was missing, and slid the tube through, carefully pushing it along the ground as far as I could towards one of the heavy tyres, which were now almost touching the barn wall. Give it another few seconds and the truck would be past my position and beyond reach. The noise from the nearest tyre scraping on the stones was high-pitched, rising above the clatter of the exhaust and the metronomic blipping of the engine as the driver became impatient to go.

I moved the selector to single shot and waited, timing the revs. One. Two-three. One. Two-three. One. Two-three. One—

I squeezed the trigger.

Some of the report came back up the tube, but most of it was lost in the roar of the truck's engine. The crude suppressor worked, but the sound of the tyre going was much louder, the released air pressure battering the planks close to my head. I yanked the tube back and cast it aside, then moved to the back of the barn and waited.

There was instant pandemonium from inside the truck. I heard the thump of boots hitting the ground and movement against the light as figures came to investigate the noise. Somebody swore about how a shit piece of rubber crap from Romania should have been replaced months ago and what the hell could they do now?

I gave it a few seconds until I heard a voice ordering the tyre to be changed and double-quick. I didn't know how good these guys were at changing truck tyres, but at the very least the driver had to know what he was doing. Either way, I didn't have time to waste.

I left them to it and moved out of the barn, jogging back to my earlier station behind the wooden fence.

My timing couldn't have been closer. As I ducked behind cover, the jeep arrived, throwing up a plume of dust as it came blasting along the street. It shot past the truck and squealed to a stop at the front of the apartment block. Grey Suit was putting on a show for the troops, and I wondered how long it would take his second-in-command in the truck to admit that they were temporarily disabled.

Moments later, one of the soldiers from the jeep appeared at the corner and ran past me, heading for a rear door in the wall. He was wearing a comms headset and armed with a Bison submachine gun and moved like he knew what he was doing.

When I heard shouting from the front of the building and the first crash of a door going in hard on the inside, that was my signal to move.

I ran across the road and through the open door, and found a pitted concrete path leading to the rear of the building through a neglected patch of disordered flower beds and rough grass.

The soldier was right in front of me, kneeling on the path and waiting for orders, one hand clamped to his headset. I was on him before he could register the fact and hit him behind the ear with the butt of the Ero. He fell face down and didn't move. I stepped over him and kicked the Bison out of his reach, and ran along the path and up two steps through a rear door into a darkened corridor.

More voices from upstairs and the sound of wood splintering. A dog began barking furiously and someone screamed. I ducked along the corridor towards the front door, hoping Grey Suit had taken at least one man with him. The more the odds were reduced the better I liked it.

I stepped outside the front door and saw Travis sitting disconsolately in the back of the jeep, with only one soldier keeping guard. It gave me an edge and I had the element of surprise in my favour, but I wasn't keen on the idea of stepping out there and being spotted by the backup troops in the truck.

There was no option; I had to go for broke. I walked out to the road with the Ero under my jacket, the selector on single-shot. The soldier watched me approach, eyes flicking to the building behind me, assessing the situation. He was probably wondering why I was sticking my head out here when the building was clearly being raided and every other normal resident was staying indoors out of the way. When it finally hit him that I didn't fit the picture of anything normal, it was too late. I yanked the door open and leaned in before he could move, and jacked my right elbow hard under his chin, clicking his teeth together. As he slumped backwards I lifted a pistol from a holster on his belt and threw it in the back of the jeep, then turned to Travis, who was looking stunned.

'Travis, this is your only chance of getting out of here in one piece. So move. Follow me and don't ask questions.'

Of course he couldn't do both; that would have been too much to expect. 'Who are you?' he yelped, staring at the soldier rolling around in his seat. But at least he was moving while he said it, climbing out of the back seat like his pants were on fire.

I checked out the army truck. It was too far away to see any detail, but I got the impression the figure in the passenger seat was staring at me and mouthing something.

Oh-oh.

Commotion. Lots of it. I heard the tailgate of the truck slam down, and two men appeared, unslinging automatic rifles. Time to rock and roll. I stepped out into the road where they could see me, lifting the Ero towards them. Soldiers know the dangers in facing a fully automatic weapon, and that standing up against one fitted with an extended magazine is like being in a duck shoot. The men fell back out of sight and the front-seat passenger disappeared below the level of the dashboard. But I wasn't about to squirt the full load. Instead I fired three careful shots at the truck's radiator. Engine blocks will stop all but armour-piercing shells, but they will take some damage in doing so. One of the shots must have punched the release mechanism, because suddenly the hood flew up and they were flying blind.

It was all the advantage I was going to get. I turned and put a bullet into the engine of the jeep and shouted, 'Come on,' grabbing Travis by the arm and hustling him back through the front door into the building.

I could hear the sound of boots pounding down the stairs and a voice yelling instructions in the background. Grey Suit was pissed at finding nobody home and was now wondering what the hell was happening outside. We had seconds to get away from here. I pushed Travis towards the back door and waited for the telltale clatter of boots on the stairs, then stepped out and fired two shots into the wall. Chunks of plaster rained down and the soldier coming down swore and scrambled back the way he'd come.

As we ran down the path to the door at the rear, we passed the man I'd hit coming in. He was rolling around in a daze but still out of it. I ignored him and led the way out into the back run and across to the car. Things were in danger of hotting up; I could hear Grey Suit screaming for the troops in the truck and calling for the area to be sealed off.

I headed west. I had a rough idea of how to get to Vokzal'na Square, and hoped the troops weren't organized enough to be able to close down the entire area west of the city before we got out of here.

'Where are we going?' Travis said at last. He kept looking at me as though I'd landed from a spacecraft, which, considering he'd just been pulled out of a threatening situation, was no surprise. 'Who the hell are you?'

'Doesn't matter who I am,' I told him, and handed him my cell phone. 'Call up Vokzal'na Square on the map; we need to get there double quick if you want to get home in one piece.'

He finally figured out that his options were limited and clamped his mouth shut. He fed in the name and gave me directions, and we drove without speaking other than to confirm our route.

Eventually I had to ask him the big question. 'Did you tell them the address?'

'What?' He seemed surprised, even stunned, that I'd asked. Then he homed in on my accent. 'You're American. Are there more of you?'

'The address of the cut-out,' I repeated. I prodded him on the arm to focus his mind, narrowly missing being sideswiped by a small truck careering out of a side street without looking. 'Did you give the man in the grey suit that address? This is serious.'

'Wha— No! I didn't. Christ, why would I do that?'

He sounded sincere and I believed him. But I wished I didn't. Because it left me wondering whether the SMS from Travis's bosses had been picked up and read by the authorities, or if there was another leak along the line. I believe in things occurring at random, but some events are simply too remote to fall into that category. People die randomly, but not always. Buildings catch fire for no reason, but some get a bit of help along the way. Secrets sometimes fall into the open air by chance. But not always.

'Did you keep the address on your cell phone?' His cell had been confiscated; another source of leakage.

'No. I committed it to memory and wiped it. I was with Military Intelligence – I know the rules.' He sounded offended at the implication that he'd been careless and I figured that with his kind of military background he would know more about being in a sensitive zone than most ordinary grunts.

Vokzal'na Square was a travel hub for the people of Donetsk, with trains, trams and buses all arriving in and leaving from there. The square itself, with the station at the far end, was wide open and spacious, with the road looping in and out like the eye of a needle and stops for trams and buses dotted around the outside perimeter. It boasted a handful of simple shops and eating places, and a brilliant white church with golden domes. It also had a lot of people standing around like refugees, waiting for their transport. But I spotted 24d immediately, a frail figure with a bucket-load of courage huddled under an advertising hoarding. He seemed to be alone and clear but I drove round twice before I was satisfied the area was secure.

'This is where you get out,' I told Travis, pulling into the side. I pointed at 24d, who had already spotted us. 'Go with that man. He'll hand you over to the next in line. You were briefed on the use of cut-outs. You know what their job is, right?'

He nodded. He seemed calm enough, if a little pale. But the fact was, in spite of any past military service, he was now a desk man and what he'd been through must have seemed like the beginnings of a nightmare. He hadn't said much since I'd grilled him about the address, and I was hoping it was his training keeping his questions and emotions in check. If he was about to freak out, it was better if he did it now while I had him under my control. I wasn't sure 24d, who had massive problems of his own ahead of him, would be able to handle that, nor could I expect him to do so.

'Where will I be going?' was all he said.

'Down the line. I'll be monitoring your progress, so just do what you're instructed to by the cut-outs, stay off the phone, even if you think it's safe to call, and you'll be home in time for tea.' It wasn't quite as simple as that, which he would have known by now, but it seemed something nice to aim for.

'Why can't you take me? You're here; we could simply head out of the country. It's safer heading west, isn't it? We could just drive out.'

He was right. We could do that. But if we ran into trouble we'd be sunk. Two Americans being caught up in this kind of volatile situation wasn't something Callahan or his bosses would be able to explain away. Travis at least had the veneer of being a State Department envoy, which might give him some small measure of protection after all the arguing and political point-scoring over why he had come in was done. But my role wasn't so easily brushed off. Worse, it would reflect badly on him.

'We have to do it this way,' I told him. 'I'll be watching your back, don't worry.'

He didn't look convinced, but he thanked me and got out of the car. I watched him approach 24d and shake hands. Then the two of them turned and walked over to a black battle-scarred VW Polo with a bumble-bee sticker on the rear window and climbed in.

I followed the Polo out of the square and called Langley. 24d was probably heading for the M04 road leading west to Pavlohrad, which was where Travis would be handed over to his next in line. If they didn't run into trouble from the various separatists or Ukrainian military they should be fine, but there were never any guarantees in this game.

'Travis is out, clear and on his way,' I said, when the woman answered. 'I'll call again later.'

'Understood, Watchman.' She clicked off without further comment and I realized I didn't yet know her name. Maybe now I never would.

Because I suddenly realized I was being followed.

NINETEEN

I stayed on course while checking the vehicles behind me. It's not as easy to do as they make out in films, especially on crowded streets with shifting traffic. It's as much a process of identifying a specific vehicle as gut feel, but I was certain I hadn't picked up a tail after leaving Obluskva Street; the roads out of there had been too quiet and I'd have spotted a car hanging on to me for too long. But when my antennae started quivering as soon as I drove out of Vokzal'na Square and turned south, I couldn't ignore the warning.

I must have been spotted at random; it was the only thing I could think of. And if that had come down to somebody trawling the streets for a red Toyota Land Cruiser, I figured it had to be Ivkanoy or one of his men.

You read a lot about checking a tail by making a series of turns, doubling back, varying your speed and hoping the other driver makes a mistake and blows his cover. Mostly all you do is warn your follower that you're on to him. I didn't want that; I wanted to identify whether they were actually interested in me or had latched on to 24d and the black Polo.

If it was me, I could handle it. It would be inconvenient but not a drama. If it was 24d they wanted, it was official. All they had to do was sit on his tail and keep radio contact with other units and they'd have Travis in the bag at their own time and place of choosing.

Either way I had to take them out in some way. It meant not being able to keep tabs on the Polo, but I knew where 24d was taking him and as long as he didn't make a wrong turn or get lost or picked up by security police or a stray militia group, I could catch up with him later.

Losing sight of the man I was here to protect was far from ideal, but it was a risk I had to take before we went any further.

Identifying the tail was a process of elimination, discounting each vehicle as it turned off or stopped until it came down to three possibles: a dark sedan with a roof aerial, a small blue Datsun and a scrubby-looking white Isuzu with an extended cab. Any one of them could be a surveillance unit, but I had to find out which one and who they were following: me or the Polo? I slowed down, allowing the Polo to get some way ahead, then braked and hung a right at an intersection, making like an out-of-towner checking addresses and street numbers while keeping an eye on my rear-view mirror.

The sedan, Datsun and Isuzu came with me. So I was the target.

I put my money on the sedan with the aerial. Aerials mean cops or security police. Was this Toyota hot after all? Did Ivkanoy have some juice with the local police department and they'd put out an all-points watch for the car? Or was I about to be stopped by security police working on a hunch?

After a couple of turns the Datsun was gone. One down, two to go.

Two more turns and the sedan and the Isuzu were still there. The sedan had two men in the front, both stony-faced, solid, dressed in shirts and ties. To me they had the look of cops. I couldn't make out the Isuzu but it looked as if it contained just the driver.

I headed out towards the south-western suburbs and the H15 road. The sooner I got out of Donetsk the better. Quite apart from my follower, the possibility of Ivkanoy and his cue-wielding pal being on the lookout for the car and my skin, and the risk of running into inquisitive or jumpy militiamen, was too great. I'd already seen too many light military vehicles and APCs – armoured personnel carriers – stationed at junctions, and it seemed evident that a serious situation was brewing and about ready to explode.

The H15 looped south out of the city and was an alternative route to Pavlohrad. It was a two-lane highway bordered by twin lines of trees, and had an ageing, pitted surface that forced drivers out towards the centre line. It would take longer to reach Pavlohrad than the northern M04 road, which 24d and Travis were taking, but it would allow me more time and space to watch my back and look out for trouble ahead.

And to ditch the trouble coming up behind.

I drove for twenty minutes, frog-hopping lumbering trucks and ratty old cars, with the sedan and the Isuzu never far behind. I occasionally put on a burst of speed but didn't make enough headway to lose them completely without making it obvious.

The traffic was mostly military or haulage, with a sprinkling of private cars and pickups. A troop carrier came blasting up behind, spreading exhaust smoke and shouldering its way through by sheer size and velocity. I let it go by. An old Range Rover decided to follow, overtaking on a suicide course and earning an angry blast from the Isuzu, before pulling in right behind me. It was full of kids with spiky hair and face jewellery, and they looked like they were having too much of a ball to care. I let them go, too. Somewhere in the mix of engines when we got bunched up close I could hear the raspy roar of a holed muffler.

The troop carrier ahead of me signalled right and I saw the sign to a truck-stop ahead. It was time to push the envelope. It was a risky strategy but I was pretty sure if the guys behind me were friends of Ivkanoy and had plans to take me out, they wouldn't do it in front of a bunch of armed soldiers.

If they were official, and had already got my number, then it wouldn't make any difference.

I followed the troop carrier in and parked at the side of the building and waited. I watched the sedan go on by. The passenger turned his head to look, but not at me. The Isuzu followed, the muffler noise going with him, but the driver was intent on the road.

I checked the café, which was busy, and went inside. I needed to get some food while I had the chance, and to see if anybody took an interest in the car.

The other customers were hunched over their plates, intent on their meals and getting back out on the road, truckers and co-drivers with a job to do and schedules to meet. The situation to the east had cast a cloud over everyone no matter where they were, and was inevitably affecting non-essential movements. That could be a problem if any local cops took an interest in non-military or non-haulage travellers, and gave me another reason to stay off the main roads as much as I could. I went back to the car and called up an app of the area on my cell phone to check the alternatives.

They were few in number. Other than the road I was on, there was the mirror route to the north – the M04 to Pavlohrad – with a thin network of roads and tracks connecting the two across an open expanse of fields, rolling hills, lakes and rough terrain.

I checked I had plenty of fuel and decided to take off. Three miles down the road I took a right turn and found myself on an unmarked metalled surface heading directly north into open country. If my map was accurate, this would lead eventually to the M04. If I didn't like the look of that I could turn left and burrow deeper into the countryside until I reached Pavlohrad on back roads.

The houses or farms were few in number and scattered; low, small structures on plots surrounded by crumbling walls or wooden picket fences, it was like stepping back in time. I saw a couple of old people, mostly weather-worn and stooped, who watched me go by without expression, but that was it.

After an hour of rough, potholed road, I came up and over an escarpment dotted with a few straggly trees and saw the ground ahead drop away in front of me like diving off a cliff. I stamped on the brakes.

Doesn't matter who you are, in this game you don't go over a brow in unknown terrain without first checking your route is clear.

Once I'd made sure there were no surprises waiting for me on the other side, I got back in and began a long ride downhill. The road was narrow here, bordered either side by rough ground and rocks, with overgrown gullies where old river courses had carved their way through the earth from the higher ground.

As I picked up speed, I heard a loud bang and my world went crazy.

TWENTY

I came to after a few seconds and found I was hanging upside down with the seat belt across my throat, slowly choking me. The interior of the car was clouded with dust from the airbag, and I could smell fuel in the air and the sourness of ingrained car dirt, and my mouth was gritty with God knew what accumulated crap thrown off the floor. I braced myself with one hand on the roof and pushed the belt release catch, rolling into a ball to cushion my impact. I kicked hard at the driver's door, which was partially open. No go. It was wedged tight with a screen of coarse grass and dirt flattened against the outside of the glass.

I squirrelled round and looked through the windscreen. The view wasn't great, and starred with a crazy network of cracks. I breathed deeply, fighting back a sense of panic. If the bang I'd heard was a tyre being shot out, and I couldn't get out right now, I was in deep trouble.

I forced myself to apply cool logic. There was no way anybody could have got into a position ahead of me to shoot out a tyre this soon. They wouldn't have known I was going to take this route because until I saw it, even I didn't know. And if I had been shot at, there would have most likely been at least one follow-up shot to make sure of a kill. So far there hadn't been any.

That left a simple blow-out; one of those things that happens on rough country roads, the inevitable result of sharp stones meeting worn tyre walls. Circumstance and randomness coming together to play games with the best-laid plans.

I found my overnight bag and checked my surroundings. I appeared to be in a gulley facing downhill. A fine mist was being blown from beneath the hood and ghosting across the cracked glass, feeding into the car through a couple of small holes. The smell raised the hairs on the back of my neck.

Smoke.

There was no way out through the front, so I checked the passenger door. It was badly buckled around the lock, but didn't appear to have anything blocking my way out.

I swivelled my hips and smashed both feet against the passenger window. It took three attempts in the cramped space, and I prayed the vibration against the door wouldn't cause the side pillar to buckle and collapse. The glass finally blew out with a crash and I followed fast, dragging myself through the hole and up the side of the car to the rear, where I rolled clear.

I lay on my back for a few seconds, winded and bruised, then rolled over again and prayed the Toyota didn't blow, while I studied the road above me and the grassland below. If my logic was all wrong and the tyre had been shot out, rushing out into the open to avoid the car blowing could be the last thing I ever did.

But there was nothing. No vehicles, no voices, no sounds of anyone approaching. No shots. Just a vague sigh of wind ghosting across the grass, and high above me the innocent sound of a bird.

I got to my feet and checked myself over for breaks or cuts. I'd been lucky – or maybe the factory had turned out an especially good car that day. I'd come out of a major crash with nothing more than a couple of bruises and a hair full of someone else's car crap.

I approached the car with caution to check it out. It was surrounded by a white veil of steam and smoke and the rank smell of burning rubber, but didn't look in imminent danger of blowing up. I checked the tyres and saw the front left had a long tear in the sidewall where the fabric looked perished through age and neglect.

Just as I'd thought. Random.

I was moving away in case whatever was burning under the hood took hold and the tank blew, when I heard the growl of an engine being driven hard. It sounded high-performance, like the noise you get at a cross-country rally.

Which was all wrong for all kinds of reasons.

I dropped down off the road and ran at a crouch towards a large clump of rocks in dead ground two hundred yards away. Instinct told me the new arrival wasn't going to be a local farmer willing to give me a ride out of here. In my limited experience, country farmers don't drive hard and fast unless they have a prize pig to sell.

I watched as the car pulled to a stop a few yards before the top ᶠ a rise. It was precisely where I'd stopped to check the road and all I needed to know.

as the Isuzu. Off-white and beat-up, it carried the clatter of a holed muffler and was streaked with mud down the sides. So much for sedans with aerials. This was too much of a coincidence.

I ignored what were merely outward signs; mufflers get broken all the time on bad roads and beat-up is a look nobody notices. And for some of us that's the whole idea; it's called blending in. But more than anything the speed he'd been travelling told me the car was no junkyard hand-me-down driven by a tanked-up kid on a joy ride. Pros don't use tools that aren't up to the job. And this one had been following me for a while now.

I watched the driver climb out of the car and ease his back. He walked once round the vehicle, stamping his feet to get the circulation going the way people do after a long session behind the wheel with nothing to do but drive and watch the road. He looked small and wiry, and was wearing a brown leather coat and a cap with ear flaps that hid his face, and moved like he was tired or old – maybe both. He might have been an ordinary traveller on this deserted back road who'd just happened on something he didn't want to see.

When he got back level with the hood he held something up to his eye which caught the light. I knew then that he was trouble. Ordinary travellers don't carry spyglasses – or what I guessed was more likely an optical gun-sight. He was checking out my dead Toyota and the surrounding landscape to see if I was out and in one piece.

When he got back to the driver's door he leaned in and hauled something heavy out of the back seat, fiddled with it for a second, then positioned himself over the hood in a stance that I recognized only too well.

Sniper.

I eased down behind a large piece of moss-covered granite and waited. I didn't need to stick my head up for a second look to see what he was doing; I'd seen all I needed to.

The man was holding what looked like an OSV-96 long-range sniper's rifle. It was hard to be sure at that distance, but by its length and the way he hefted it, if I was correct it was capable of taking out man, beast or vehicle at anything up to a kilometre. And when fitted with the optical gun-sight he'd be able to shoot the pimples off a target's face.

The target being me.

I looked across at the Toyota. From his elevated position the shooter would have a grand-stand view of the vehicle. He'd be a himself if I was still inside, was I banged up and trapped. Or dead. Even as I thought it, he decided to check it out the only way he knew how.

The crack of a shot rolled across the open ground like small thunder.

I ducked involuntarily. But the shot wasn't aimed at me; instead the rear window of the Toyota blew out in a spray of glass on the driver's side, and a ragged piece of the radiator grill zinged off into the distance from the other end. Heavy gauge shells do that; they go right on through, mashing up whatever gets in their way. Fabric. Metal. Skin.

Another shot and the same thing happened, this time on the passenger side. He was playing now, but making sure at the same time, drilling the car on both sides. A third shot rang out and the car was toast.

Incendiary round. Intended for light-armoured vehicles and buildings, and certain death for a light-skinned 4WD, especially when aimed at the fuel tank.

I gave it a count of ten while I watched the burning car push a column of thickening black smoke into the air, accompanied by the popping of the three remaining tyres and the clank of overheated metal. Then I risked a quick look. The Isuzu was still in place on the rise.

But the shooter had disappeared.

I rolled away, keeping the rock between us, and slid into the gulley. There was no point going back to the car, so I grabbed my bag and began running up the gulley towards the rise. I had no massive plan in mind; this was all or nothing. But one way of facing off danger is to do what is least expected and run towards it. The man with the rifle had the upper hand at whatever distance he chose, and there was no way I could outrun him. So going out into open country was pointless. All I had was my overnight kit, a small pair of binoculars and a powerful desire to keep living.

tough going. I was still dizzy from the crash and found difficult to navigate underfoot. And the need to the waist to prevent breaking cover was enough to catch my breath.

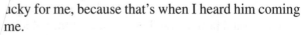

cky for me, because that's when I heard him coming me.

He'd reached a particularly steep part of the terrain and his momentum, coupled I guessed with the idea that I was being roasted in the upturned vehicle, had made him careless; he was also moving too fast and kicking up dirt underfoot which pinpointed his position and progress. He'd moved up on to higher ground at the side of the gulley to get a better view, so I hugged the ground beneath an overhang of earth and coarse grass and waited, counting the seconds to help me focus.

As his shadow appeared above me, I launched myself upwards over the lip of the gulley and hit him with my shoulder at waist level. It was all or nothing.

It took him by surprise. He gave a whoosh of expelled air and I felt him lift off his feet with the impact. But he had good instincts and I felt the butt of the heavy rifle slam into the small of my back. He was also fitter than he'd looked earlier, with the wiry strength of someone accustomed to extremes of exercise. I held on to him in desperation, my fingers curled into the soft leather of his coat. If he got free and stepped back with the rifle, I was dead meat. I did the only thing I could: I flipped backwards and dragged him down into the gulley, making him grunt as we crashed against a lump of granite. I tried rolling him beneath me to smother him with my weight, but he knew all the moves. He pushed the rifle clear and used the flat of his hands to keep himself level, before twisting violently sideways and getting one hand between us.

It didn't matter whether he was reaching for a knife or a handgun; the outcome if he succeeded would be the same.

I let go with one hand and slammed my fist between the ear flaps. There was a crunch of cartilage giving way and he grunted, blowing out a gust of air and a splatter of blood. I hit him again, this time feeling him go limp against me. But I wasn't taking chances. I rolled him on to his front and knelt on his back, pressing his body into the grass beneath and pulling his head back until he gurgled and began to kick violently as his throat became too constricted to breath. Another few seconds and he'd stop breathing altogether.

I eased off at the last moment and pushed his head down, and knelt on his back between his shoulder blades. Then I did a quick check of his pockets while he gulped for air. I found an ID card, some cash and a cheap cell phone. In his outside jacket pocket was a Grach 9mm semi-automatic pistol, and tucked in his waist was a knife in a sheath; commando-style, rubber handle grip, sharp as a razor.

But there was something else that almost threw me.

He was a woman.

TWENTY-ONE

'Are we secure?'

Howard Benson had just entered the private library of the prestigious Washington law firm of Chapin, Wilde and Langstone. Already seated were four other men, three of them members of a privately financed think-tank calling themselves the Dupont Circle Group.

'Of course we're secure, Howard,' Vernon Chapin muttered. 'I have the place swept every day and twice on Sundays. What have you got for us? I was hoping for an early round of golf. Then I have to visit my consultant.' He waved a vague hand at their raised eyebrows. 'He thinks I might be dying, but he's an idiot.' A senior member of the law firm bearing his name and a former member of Military Intelligence back when the Cold War was dribbling to an end and Soviet president Mikhail Gorbachev was ushering in a new age of liberalization, Chapin had forgotten more about security than most people could even begin to know, and shared much of Benson's dislike of the CIA. He also despised health consultants as charlatans until they proved themselves otherwise.

The hum of subdued and orderly activity in the offices outside the library was barely detectable, but in any case an electronic net embedded in the partition walls ensured that whatever was discussed within the room stayed there. It was why this place had been chosen for their meetings.

'Travis, the man the State Department sent in to talk with the various factions in Ukraine and elsewhere,' Benson began, 'has run into a shit storm. He's under virtual house arrest and has been told that if he leaves his hotel, he'll be shot. The State Department's frightened he'll be accused of conducting a spying trip under orders from the White House, and have asked Langley to get him out of there with immediate effect. They've sent in a private contractor under cover to escort him out.'

'My God, gun-boat diplomacy?' Ambrose Teller, a retired banker and private investor, and a former officer with the now subsumed

National Intelligence Agency, gave a wry chuckle. 'I thought that stuff went out of fashion with the Brits and Margaret Thatcher.'

'I cancelled a round of golf for that?' Chapin looked mildly ticked off, but his tone was intrigued. He glanced at a slim, dour-looking man sitting to his right. 'What's your information on this, Walter? Anything we should know?'

A senior White House staffer with a host of hot contacts in government, Conkley was an ambitious and invaluable source of inside information for political movers and shakers like these. Although not an inside member of the Dupont Group, his seat at National Security Council meetings chaired by the president, and his willingness to spill details for financial return, automatically guaranteed him a chair here.

'It's a serious threat and the action suggested is entirely reasonable,' Conkley announced loftily. If he'd expected a moment of hushed awe at the comment, he was disappointed. After a moment of silence he continued. 'The original idea was for Travis to initiate talks with the affected parties while they were still in a position to do so freely and without interference from Moscow. But someone appears to have taken him out of circulation.'

'Do we know who?' said Teller.

'We don't, not yet. It could be one of the nationalist organizations opposed to closer ties with Moscow, stirring up trouble between us; it could even be one of the separatist groups on orders from Moscow, irritated by what they see as interference. We're not exactly short of suspects in the region.'

Teller shook his head. 'I may be naïve in these matters, and you'll have to forgive me for that, but why can't this Travis simply go to the embassy in – Kiev, is it? He'd be safe there, surely.'

'Ordinarily, yes,' Conkley agreed. 'But the situation over there is fragile. Using the embassy might compromise their position beyond retrieval.'

Benson grunted. 'Especially now Travis has a CIA hired gun in tow.'

Conkley nodded. 'That's unfortunate, I agree. Also the government in Ukraine is losing control by the day with pro-Russian elements taking control of official buildings and the police, especially in the east around the Donetsk and Luhansk areas. But it doesn't stop there; there's a real concern that the situation could get worse with signs of political unrest building in other countries, like Moldova.'

'Is that likely?' Teller asked.

'It's possible, yes. We've had reliable reports of Russian troops in unmarked uniforms operating in various locations throughout the region, but especially close to main roads, airports and border crossings. President Putin has made no secret of his long-term intentions to win back what were satellite states, and he's not without support within some of those countries where there is a substantial pro-Russian population who would welcome closer ties with Moscow.' He hesitated, then added for emphasis, 'And I mean much closer ties. The main fear is that he could do what he did once before with Ukraine; he could restrict or cut off completely supplies of oil and gas.'

Teller looked bored. 'Why would that bother us?'

'Because,' Benson said, 'it would destabilize the entire region, including large parts of mainland Europe. And that should certainly concern us all.'

'Explain,' said Chapin.

'Ukraine isn't the only big user of Russian energy. Germany is a big net buyer of natural gas, with other European states to a lesser degree. They rely on a number of pipelines which pass through Ukrainian territory. If this situation blows up further and Putin tightens his grip on those supplies long enough, those countries could end up going dark for long periods until they source other supplies. That would take time. It would cost them dear to source other supplies . . . but they'd have no choice.'

'Why would Putin risk doing that? He must know he'd earn international opprobrium.'

'He probably does, but I doubt he really cares. As far as he's concerned, it's nothing to do with him; civil unrest in other states is beyond his control and pipelines are vulnerable to attack by extremists.'

Teller nodded impatiently. 'But that's a political problem. How does it affect *us*?'

'Simple. Look what happened in the Middle East when the pipelines and installations were interrupted. Oil prices went through the ceiling.'

'Amen to that,' Teller murmured softly, with a dreamy look on his face. 'And may the good times roll again.' He only realized what he had said when he became aware of an uncomfortable silence and saw the warning looks thrown at him by Benson and Chapin.

But it was too late. Walter Conkley was staring at him.

'Why do you say that?' the staffer asked. 'The good times? For who?'

'Just a joke, Walter,' Benson suggested mildly, but glaring at Teller to shut him up before he said anything else. 'A bad one at that.'

'Was it?' Conkley looked around the table at the assembled faces, but appeared to find nothing there to reassure him. He turned back to Teller. 'Didn't you once tell me that you had developed extensive energy portfolios during and after the Gulf War?'

'I really don't recall. I may have had. Is it important?' Teller sound calm, but he looked uncomfortable under the poisonous looks his friends were giving him.

Benson jumped in before anyone else could speak. 'Forget it, Walter. Like I said, it was a bad joke. On a more serious note, we're merely laying out the scenarios if this situation deteriorates further. People ask our advice, you know that. We have to know what the big picture might be. That's where you come in.'

It was naked flattery, but Conkley looked unconvinced. 'Well, I don't know, Senator. I've been coming here and giving you information – most of it open, I know that – but still, it's information not available to everyone and frankly, some of it is stuff I shouldn't be discussing.' His voice had taken on a wheedling tone, and he was looking like a rabbit in the headlights. 'I hope none of it is going to be misused in any way.'

'Of course not. And we appreciate your valuable input, Walter, we really do. I think you know how much, too.' He smiled as he delivered this unsubtle reminder, in case anyone had forgotten, that Conkley was well paid for any 'input' he placed their way.

He swallowed and nodded. 'Of course. I didn't mean to suggest . . .'

'No, of course not.' Benson's face was genial but to anyone who knew him, it was just a mask. Inside he was seething at Teller's stupidity. But he smiled warmly and said, 'I think we can allow you to get back to your office now, Walter. You'll keep us informed of further developments at your end, of course?'

It was a dismissal and they all knew it, Conkley most of all. He was sufficiently versed in the subtleties of atmosphere to know when it was time to leave. It had happened before with these men, but he'd chosen to look on it as part of their secret games, nothing more. A gathering of old men with long memories and more snap than teeth, they at least had a talent for analysing world events that proved occasionally useful for the administration. He stood up and buttoned his jacket, then left without a word.

TWENTY-TWO

C hapin looked at Benson in surprise. 'What the hell was that about? The man's a self-serving weasel, we all know that, but did you have to be so rude?'

'Blame Ambrose, not me,' Benson snarled, and turned on Teller, who wilted under his gaze. 'Jesus, could you have been any more open? That little schmuck is not stupid; he knew what you were suggesting – what we're all thinking right now. If this gets out that we were planning on using inside knowledge about energy movements, we'll be finished.' He took a sip of water and wondered how much damage had been done. If Conkley panicked and let it be known that he was paid to come here and spill details of matters discussed in the seat of government, and that some of that information was being used to line the pockets of a handful of speculators, they would likely end up in jail.

'Come on, Howard,' Chapin muttered soothingly, 'calm down. Conkley won't talk; I've known him for years. He's got too much to lose. Now, if you've got something on your tricky little mind, let's hear it before we all grow a day older.'

Benson nodded and breathed deeply to restore a sense of calm. Perhaps he had overreacted and Chapin was right; Conkley was a typical civil servant, with a love of meetings, paperwork and procedure, and a prudish distaste for anything too adventurous. 'You're right,' he agreed. 'I'm sorry.' He held up two fingers. 'Two points I wanted to raise: one is at the forefront of all our minds: the reversal of budget cuts to the intelligence agencies and the continuation of their position in fighting terrorism and securing information from our enemies. We've all been in this game too long to enjoy seeing the numbers going down, the budgets slashed and our hands tied by the idiots currently in charge.'

'I agree,' Chapin murmured, but he was frowning as if he failed to see the direction Benson was going.

'But it's not entirely their fault; there was a time when intelligence gathering produced real results. But that was in the past, before the CIA was taken over by hoodlums who seem to think they're above the law. Their record of inappropriate and, frankly, illegal activities over the past twenty years, such as hiring private armies of mercenaries, kidnappings, black flights, God knows what else, has ruined the good work of other agencies; agencies who are better equipped to put the fight on a level above the gunfighter mentality.' He hesitated while his message sank in, noting the nods as the others gave their agreement. 'I'm talking about electronic intelligence gathering, and it's time we got back to that situation. This could be our chance.'

'You'll get no argument from me there,' Teller murmured. Like the others, many of his investments were in the electronics industry where much of the equipment and expertise Benson was talking about was produced. Any change in government spending in these areas would affect them all directly.

Chapin nodded. 'Good. And point two?'

Benson smiled and in response looked down the table at the fourth man present, who had so far said nothing. 'I'm sure Burman can see where I'm going.'

'I can indeed.' With heavily veined hands and a shock of white hair, Burman Cassler crouched in his chair as if being pressed downwards by an invisible burden, using the power of his eyes to draw the attention of the other men. Thought by many in Washington to be long dead or retired to his country estate in New Hampshire, he was still a big hitter in industrial and banking circles. He had served briefly in the US State Department before finding an outlet for his razor-sharp brain in Wall Street, with a leaning towards military and defence production, and it was his talent for spotting and using investment opportunities that had drawn him to this group, allying their insider knowledge to his ability to play the markets. 'Where there's a war,' he continued, 'there's a percentage. The drawdown of US personnel and commitment in Afghanistan is already showing a shortfall in military spending; a situation where we all stand to lose out. Frankly, if we don't find an alternative somewhere else, we could get our fingers burned.'

'So how does Europe allow us to make that up?' Teller queried. 'There's already an over-supply of weapons in Eastern Europe, with old Russian arsenals being discovered and ripped open all the time and the contents sold off to the highest bidder. That market is saturated.'

Cassler nodded. 'True enough. However, I'm not talking about

AK-47s or missiles. As Howard said earlier, there's a growing energy-supply problem over there. G7 is already threatening sanctions against Russian interference in Ukraine. If Moscow calls their bluff and shuts down the pipelines, somebody will have to step in.' He looked around at the other faces as realization began to build. 'It might as well be us.'

Chapin nodded. 'All we need to do is get Congress to loosen export restrictions and we can get more natural gas on to the market.'

'Aren't they already planning on issuing licences?' asked Teller.

'Correct.' Benson nodded. 'But they don't take effect until later this year. We need it to happen now.'

'So what do we do? We can't put pressure on the Department of Energy; that would be stating our interest too openly.'

'Maybe so. But if the situation in Eastern Europe is seen to worsen, that might work in our favour. We just have to be in a position to do something about it.' Benson got to his feet. 'It doesn't mean we have to be overt; a few well-placed suggestions to the right people should do it. Let the momentum gather from there.'

Cassler smiled. 'Excellent idea. There will be many who will want to be seen as the instigators in helping out those unfortunates caught up in fuel shortages.'

Benson didn't need to say anything more. His tactic had worked. These men were better at chewing over the fine details than he was. Right now he needed to check on some things with Langley. He moved towards the door. 'You'll have to excuse me, gentlemen, but I have some business to attend to.'

'Of course,' Chapin said. 'We meet again in twelve hours.'

Once outside, Benson made a call. He was still feeling sour at Teller's crass stupidity; by his thoughtless comment he'd put them all in an invidious position. As far as Conkley should have been aware, the Dupont Circle Group was one of several independent think-tanks in the Washington arena and, as such, had no conflicts of interest with situations coming under their radar. Teller's remark had now blown that notion right out of the water, exposing himself and the others as nothing more than a clique of heavy investors on the international markets with an eye to the main chance. And Conkley had instantly picked up on it.

Benson didn't want to take any unnecessary action, but neither was he prepared to sit back and allow matters to get out of hand.

If Conkley decided to talk about what he'd heard, they would all be finished. In this town you didn't have to show absolute proof of wrongdoing to become a focus for damaging and ruinous attention from the press or enemies in the corridors of power; the accusation was often enough to last a lifetime.

The very idea filled Benson with horror. He had too much of a stake in this, both financially and with his position in government, and the thought of losing both was too terrifying to contemplate.

'Two-One. Go ahead.' The voice was, as usual, brisk and devoid of emotion.

'I need you to monitor Walter Conkley. He's on the White House staff list. Who he meets, who he talks to over the next three days. Conversations, phone calls, emails – the lot.'

'No problem. How deep?'

'Deep as you can. Stick a bug up his ass if you have to; I want to know everything. And if he so much as smiles in the direction of anyone in security, call me immediately.'

TWENTY-THREE

I don't get surprised by much. Not after the stuff I've seen. But a woman sniper isn't something you come across every day, although clearly they exist. This one was even more surprising because I put her age at somewhere in the late forties or early fifties – which is high for anyone in that profession.

The name on the ID card was Olena Prokyeva. She had experience and pain in her eyes – although the latter might have been entirely due to the damage I'd done to her nose – along with a coldness that was entirely focussed on me. Even though I had the upper hand it didn't seem to bother her much.

If I'd been looking for trouble, the look told me, I'd found it in spades and had better watch my back.

'Well, I know your name,' I said, and got to my feet, gesturing with the Grach for her to sit up. Nobody can talk easily lying on their back, not when they're suffering a blunt-nose trauma and impaired breathing. 'But why are you trying to kill me?'

She didn't reply. Just stared at me and waited, then slowly sat upright. She was rail-thin and whippy, with weathered skin and a sideways slant to her jawline as if she'd been hit hard and the bone hadn't been set right. With the swelling around her nose and eyes, she wasn't going to be winning beauty contests anytime soon. She looked as if she'd lived a hard life and I wondered what had brought her to this point. I was guessing she was a gun for hire.

'Who sent you?' I asked. I had to get something out of her, but it was better if she gave it voluntarily.

She still didn't reply and I realized she wasn't even looking at me, but at a point over my shoulder. Then I saw a flicker in her eyes. It was a 'tell' – the giveaway that something was going on behind me. Something I wouldn't like.

I hit the ground a split second before the crack of a high-velocity round split the air right where my head had been.

Shooter number two. She hadn't come alone.

I twisted round and found I was half lying on her rifle. I'd called it right: it was an OSV, a beast of a weapon for long-range work.

It was coated in dirt and bits of grass from where it had hit the ground, but was still good to go. I stuffed the pistol in my pocket and lifted the rifle, which made my shoulder muscles crack, and checked the load. She had loaded a fresh five-round magazine after taking her shots. I inched my way up to the lip of the gulley and took a look around.

Her partner had to be on high ground if he wanted to reach me, so I checked the ridge where it ran away to my right, jagged and untamed like a line of broken teeth against the skyline. The big bits were rocks the size of cars, easy to hide behind and a good platform for a long-range shot.

Except he'd missed with the first one and now wouldn't be feeling so cocky. He – or maybe another she – would have to play duck-and-dive because they would know I was still in play and now in a position to go on the offensive.

A second shot slammed into a rock thirty yards away, and a rabbit skipped out of cover and streaked away across the grass. With it went another dent to the shooter's confidence. I heard the woman swear softly behind me and smiled. What she said wasn't complimentary about the other hired help.

That told me the second shooter wasn't the primary gun. The woman had come down first, confidant of having an easy target, leaving the other gun in the back of the Isuzu just in case. Only he hadn't been up to the job.

The move had been clumsy on both parts and she knew it. I smiled at her and nodded up the slope towards the ridge. 'Friend of yours? Someone you value?'

She shook her head and told me to go screw myself.

I eased my head back up to the lip and saw a movement two hundred yards away. It was very brief before disappearing, but if it was another rabbit it was wearing an old style camouflage smock and a beanie hat. It was also carrying a rifle fitted with a big scope. Smaller than the OSV but just as deadly in the right hands.

I waited, reading the situation ahead and knowing what was unfolding. The shooter was thinking tactical. He knew where we were and was making his way down and round to my flank, where lower ground would give him a view up the gulley. He was also thinking I'd expect him to stay on higher ground where he had the advantage.

I stayed where I was, eyes on the ridge and the ground below it, nestling the rifle on a piece of out-jutting rock for a firing platform. He'd find some dead ground, a smaller gulley or a fold in the land, which he'd use like a fairground slide to take him downhill fast and safe. He'd have already picked out a spot from his higher position where he would stop and find a safe firing point.

If I allowed him that much leeway, he'd have me in a corner and I'd be dead.

I shuffled over to the woman, keeping low, slapping her hand away as she tried to punch me, and pulled her across to lie on the ground. I pulled out one of her bootlaces and tied her little pinkies together, then shuffled back to the rifle and took up a firing position.

I was now looking over her head at the ground beyond.

She took one look and the stiffness in her shoulders said it all. She saw immediately that if her partner did what we both knew he was going to do, which was to come up shooting, she would be right in his line of fire with no way out. She threw me an angry glance but other than tugging futilely at the bootlace, she didn't move. She certainly had some guts.

'Go back,' I said, pointing to her original position. I wanted her to know that I had complete control over the next few minutes in her life, just as she'd thought about mine as she descended off the ridge and tracked me down the gulley.

She hesitated, fearful of a trick, then ducked her head and rolled over and over until she was behind cover.

I counted slowly to thirty, eyes on a small rise in the ground where the gulley followed the line of the slope. He was being cautious, but I figured he was also in a hurry to prove himself. Number twos always have their eyes on the top spot; it's human nature, especially in a competitive industry. Nobody likes being second best.

A flicker of movement came six feet away from where I expected it, and the ground twenty feet in front of me was churned up by a volley of shots, throwing up grass, mud and chunks of granite. One round passed too close for comfort but it wasn't aimed; none of them were. But a stray bullet would have been curtains just the same.

'He didn't even check his target area,' I told her, nodding at the torn-up ground. It was exactly where she'd been lying moments before. 'That would have been you.'

She said nothing, but looked away, her jaw clenching as the truth sank home. So I focussed on waiting for the other shooter to stand up. One. Two Three.

And he did just that, rifle at his shoulder, but several degrees off the mark. When he finally saw me, his mouth dropped open in surprise.

I centred on his body mass. Squeezed the trigger.

Using a strange rifle without firing a test shot is always risky. But I figured the woman was professional enough to have looked after her weapon and kept the sights zeroed in.

The punch of the recoil was a surprise, but nothing like the shock the other man would have felt if his nervous system had been fast enough to pass on the message that he'd been shot. He flipped over like he'd been hit by a truck and went down, his rifle flying clear.

I didn't need to inspect the result, but I jogged over and looked down at the body anyway. It pays to be sure.

It was a man. Somewhere in his thirties, unshaven, gaunt and dressed in rough weather clothing, he had a ring on one finger which looked like heavy gold. I pulled back one sleeve and checked what remained of his chest. Tattoos. Difficult to see what they were now, but one on his arm was a large spider. I didn't know the significance of that but it pointed at a possible gang involvement or a contract shooter. Ivkanoy. It had to be.

I checked his pockets. He had nothing. No wallet, no papers. Clean.

A pro, like the woman, but less experienced. Now dead.

TWENTY-FOUR

I walked back and found the woman lying where I'd left her. She wasn't trying to get loose, but staring up at the sky, face blank, numbed. Waiting.

I'd seen this kind of reaction before in defeated fighters; it's a mixture of shock, of fear, of wounded pride, of not knowing what to expect next. And of judging by their own standard of life that their options were strictly limited. Even so I wasn't writing her off as a spent force; there was a glimmer of something still present in her that told me if I let her, she'd be all over me.

'What was your assignment, Olena?' If she was in any way official, such as part of any government agency, I was royally screwed and had no time to mess around. It meant my presence had been blown and I was going to have to hustle out of here. But to do that I had to know which way to run.

She shook her head, lips tight, then spat out a gobbet of blood. This wasn't going anywhere.

I knelt down beside her, getting right in her line of sight so she'd have to look at me. I wasn't trying to intimidate her – I figured that wasn't going to work. But she couldn't ignore me completely and it might make her say something unguarded. I noticed she was wearing ear-buds to drown out the noise of the rifle shot, so I flipped them out. She'd heard me plainly enough but I wanted to show her I had control.

'You had orders to kill me. Who from? You don't have to say, but I'm kind of interested.'

She told me to go screw a goat. Mildly creative but not helpful.

I said softly, 'Thank you. Your colleague is dead. You want to join him?'

There were no more insults this time and she blinked in spite of herself. If I'd raged and threatened her, it might have been different. Nobody likes to be asked that kind of question, especially in a soft voice. It carries an air of finality, as if a line has been crossed and there's no going back.

The silence was enough. Tough as she was, she wanted to live.

'Your choice,' I said, and swung the rifle barrel round to point at her. I held it steady just an inch from her left eye.

She blinked with shock. It must have been like staring down a rail tunnel. She hesitated for three seconds, then began to talk, speaking softly, as if worried somebody might hear. She was a former army sniper, she told me, now employed on a contract basis. When I pressed her she said it meant anyone who could afford to pay for her services, mostly private clients with enemies they wished to eliminate. It happens a lot in Eastern Europe, where competition for power and influence is brutal and the means to blast your way to the top of the heap are there if you have the money and the ambition.

I asked her why me.

'I do not know. We were told to find you and stop you for good. I get paid to do this work, not to ask questions.' She shrugged. 'It's my job.'

'So who gave you your orders?' It was a vain hope but you never know.

'Ivkanoy. It was Ivkanoy.'

Surprise, surprise. The fat man with the attitude problem. Max had been right; Ivkanoy really was pissed. So much so he'd sent a couple of contract shooters to kill me.

Ivkanoy was a big man in the region, she said. He had 'friends' all over, including across the border. I didn't need to ask which border; Max had already told me that. She'd done work like this for Ivkanoy before, she admitted. Her mouth turned down at that. I couldn't figure out if it was a grimace at the memory or if she was nervous at how this chat was going to turn out for her.

'How did you find me?'

They had been checking all routes west out of Donetsk, she said, and had struck lucky as I pulled out of Vokzal'na Square. They had recognized the car immediately; it was one of Ivkanoy's pool cars and used for clean jobs around the city. The plates didn't match the originals, she'd noticed, but how many red Toyota Land Cruisers do you come across in this part of the world? They had tucked in behind me until I'd pulled in at the truck stop and they'd been forced to go on by. They had stopped further on, but when I failed to show, they knew I must have taken a different route. By the time they got back to the truck stop, I was gone. But it didn't take a rocket scientist to figure out where I must have pulled off the main road and they'd set off after me.

'So what does Ivkanoy want with me?'

She looked puzzled and shook her head. 'He said you stole the car. We had to find you, no matter how long it took. He was real mad. He put out calls all over to watch for you. He said you would have already left the city, but we were the ones who got lucky.' She glanced towards the gulley at her late colleague, who I guessed wouldn't have agreed with her. 'Where I come from red is a bad colour.'

'Well, I hope he doesn't want it back.'

'He doesn't give shit about the car.'

So it was all pride. Nothing to do with Travis or my reason for being here. He wanted to show that he wouldn't take what I'd done to him lying down. At least that was something good; it meant the mission wasn't yet a complete bust.

I made a mental note never to drive a red car again, though.

'What else did you do to piss on his feet?' She had a sly look on her face in spite of the gun. 'Make him lose face? Sleep with his mistress?'

'He didn't tell you?'

She shook her head. 'He does not have to explain.'

'There was no "else" about it. He tried to cheat me, spat in my face, so I kicked his ass and broke his finger. It happens when you don't play straight.'

She agreed that it probably did and glanced towards the burning Toyota and the coil of dark smoke rolling across the grassland. 'Actually, I think he's going to be madder than ever when he sees that. He liked the car.' She didn't seem too distraught at the idea, and I figured Ivkanoy wasn't her favourite employer.

I relaxed a little. At least the mission hadn't been compromised. The number of people who knew what I was doing was no more than four or five, maximum. To have been able to find me so easily in a country this size meant they would have had to know my coordinates, description – everything. And they didn't.

'So what were your orders? Precisely.'

She looked at me pityingly, before nodding out at the grassland around us. 'There are pools here. Bogs. Very deep. You go in, you never come up again.'

That was pretty terminal. I nodded and thanked her, but she didn't respond. She wasn't happy about having talked so easily and I guessed in another life she'd be on my tail again to finish the job so nobody ever found out. Longevity in her kind of game meant being trusted never to talk even under pressure. Talkers were a liability and usually ended up dead.

I stood up and lifted the rifle. She turned her head away and waited.

I used the rifle butt to break her ankle. It was a kinder fate than the one she'd planned for me, or that one in her profession might have expected. But it would slow her down until somebody came along the road. More importantly it would get her off my tail. I didn't need to kill her to accomplish that.

She hissed sharply but never uttered a word. She was a tough cookie all right.

I smashed her cellphone and collected my bag, then walked up the ridge to the Isuzu. The most urgent task was to call in and tell support. Callahan would have to know about any potential police activity arising out of the past few hours. Even if the incident at 24 Obluskva was put down to the political situation, a dead body and a burning vehicle out here would cause comment. And that might spread ripples out to a wider area. Before speaking to Callahan, though, I needed to put some mileage between me and this place.

TWENTY-FIVE

After an hour's hard driving I pulled in to the side of the road and gave the Isuzu a careful going-over. I didn't know the female shooter's status or if she had other colleagues in the area. But I found no bugs, no tracking devices or unusual little electronic boxes beneath the hood or in the trunk, nothing to tell me that I might soon have a backup team all over me like a rash.

The back seat in the extended cab had a sleeping bag where I figured the second shooter had been asleep while the woman drove. There were two bags containing a change of clothes – one small female, one larger male – and some basic field-type rations typical for the kind of track-and-stop operation they had been on, and which wasn't expected to take more than a day or two. The woman's bag held extra magazines for the OSV and the Grach, which I pocketed. The man's held a spare magazine for his rifle. I left that there but took a hat with ear flaps and dumped the rest behind some bushes. Then I took out my cell phone and keyed the speed-dial for Callahan and waited.

A woman's voice answered. 'Go ahead, Watchman.'

'I need to speak to Callahan.'

'Sorry, he's not available right now. You can report to me and I'll see he gets it soonest.'

'You'll take it to him yourself?' There's an etiquette regarding operatives in the field; they get top priority no matter what. It's the nature of the game. If their prime nominated contact – and for me that was Callahan – isn't available, they get handed to the next in line, usually another duty officer of similar or appropriate rank. It's how decisions that might involve life or death situations get made promptly and nobody gets left hanging.

Being left hanging is a form of slow torture.

'If I have to. But I'm your primary communications link from here on in. I'm recording, so please speak when ready.' Her words were crisp and confidant with no superfluous chatter. She'd been well trained.

'What's your name?' It probably wasn't approved procedure, but neither time nor circumstance were in abundance. I needed this faceless woman on my side, and having a name – even a temporary one – would help us both establish a professional rapport.

'Lindsay. With an "A".'

'First or last?'

'First.' Something about the way she had said it told me it was real. But I like to check. Most of us use our own names with a faint hesitation, unless you're a call-centre operator and hitting numbers eight hours a day trying to sell finance or auto wax. Then it's just another word. I did the job once working undercover. Never again.

'Nice name.'

'My mom thought so. Dad not so much.' The hint of humour made me wonder if she knew anything about where I was right now and what I was doing. I knew she would have been thoroughly briefed, but the level of information given out about operatives and assets depended a lot on the ops officer and his trust in the people he was using. And Callahan had told me they would be using someone off the trainee program.

I gave her a summary of the run-in with Ivkanoy and the two shooters he'd sent after me. I left out the fine details; it wasn't necessary and bragging about a kill ratio isn't cool. If Callahan wanted to know more I'd tell him later. For now it was over and done with.

'Are you free and mobile?' She meant was I in one piece.

'I am.' The one thing a comms officer has to know is the condition and viability of an operative in the field. I confirmed my approximate position and direction of travel, and she listened without interruption. I could hear the soft rattle of a keyboard in the background as she made notes.

When I finished she said, 'What's your position relevant to Travis?'

'I'm an hour behind him. He's being taken to the first hand-over. That's if it hasn't already been raided.'

'I understand. We're having them checked out independently. Do you expect any interference from the two from Donetsk?'

She was asking if the shooters were likely to pose an imminent threat to me keeping an eye on Travis. She had a sharp ear for detail, and I was relieved; having someone on the other end of the line who was focused meant I didn't have to repeat myself.

'That situation is resolved.' It was as oblique as I could manage and as vague as she was going to get. I wasn't concerned about anyone listening in so much as not wanting to give out details I might later come to regret.

'Can you confirm any ID?' She was covering all the bases, just in case Callahan wanted to run a check through local contacts to make sure the field wasn't being flooded with opposition forces or cops on the look-out.

'One was named Olena Prokyeva – a freelance pro. It was a local thing; gang-related. Nothing to do with our situation.'

That wasn't entirely correct, and Callahan would know it. The fact of my passing through the region was now on the board, even if known only by a local ticked-off gangster. As far as the troops in Obluskva Street knew, I was an unknown quantity who'd got in the way and snatched Travis from under their noses. I'd left no footprint, so I didn't think that was serious. But sooner or later somebody would happen on the Toyota and the two shooters, drawn by the sight of smoke in an otherwise open landscape. What happened after that was anybody's guess.

'I'll get her checked out,' Lindsay said. 'And the other person?'

'He wasn't saying.'

She didn't miss a beat. It showed remarkable cool and I admired her for it. Even the mention of a woman shooter in opposition hadn't surprised her.

'I understand. Anything else?'

'Just one thing. I know you've got approved speech procedure. But we should keep it casual.'

'I'm not sure I understand.'

'The terminology. If there's a monitoring station in the area, they could pick up and recognize key words.'

Key words: the bane of anyone wanting to stay off the grid, yet forced to use technology for what it was. Government agencies use key words for information searches and listening in to phone calls – even encrypted ones. All it needs is one – among the biggest are 'terrorist' and 'bomb' – and electronic tracking does the rest. The US has the National Security Agency (NSA) and the British have the Government Communications Headquarters (GCHQ). But they'd be foolish to think they were the only ones using such powerful, high-tech systems. Russia has a reputedly much-diminished Third

Directorate, which does similar work, but nobody assumes they're anywhere near powerless.

At least, I don't.

'I gotcha. Will that do you for now?'

I laughed. Lindsay with an 'A' caught on fast.

TWENTY-SIX

W alter Conkley was in a blue funk. Ever since the meeting with Chapin, Cassler, Teller and the brutally threatening Howard J. Benson, he'd been looking over his shoulder. He had no illusions about his position relative to their activities, and was aware that he was allowed into their circle solely because of the level and nature of the information he could bring them from his place at the seat of government. He was also aware that the four men clearly had interests that went far beyond their think-tank status and their stated interests in the intelligence and security apparatus or, as it now seemed, the welfare of their country.

After what he'd heard Teller say earlier, he knew that there had been a subtle shift in his situation, and that there was no going back. Making profits out of war was nothing new; men had done so over the years, both in and out of government. But it was mostly unsaid and understood to be the prerogative of a few ruthless – and mostly nameless – entrepreneurs. What Teller had inadvertently opened the door to was the idea that this small group had plans which were not solely centred on the continued welfare of the Intelligence Community, as they pretended, but on their own financial interests. That their patriotic support of that community and the future of American foreign policy had been little more than a front for their own plans.

He wasn't a friend of such men, but he knew enough about them to have instantly divined where their discussion regarding European fuel and energy problems was taking them. And the idea of being caught up in that kind of deal worried him.

But not as much as the knowledge that he was now a marked man.

That had become evident in the seconds following Teller's comment, when Conkley had seen a glint of something in Benson's eyes; something that had sent a shiver right through him. Working alongside the most powerful men and women in the United States, individuals with the ability to make things happen that could shake the entire world, had become something of a norm. He'd been impressed, even intimidated by their personalities and the aura surrounding the real movers and shakers, but that had diminished over time at the knowledge that it was merely politics, and that the power was usually aimed at others far away.

However, the look Benson had thrown at him was something he'd never seen before. It was a malevolence that had come out of nowhere and aimed right at himself.

The look of a predator.

And Conkley was the prey.

He checked the ATM slip in his hand. It showed the balance of the secret account he had set up when first suborned into providing information for the Dupont Group; the account where regular payments were deposited that would go some way, he hoped, to cushioning a retirement against the privations of an inadequate pension and a depressing future. He had no idea which of the four men physically paid him the money, only that it came with the unspoken proviso that it guaranteed his absolute discretion and lack of curiosity about their work.

Well, he'd certainly come as close as he'd ever imagined to blowing that proviso out of the water. But there was nothing he could do about that now. He scrunched up the ATM slip and threw it in a nearby trash can. Then in a moment of panic snatched it out again and tore it into tiny pieces. In a town where guarding secrecy was a way of life, paper trails were every bit as useable as electronic ones. And the amount on the slip was substantial enough to cause an instant investigation by Justice Department officials and the FBI if it was ever revealed.

He checked his watch. Several hours had gone by since the meeting. There had been no follow-up from Benson or the others, which was a bad sign. Common sense and a civil servant's in-bred instinct for survival told him he should talk to somebody; somebody with a Teflon disregard for the kind of power people like Benson could wield. But that encompassed a very small and select group of individuals and would mean signing off the end to his career. Guilt by association was a hard charge to shake off – but possible given the right support. However, taking financial fees – payoffs – for the unauthorized disclosure of confidential government information was covered by all manner of secrecy regulations, and would settle around his head like a black cloud.

It would mean jail time.

He imagined the alternatives, toying with options and trying to convince himself that he was overreacting. If he kept quiet, maybe the problem would simply go away. What if he'd imagined the look in Benson's eyes as being nothing more than annoyance with his friend and talkative co-schemer, Teller? Maybe Benson had been embarrassed, and the look had been nothing more than that of a man trying to cover up a friend's indiscretion.

But the idea refused to go away and he felt sick with indecision.

Traffic was light, so he decided to walk. Clearing his head through exercise and fresh air would allow him time to think about what he should do next. He waited for a gap in the traffic and turned across the street towards a small park bordered by trees. Trees brought calm and serenity.

He took out his cell phone and scrolled through his address book. His mind was made up. It was too late for regrets; all he could do was make sure that he maximized the potential of the situation.

Over the years he had amassed an impressive roll of contacts throughout government and the private sector, including the media. Maybe it was time to consider the fourth estate to help resolve his fears, just in case a backup plan was required and he needed some protection.

After all, there were plenty of journalists out there who would give their mother's right arm to be able to bring down a self-important and overbearing bully like Senator Howard Benson. All they needed was a nice juicy scandal. Sex used to be good, but Clinton had rubbed the magic stone on that one and reduced its effect. Financial, then. Like most politicians Benson had enemies; you didn't get to the top of a local, state or national tree without stamping on toes, and some people never forgot an injustice. And if self-interest and financial gain while in high office were part of the mix, that would be enough for the knives to come out.

All Conkley had to do was find the right media person – one who would relish the opportunity to get his or her own back on one of the big beasts of Washington. Someone who would pay for the privilege and add to his secret account. Then he had to work out how to keep his own name out of the spotlight and his hands clean.

TWENTY-SEVEN

Senator Howard J. Benson sat in his office and studied a list of scribbles in his notebook. It wasn't as complete as he would have liked, and possibly not entirely accurate. But he'd only had a few seconds to look at the original, which was in an open mission file on Assistant Director Sewell's desk. He'd managed to take a quick look when Sewell had excused himself to take an incoming call. Fortunately, Benson had been blessed with a politician's memory. He'd made the notes after excusing himself to go to the washroom.

He now had something he could use to put a stop to Callahan's private gun-for-hire.

A call came in. The number was unlisted. It was the man he knew as Two-One.

'What have you got?'

'You were right about Brian Callahan.'

'How so?'

'He rarely moves far from the Langley bubble. But six days ago he travelled to New York City. He checked in to a CIA front office at ten-fifteen New York time and thirty minutes later he was joined in a secure room by a civilian. They spent forty minutes together, which went unrecorded, then went their separate ways. That was Callahan's only trip out of Langley other than family business.'

'Did you get a name for this civilian?'

'Yes, sir. He booked in as Marc Stuart Portman, a resident of New York. I got a photo from the security camera which I've just sent over. A passport check makes him a holder of dual US–British nationalities. I checked with a few places and he has almost no profile, which takes some doing. This guy's a pro.'

'That much I gathered. So what exactly do you have on him?'

'He's a contractor, obviously. Moves around, is known to have used at least one cover name, with addresses in New York, London and Paris. He has had contact with various agencies here and possibly overseas, but I can't prove that for sure without further digging.'

'Is that a problem?'

'It could take time and cause ripples. Are you ready for that?'

'Make it as fast as you can but don't trip any alarms. What else?'

'The rest is supposition. He's ex-military; he has to be.'

'Official records?'

'I tried that but I haven't found a link yet. He may have been enlisted for only a brief period and got busted or discharged, so there's nothing of significance to show up.'

'This is not helpful. The man can't be a ghost.'

'Actually, that's not strictly true.'

'What does that mean?' Benson's voice was a snap. He was fast becoming frustrated at the lack of detail. He knew the extent and depth of modern military records, and knew that very little managed to sink without trace. There had to be something somewhere that would give him some leverage on this mystery Watchman; leverage that could help him undermine Callahan's faith and reliance in the one man he believed could get Travis out safely.

'Well, I found one hint on a file, no more than that, that he might be former French Foreign Legion. But that's unconfirmed.'

'Can't you find out from the French?'

'No. They're not in the habit of disclosing information about former personnel – to anybody. Portman isn't like most of the contractors out there, I can tell you that. He keeps his head down and doesn't mix with any of the regular guys I spoke with, doesn't go to any of the usual hangouts to trade war stories. In fact, none of them had heard of him save for one former SEAL who said he'd done a job in Peru with a guy named Portman once and he said he was right up there.'

'I take it that's some kind of sub-level alpha-male compliment?'

'I would say so. Coming from a SEAL, it means Portman's something special.'

'Christ, you sound as if you admire the man.'

'I know the type, that's all. It comes back to the ghost thing.'

'How?'

'If he's as good as he seems to be, and he's worked for the CIA or other agencies before, my guess is his records could have been blanked out.'

'How do we confirm that?'

'We don't. I've tried before. If agencies want a former member of the military to disappear, that's what happens – they disappear.'

'You mean their specialists?'

'Those and others they use on a freelance basis, yes. The kind of people they want with no footprint.'

'So he is a ghost.'

'As good as.'

'Let me know as soon as you have something. Anything.'

Benson cut the call. This was a waste of time. It was yet more evidence of the CIA's cavalier attitude and their willingness to impose their own rules on established procedures. He had come across mentions before of former special forces personnel 'disappearing' from the records on a temporary basis, presumably allowing them to be used thereafter as unattached personnel to prevent any trail coming back to the US government. He had even been persuaded against his instincts of the usefulness of such ploys, but now saw it as further proof that the CIA was capable of almost anything in the furtherance of their 'missions', adding to the established stories of extraordinary rendition and so-called torture flights.

His incoming mail beeped. He found a file containing a single photo. It was a black and white face-on shot and showed a slim man with short dark hair and dark eyes. He was entering the CIA front office in New York. Dressed in a sport jacket and plain pants, he could have been anybody off the street. He looked about medium height and might have been of Spanish or Italian stock, but it was hard to tell. He had the compact appearance of a man who kept himself fit, the type Benson had seen many times over the years connected to the CIA and other agencies.

Benson had an uncomfortable feeling taking hold deep in his gut. The fact that this Watchman a.k.a. Portman was a professional was bad enough; but having dual nationality and addresses in other countries put him way beyond the normal level of contractors and second-hand soldiers for hire. With what Benson and the Dupont Circle Group were hoping for as an outcome with Edwin Travis, a pro with a Navy SEAL's mark of approval could pose a serious problem if he was successful in his assignment.

Still, he had a plan for that. All it would take was the decisiveness and courage to make another phone call. Only this one was way off the board of acceptability in normal terms, and would be regarded as treachery of the highest order in most quarters if it ever came to light.

He considered the probability of that ever happening, and dismissed it as unlikely. But what would happen if he took no action and allowed Portman to bring Travis home? Good for Travis, of course, and a hero's return for Portman if his name ever got into the spotlight. But after patting themselves on the back and thanking their lucky stars that they had retrieved the situation, the idiots in the State Department and the White House would go back to watching and waiting while other countries stepped in and took the initiative. And the spoils.

No. What he was planning would see the budgets and power return to the US Intelligence Community where it belonged, although not necessarily the CIA, not after he'd finished with them. It would cement in the eyes of the outside world at least, his reputation as an impartial advocate for the protection of the country, while being a hard-hitting monitor of illegal activities carried out in the name of the state. On the back of that, there would be an inevitable pressure on Congress and the Department of Energy to ease exports of energy to the European market.

Which would play right into the hands of the Dupont Group.

He took another cell phone from his desk. This was a disposable device and one he used very rarely. He dialled a Washington number and waited for it to answer. He could picture the room where it would be ringing, see the man sitting behind the ornate desk. A man with all the appearance and trappings of Washington affluence, an East Coast accent and great teeth, but with his heart and soul, along with a host of useful contacts, directly inside the Russian intelligence network.

While waiting, he studied the photo of the contractor named Portman, trying to read into his soul. He wondered what made such a person tick. Was it money? Patriotism? Honour? Kicks? A death wish?

He hoped it was the last one. Give it a few hours and Portman would have his wish granted in spades.

TWENTY-EIGHT

I was close to the intersection with the M04 to Pavlohrad when my cell phone call light flickered. I stopped by a clutch of trees at the side of the road and picked up.

It was Lindsay with an 'A'.

'How you doing?' she said. She sounded chirpy. Casual. But behind it was a rigid professionalism.

'I'm good. What've you got?'

It was an update from Callahan. Donetsk International Airport had just shut down, a victim of the unrest. Closed until further notice. Even if I'd wanted to, flying out from there was no longer an option.

It didn't matter. I hadn't planned on going out that way, anyway. Turning back east would be like walking into a sack. But it gave me a feel for the way things were going locally. With the airport closed, the mood of isolation and unrest would spread quickly to other parts of the region. There would be the inevitable ramping up of police and military activity, of curfews and the restriction of movements. If it spread far enough and encompassed the west of the country, getting Travis out might be a problem.

'There are no reports so far in the national media or via any of the state security links we have access to that could be related to your presence. There was a brief reference to an attack on security members in the Kyiv'ski District, but it was dismissed as the isolated work of criminals and no arrests have been made.'

'Nice to know that's what I am.'

'I have an update regarding the next cut-out. She's been contacted and will store Travis overnight at a local hotel where she's the deputy manager. Her husband has strong pro-Russian family links, so she feels Travis will be safer in the hotel out of the way. It's called the Tipol, close to the river. I checked the website and the building's big enough so he can be anonymous if he keeps his head down.'

'Good work. Anything else?'

'How's your status?' She was probably thinking about the two shooters. It was nice of her to ask, but it was standard procedure. A field operative who has specific fears he can't or won't express is a danger to himself and his assignment if those fears are unresolved for too long. It's the job of the handlers to tease out any such issues. They might not be able to do much about them, but talking helps. If that fails, the extreme is intervention.

'My status is fine. I'm staying on the move.' If Olena Prokyeva had managed to get word to Ivkanoy about what had happened, the chances are he would be even more on my case and would have more people out looking for me. The biggest danger for me lay in new faces, especially in built-up areas; I simply might not see them coming. Out here it wouldn't be so easy for them, but the threat was still real.

Lindsay was ahead of me. 'I did some checking,' she said, 'on the man Ivkanoy. Interpol and the Ukrainian Ministry of Internal Affairs have files on him. He also shows up in their State Prison Service records. He seems not to have a first name – at least there's nothing on record. He's done time for numerous offences, including murder and extortion. So not a nice man.'

'Good to know. And the shooter?'

'Olena Prokyeva. She has an interesting history. She completed military service and was stand-by on the Russian Olympic shooting team in 1988 and again in 1992. It was reported that she should have been in their first team but lost out because she was Ukrainian and had an attitude problem.'

'They got that right. Where did she serve in the military?'

'Afghanistan in 1989. That was right at the end of their involvement. She appears to have gone off the rails after that and dropped off the radar. Until now.'

'Good to know.'

'That's not all. Ivkanoy has extended family across southern and eastern Ukraine and over the border into Russia. One of his cousins is Yuri Beltranov, named recently as a leader of a separatist pro-Moscow group in the Luhansk district. Ivkanoy is rumoured to be one of his sponsors for political position in any new administration.'

'You've been busy. Thank you.' The last bit of information didn't exactly add to my feeling of well-being, but it was good to know where I stood. It also explained why and how Ivkanoy was able to send two shooters after me so casually; he didn't fear being implicated because his cousin the separatist leader would be his protector.

'How's the work?' I asked, watching a long line of army trucks thudding east. They were full of troops and equipment, and had an APC at the head of the column ready to clear the way. They looked like they meant business. A military chopper was keeping station overhead, jinking back and forth to study the landscape. It all looked a little unreal, like military convoys so often do.

'Quiet. I get to see even fewer people than you do.' There was a smile in the voice and I guessed she was in some kind of isolated room surrounded by electronic equipment and cut off from visitors. Like being in a hospital room only without the smell of medicines. I sensed a reserve, too, as if she wanted to say something but couldn't.

'You OK?'

'I'm good, thanks. Speak later?'

I signed off and got back on the road. If something was bothering her she was too professional to let it out, and I had other things to do.

I found myself in a steady stream of traffic heading west, with bunches of military vehicles and lines of trucks parked at the side of the road. It seemed as if the entire Ukrainian army was on the move, heading towards the east and the separatist militias waiting for them. The soldiers here were standing around smoking and waving encouragement to a few going the other way. None of them looked as if they were relishing the part they were going to play, but they were doing what soldiers do everywhere, which was waiting for the next list of orders from the high command.

The countryside here was flatter than I'd seen before, with gently rolling fields heading off into the distance and not much in the way of trees, other than a long line bordering a rail track heading, I guessed, to Pavlohrad.

As I was taking in the detail, I heard a car horn to my left. A military jeep loaded with armed men was sitting right alongside me. The driver didn't have a whole lot of room, but he was flashing oncoming drivers to get them out of the way and they weren't arguing. The front seat passenger flipped a hand for me to pull over and stop, while the rear seat passenger had a grim smile on his face and an AK-74 pointed at my head.

TWENTY-NINE

I pulled over and rolled to a stop on the grass verge. The jeep pulled over with me and stopped in front, blocking any escape. Seconds later I was out of the car and standing against the hood, with the rest of the traffic thundering by a few feet away. The two men from the back of the jeep stood guard, while the front seat passenger strutted his stuff and demanded to know who I was and where I was going.

I was worried this might be another Rambo-style vehicle check, but it quickly became obvious that there was something too efficient about the officer and his men, and that they weren't playing at being traffic cops just for the hell of it.

I told him I was from Germany and that I had a family to feed and was looking for work. I'd heard about some kind of government hostel hiring a maintenance man in Pavlohrad and was hoping to get the position.

He nodded like he was familiar with the place and peered into the car. I held my breath. If he saw the sniper's rifle I was in a whole world of trouble. He took an age walking round the car, tapping on the roof as if deep in thought. All the while I waited for him to open the doors and for the hammer to fall.

But he didn't. Instead he turned back and began flipping through my papers. I relaxed a little. I knew the address was a blind and even if he had the time or inclination to check it out, it would come up good.

'You're a long way from home. And Germany is a rich country.' He meant why was I wasting time looking for work in a poorer economy that was in danger of disintegrating into civil war any day now.

'I heard things were good here for people willing to work hard. I want to set up a business, employ others.' I shrugged. 'It's not good right now but you have to take a chance and run with it, right?'

He grunted with scepticism and I knew why. The kind of chances the military takes bear no resemblance to those in civilian life. Guns and ammunition present a more final and binding solution than spreadsheets, order books or corporate rules, and risk for civilians is measured purely in economic terms, not life and death. 'It sounds a good plan, but you should pay more attention to news reports. What kind of work do you do?'

'Electrician, plumber, carpenter . . . whatever you want me to do, captain,' I replied. He was a junior lieutenant but he didn't take offence at the promotion. His mouth twitched and he handed the papers back and nodded at the rear of the Isuzu. 'If you're so good with your hands, get your stop light fixed – it's flickering like a welcome sign on a Black Sea whorehouse.'

A burst of chatter from his car radio interrupted any further discussion. He listened, head cocked to one side. Whatever was said galvanized him into action. He gave a brief signal to his men and said to me, 'You can go.' With that, they all jumped aboard and were gone.

I let out my breath and got back in the car. It had been a random stop, but served as a timely reminder of just how fragile my presence here was.

Pavlohrad was quiet, with wide roads and not much in the way of traffic to fill them. I guess anyone who didn't need to travel was keeping their heads down. The elegant gold mushroom domes of the orthodox Christian churches flashed in the light, and after all the signs I'd seen of military activity, the town was indisputably civilian in tone and appearance, with an understated elegance to the buildings.

I followed the main road in and passed a large IS-3 Russian heavy tank sitting on a plinth. It was a memorial to the liberation of Pavlohrad in 1943 and a simultaneous reminder of the country's past and its links to its vast neighbour to the east.

I turned off the road before crossing the river Vovcha, which snakes its way through the town from north to south, and stopped to look at the map. I'd decided to check out the address of the cut-out first before going to the Hotel Tipol, where Travis was staying, just so I had a picture of the layout. Knowing where all the players were located was a must.

I checked the list on my cell phone. Apt 5, 12, Terkova Street. According to the map it was close by. I drove slowly, relieved to have caught up with Travis again. I'd make sure he was OK, then step back and wait for Callahan to make the next move. If the original plan went ahead, Travis would be handed over to someone else and be on his way.

The address I'd been given was in a small, three-storey apartment block over a row of shops not far from the river. It was a quiet area with little traffic and few pedestrians, and darkness was setting in. I'd been so focussed on getting here that I hadn't even noticed how the day had slipped by so fast.

I parked a hundred yards down the street and walked back towards the apartment block, conscious of being watched every step of the way, even if only out of innocent curiosity. It's a familiar feeling when operating in hostile areas. You have to learn to deal with it, even if you can never entirely dismiss it; having that little bit of nervous edge is what keeps you alert and out of trouble.

I stopped at a small store across the way. It smelled of cooked meats, fruit and vegetables, and had a trio of elderly ladies in head-scarves exchanging some local gossip. They stopped talking when I walked in, but started up again once they figured I was harmless. I bought some fruit and a bottle of water, taking my time as I kept an eye on the apartment building across the way to see if anything bad was playing out. When I was satisfied nothing was, I paid up and left, carrying a plastic bag. At least now I was just another local making his way home.

I walked past the building, chewing on an apple and watching for signs that I wasn't about to walk into a trap. An old man was sweeping some dirt on to the street and a dog was sitting watching him. Above them a curtain twitched and an old lady flicked a duster against the window.

The street was quiet so I walked on, taking my time and tuning in to my surroundings. If there were police or army here, there would be something in the atmosphere – a tension like no other. But I couldn't feel it. And the old ladies in the store were the kind who would have been talking their presence to death if they'd seen anything.

I continued a tour of the block, then walked back. When I reached the apartment building the old man had disappeared but the dog was still there, doing what dogs do when somebody is looking.

It was now or never. I stepped through the front door. I was in a small lobby with a flight of tiled stairs leading up right in front of me and a narrow passageway running towards the rear of the building. Two doors with numbers. 1 and 2. A bank of mail boxes stood against the wall, the slots stuffed with junk mail and newspapers.

As I walked up the stairs I felt the hairs on the back of my neck stirring. I ignored that one; it's a natural reaction to going somewhere you shouldn't, and besides, I hadn't seen anything to concern me. Sometimes you have to know when to override the instinctive signals the body and brain sends you otherwise you'd never move forward.

Number 5 was on the next floor. Three other doors shared the landing, along with a couple of bicycles, a small pram and a broken bathroom cabinet. I listened outside 5, heard the sound of a television or radio with a news update. The bit I caught didn't sound good; separatists were boasting of three government tanks set on fire and a police station blown up, but the government was denying it as lies.

A man's voice spoke, followed by a woman's laughter. But not from the television.

I backed off. If the woman was in the last thing she'd want was me stepping into her life out of nowhere, especially if her husband was unaware of her private work for the CIA. If Travis had made it this far, I'd find him at the Tipol.

I checked the hotel's location and followed the directions. It was back across the river on a broad boulevard lined by trees and a scattering of shops, houses, a gas station, another hotel and a school. I parked close by and walked past the front entrance, giving it the once over.

The Tipol was surprisingly large given the size of the town. A four-storey building with coloured fascia and lots of flower tubs, it boasted a large sign over the front door listing its many facilities including conference rooms and Wi-Fi. The car park was busy, but one vehicle stood out immediately.

An old black VW Polo with a bumble-bee sticker on the rear window.

I didn't have to look twice. It was the same car I'd followed out of Obluskva.

I walked round the block and back. No sign of surveillance, no military or cop presence. But something felt odd. Why was 24d still here? He should have been long gone into his new future – taking with him any chance of his car being spotted.

There really wasn't an option. I was going to have to go in.

I approached the reception desk. The foyer was standard hotel issue with a selection of uncomfortable looking chairs, bright posters of the local countryside and a rack of tourist brochures. The clerk was a young woman in her early twenties.

She looked up and smiled. 'Can I help you?'

'I need to speak with one of your guests,' I explained. 'The driver of a black Polo.'

She thought about it and nodded. 'I think I know the one. He arrived with another gentleman. Can I take your name?'

I ignored the question and feigned embarrassment, telling her that I'd scraped the Polo with my car and wanted to apologize to the owner, that my conscience wouldn't allow me to just drive away.

She looked impressed. 'Of course. One moment, please.' She checked her computer screen then picked up a phone and dialled a number. She waited and pulled a regretful face.

'I am sorry, sir. There's no answer. He must have gone out.'

'Might he be in the restaurant?'

'No, sir. I have just come from there. Two ladies and a man I know personally. But not Mr Travis. Can I take a message?'

Travis. He was using his real name? Jesus.

'No. Thank you. I'll be around for a while so I'll call back later.'

I got out of there and did another tour of the area, checking for stray State Department employees and blown cut-outs. But they were nowhere to be seen.

I'd been in the area enough for one day, and it was getting dark. If Travis was out with 24d, it was pointless looking for him, and sooner or later somebody would wonder why I was hanging around.

I found a quiet spot with a view of the hotel's front door and ate some fruit and drank the water. It wasn't the best meal I'd ever had but certainly not the worst. Besides, I'd found that once I was on an assignment and ready for go, so-called proper meals were something of a luxury.

By nine o'clock there was still no sign of Travis. To make sure, I walked back into the hotel, where a different receptionist was on duty. I asked if Travis was in.

She checked her screen, then rang his room extension, keeping one hand over the dial pad so I couldn't see the room extension number. All the time she managed to keep one eye on me as if I might run off with one of the uncomfortable chairs. After several rings she shook her head. 'I am sorry. Maybe he's asleep.'

I agreed that maybe he was. 'I'll call him in the morning,' I said, and left her to it.

THIRTY

E d Travis lay fully dressed, staring at the digital read-out in the base of the small television in his hotel room. It said 05.00 a.m. and he was listening to the night sounds – or were they early morning sounds? It definitely looked lighter than it had a while ago, although lack of sleep was doing strange things to his head. He focussed on the individual sounds in the hope that sleep would overtake him. There was the vague hum of the heating system, the occasional buzz of traffic passing by on the road outside, and the coughs and rumbles issuing from occupants of the rooms either side of his.

So far, as a distraction, it wasn't working. And whatever service the television was supposed to provide seemed to have been switched off and it gave out only a mushy screen of white noise, a frustrating snowstorm against a dark background.

He thought about the old man named Denys, three doors along. They had driven here from Donetsk mostly in silence, Denys steering the car with studied care and observing all the traffic rules. At times his grip on the wheel had become light and Travis had been forced to nudge his shoulder at one point when he thought he was zoning out. It was Denys who had decided to stay the night before moving on to try and get over the sickness that had settled on him. He hadn't said where he was going, only that he had a couple of people who would help him, old friends from way back.

Travis hoped he was right; he was no expert, but he'd witnessed the way his own father had faced death, and the aura that had settled around him in his final days. Denys had the same grey pall around his shoulders, the same gaunt look that no amount of medicines would put right. Nobody should have to endure that kind of solitary end in the final days of their life without someone to help and care for them.

It made him wonder what the hell he was doing here himself, so far from Beth, his wife, and his two children, Dean and Andrea. After his confinement at Donetsk Airport and being freed by the mysterious American, who had so far remained out of sight, he was now in another building, but just as disconnected from them as he had been before. At least he was free to move around within reason, without having an armed guard outside the door.

But what had he achieved coming to this country that was teetering on the brink of a civil war? He'd spoken to a few self-styled leaders, some clearly extreme in their views, some more strongly committed to real change in their country but by peaceful means. They had invariably been shouted down by others, perhaps not all provably Ukrainian, who were brutally critical of America's place in the world and demonstrably not happy at Travis's presence. The latter group were no less convinced that they wanted change, but there seemed to be no limit to what they had in mind to achieve their desired goals.

He knew which ones were doomed to fail, swept under the carpet of change by the gun rather than the political chamber; and it wasn't those with a soft line in dialogue and a desire to power-share in a new democracy.

The idea depressed him, and he found thoughts of his children laying heavy on his mind. They were too young for him to be off risking his life in foreign lands. But then so were thousands of other kids with parents in the military, or in embassies and missions all around the world, facing daily problems and dangers that could rip them away from their loved ones at a moment's notice. The temptation to pick up the phone as soon as he'd arrived had been tremendous, but he remembered what the American in Donetsk had told him. In any case he knew the dangers of calls being picked up by monitoring stations and had clamped down hard to resist reaching for the phone.

He closed his eyes, settling his breathing and deliberately trying to ease his family from his mind. If tomorrow was anything like today, he'd need all the rest and energy he could muster.

Seconds later he opened them again and realized that he'd fallen asleep. He sat up. He'd heard a noise, penetrating his consciousness in spite of his exhaustion. It hadn't been a car or a phone ringing, or the noisy heating. What then?

He heard it again. It was a thumping noise, like somebody hitting a pillow to soften it. He lay back, the explanation easy to take in, and closed his eyes.

Then somebody cried out. Short and sharp, it had the quality of a man in pain . . . or someone suffering a bad dream. After what he'd seen going on in this country, it would be amazing if some people weren't troubled by thoughts of what was happening to loved ones, to friends, to their country.

He sat on the side of the bed, now more than wide awake, and wondered if he should check on Denys. The old man was clearly in a bad way, undoubtedly a victim of poor diet and neglect. But the sudden departure from his home in Donetsk and the journey here, expecting all the time to be stopped by police or military roadblocks, had been an additional strain on a tired body already racked by ill-health. He had gone out shortly after arriving, telling Travis to stay inside and not to talk to anyone, that someone would be along in the morning to pick him up for the next stage of the journey.

Since then, nothing.

He got up and checked the grounds outside the window. Nothing moved. A few cars parked in rows, a dog – or was it a fox? – trotting along the road, and the darkness of a section of town without street lights. After what he'd seen in the east, it was oddly peaceful, serene almost.

A door opened and closed; a soft thump in the dark followed by the click of a lock. An early riser hitting the road. He heard the scuff of footsteps in the corridor. They stopped outside his door.

He stepped across the room. *Denys*. At last. Now he could be on to the next stage of the journey . . .

But it wasn't Denys. The man filling the doorway and blocking out the night-light in the corridor was big. Travis caught a glimpse of a bullet head and broad shoulders. The man was pointing at him, his arm encased in a leather jacket giving off a smell of cigarettes and body odour.

'What?'

He stopped speaking, the words congealing in his throat. The man was pointing but it wasn't a finger; he was holding the cold metal of a gun barrel against Travis's forehead.

'Back inside,' the man said softly, and prodded Travis backwards until he fetched up against the bed. The man closed the door then dropped the gun into a holster strapped under his jacket against the side of his chest.

'Where is the other man who brought you here?' The newcomer's voice was clear and precise, almost friendly. But what came next was not.

'I don't know,' Travis replied instinctively, and instantly felt a tremendous blow to his stomach that knocked him back on to the bed. He tried to roll away, his knees going weak, but fetched up against the headboard with a sickening bang. A wave of nausea rolled over him, making his head spin.

'Not the right answer, Mr Travis.' The man leaned over him and began binding his hands and legs together with a roll of packaging tape until he was immobile. 'There. That's better. Now, where is the other man?'

'I told you—'

Another body punch, this one to the chest, followed by a round-house slam to his ribs that nearly lifted him off the bed. He heard something crack and felt his stomach rebel as the pain lanced through him like a bolt of fire. There were other blows, but not nearly so hard, merely a relentless repetition, spaced out around his body, the fists sending waves of pain through him until he nearly passed out.

Eventually the beating stopped. 'I'll ask you another question, to see how we get on. Where are you going after here? What address have you been given?'

'I haven't been told that.' Travis braced himself for another blow, knowing that he couldn't sustain this level of systematic damage for long without something going badly wrong.

But the man didn't hit him. Instead he leaned closer and whispered in his ear. 'Your friend, the old man? The one whose car you were in?'

Travis coughed. The movement produced a renewed burst of agony and he wanted to be sick but didn't dare in case he choked to death. 'What . . . what about him?' This thug evidently knew about Denys, there was no point denying it. Maybe he could delay things in the hope that one of the other guests would alert the management about the noise.

'He's dead. See this?' The man produced a long, slim knife with a sharp point. 'I asked him the same questions. But he refused to talk so I provided him with an incentive. You know about incentives, Mr Travis?'

Travis couldn't speak, he was so horrified. Instead he nodded, not wanting to hear more.

'Good.' The man smiled. 'I made a large hole in his side.' He sighed dramatically, his breath hot and stale on Travis's face. 'He was a foolish old man, but a brave one. He had guts – and I saw some of them. But in the end he told me where you were.' He giggled and placed the knife blade on Travis's cheek, close to his eye. 'Now then, where shall we begin, Mr Travis? You like reading? Watching TV? Looking at your pretty wife as she takes off her clothes and gets naked for you, huh?' He pressed down on the blade without breaking the skin. 'How would you be able to do that without your eyes, do you think?'

The man suddenly moved away. He picked up the roll of tape and tore off a strip, slapping it across Travis's mouth. Then he bent and ripped out the phone wires from the handset. 'I'll give you a couple of minutes to think it over. Don't think about running anywhere, will you?'

The man left the room and closed the door and Travis felt himself losing consciousness. Oh, God, he thought, don't let it end here like this . . .

THIRTY-ONE

I woke at six with a stiff neck and the feeling that I'd missed something. I checked the hotel. All the curtains were drawn tight and the Polo was still in the car park. A delivery truck was dropping off laundry and supplies to one side, but other than a sleepy-looking driver and a woman with a clipboard and the sullen manner of an afternoon person, the place was quiet.

I left the car and walked a short distance until I found a café with a number of workmen getting ready for the day. Or maybe they were night workers stopping on their way home for coffee and what looked like brandy or white spirit – *horilka* – locally brewed and flavoured with fruit. I avoided the alcohol and settled for fried potatoes and eggs, which seemed the staple breakfast diet. The nods I got from the other customers, who shifted over to allow me to sit, told me I seemed OK.

Blending in.

I finished eating and paid up, leaving an acceptable tip, then walked back to the hotel. Most of the room curtains were now pulled back. The Polo hadn't moved. Travis had to come out sooner or later and be on his way. Unless he was waiting for the next cut-out to show up and collect him.

I waited until eight, then decided to take the initiative. The hand-over was taking too long. The more time Travis spent here the more exposed he would become and the greater was the risk he ran of being noticed.

At eight-ten I walked across the road and approached the reception desk. The clerk was male, impressively tall and snappily dressed, with four pens in his breast pocket and the manner of someone who knew what was what in the hospitality industry.

'Can I help you, sir?' He looked ready to vault the desk and do a polka. In the background I could hear the clatter of dishes and cutlery.

'I need to speak with one of your guests,' I explained again. 'The driver of a black Polo.'

He thought about it and nodded. 'Of course, sir. Is there a problem?'

I told the story again about scraping the Polo with my car.

'I see. One moment, please.' He checked his computer screen, tapped several keys, then picked up a phone and dialled a number. He waited and pulled a regretful face.

'I am sorry, sir. There's no answer. He must have stepped out early.'

'Might he be in the restaurant?'

'No, sir. I would have his meal tab. His is not one of them. Can I take a message?'

'No. Could you try his extension again? He might be in the bathroom.'

'Of course.' He went through the dialling routine again, and I watched the numbers to see which room he was calling. Twenty-eight.

Still no answer.

Alarm bells were now ringing big time. Travis had no reason to go off the plan like this. Maybe he'd taken a walk like the clerk suggested. Stress needs a form of release and he would have been feeling under plenty of that in the past few days. But sightseeing was the last thing Travis would have wanted to do – he was too keen on getting home to his family.

I thanked the clerk for his help and walked outside and round to the rear of the hotel. I hadn't seen any CCTV cameras in evidence, so I figured it was safe to take a little snoop. I found a newspaper tucked inside the pannier of a moped and grabbed it, and walked in through a back door as if I owned the place.

The stairs to the second floor were deserted, and I got to room twenty-eight without seeing anyone. The place sounded quiet save for the distant hum of a vacuum cleaner.

I tapped on the door. It opened a fraction.

I rolled the newspaper as tight as I could, with the spine edges out where the paper was thickest. As a make-do weapon at close quarters, it wasn't great but would do. I wasn't expecting Travis to go all physical at me, but the atmosphere here was wrong enough to make me think something bad had happened.

I pushed the door back until it bumped against the wall. The room was standard design, with a bed, armchair, night table, a line of hangers and a waste bin. The bed was undisturbed. As I was about to go in, I heard a clank and a maid appeared wheeling a small service trolley. She peered past me and saw the undisturbed

bed, then walked away with a shrug of her shoulders, waving a hand and muttering about guests who never turned up.

I stepped inside the room and walked across to the window. The air smelled sour and stuffy, as if the heating had been turned up too high, and there was another aroma, too. Somehow gamey, like blocked pipes. I checked the car park. The black Polo was still there.

So where was 24d?

I turned to leave, and that's when I saw him. He was in the corner, behind the armchair.

Even without checking I knew he was dead.

THIRTY-TWO

By the position of his body it was evident that his neck had broken. Whoever had killed him had curled him up tight, forcing his thin legs in against his chest and wedging them in place with the armchair. He didn't take up much space and looked even skinnier dead than alive. Killing him must have been a simple task.

I checked his pockets. They were empty. Nothing to identify him.

As I flipped back one side of his jacket, I saw a rip in his shirt. I also pinpointed the gamey smell I'd picked up earlier. He'd soiled his pants. I could see why, too. His shirt wasn't ripped – it was cut. And there was the deep black-red colour of blood soaking his hip and the carpet beneath him.

I peeled back the shirt. 24d had been tortured. Somebody had used a knife on him, jamming the blade in his side and making a hole just above the hip bone. The pain must have been unbearable. I lifted his head, wondering if he'd had a chance to cry out. But that had been impossible; the corner of a bright yellow handkerchief protruded from between his lips, with the rest stuffed down his throat.

Torture. The kind of thing people do with only two aims in mind. Information or revenge.

I discounted the second; as far as I knew, 24d was a stranger here and hadn't seemed the sort to hurt a fly. But the information he had which would have made this worthwhile was the whereabouts of Edwin Travis.

And the location of the local cut-out.

I had to get out of here. But finding Travis was a priority. Without him, my job was over. I stood up and made sure the body wasn't visible from a casual look through the door. I didn't want the maid coming back and screaming the place down before I was clear and away.

I stepped out into the corridor and three doors down almost walked into a man coming out of another room. He was tall and heavily muscled, with a bullet head. He moved like a club bouncer, all shoulders and arms, and was dressed in jeans and a leather jacket. As he turned to pull the door shut, his jacket swung open to reveal the leather strap of a shoulder harness across his chest and the butt of a semi-automatic in a holster. Then he saw me.

His mouth dropped open in surprise, and I could see him trying to compute whether I was a threat or not. Then a light came on and he lashed out with a fist like a bucket while reaching for the gun.

I didn't know how, but somehow he'd recognized my face, and that worried me.

As fast as his reactions were, my appearance had caught him off-balance. I ducked beneath the punch and turned, kicking his right knee from under him. It gave with a sharp crack of bone and he started to fall, a scream of pain building in his throat. I hit him across the side of the neck and bounced him off the wall as he went down, out for the count. Then I grabbed him under the shoulders and dragged him back into the room he'd just left and rolled him behind the bed. As I did so I heard a sound behind me and swung round, expecting trouble number two and ready to go again.

It was Ed Travis looking at me from the next bed.

His eyes were rolling imploringly above a strip of tape wrapped around his head and over his mouth, and his hands and feet were taped up tight so he could barely move. He was sweating freely and looked like a man living a nightmare.

I peeled away the tape from his mouth and he yelped as it took off some skin from his lips.

'Sorry. Who's your friend?' I asked him.

He shook his head without replying, and I saw why. His lips were dry and cracked, and he was having trouble breathing. The heavy must have had him taped up for some time without water. He also had a heavy bruise under one eye and possibly other injuries I couldn't see.

I made him stay where he was and got a glass of water from the bathroom and dribbled a little over his mouth. 'Take it easy,' I said, when he tried to grab the glass from me. 'Where are you hurt?'

He flapped a hand over his ribs. I told him not to talk and peeled back his shirt. He had some vivid bruising across his chest and stomach where he'd been punched repeatedly, and I didn't want to speculate on how much internal damage might have been done. Whatever it was, there was nothing I could do about it at the moment.

Once I was sure he'd drunk just enough to keep him going I went over to check the windows. If the unconscious man now snoring behind the bed had any colleagues about, they were out of sight. But staying here was now even more risky with a dead body down the corridor and the likelihood of someone coming up here to join the muscle-man.

I turned round just as Travis finished the water and nodded. 'It's OK. Thanks. I'm good.' He shook some feeling back into his arms and feet, and gingerly tucked his shirt in, wincing as he touched his stomach. He stared down at the thug behind the other bed. 'I thought I was dead. He threatened to kill me if I didn't tell him. He was like a madman – but controlled. Sadistic.' He took a deep breath as the shock suddenly hit him, and his face, which was already pale, went a shade of grey. He rolled off the bed and just about made the bathroom, where he threw up noisily in the sink. Sudden rehydration will do that to you.

He came back out wiping his face with a tissue and looked at me with a vacant expression. I'd seen that look before in others. It's the kind of phase a person goes through just prior to sinking into a state of severe shock. He had tear streaks down his cheeks and when he spoke his voice was shaky. 'He wouldn't believe me. He told me what he'd done to Denys and he'd do the same to me if I didn't tell him the address.'

'Hold it. Denys? Denys who?' I had to keep him talking, keep him thinking about putting words together. The alternative was for him to go catatonic.

'The man from the apartment who brought me here. His name was Denys. He wouldn't tell me his family name. You didn't know?'

'I didn't need to. What address was he talking about?'

He coughed with difficulty and cleared his throat. 'The next in line. The cut-out. I tried to tell him but he wouldn't listen—'

'Did you tell him?'

'No!' He looked offended. 'I couldn't. I was only given the first address – that was Denys'. He said it was best if I didn't know who he was delivering me to in case we ran into a roadblock. He said if that happened I should call the US Embassy in Kiev and find somewhere to hide until they could arrange a pick-up, and not to trust anybody.'

'And he left you here?'

'Yes. He said he had to go out and that I should stay inside. I

think he was going to make contact with the local asset, but I didn't
hear from him again. Oh, God, that noise.' His mouth fell open and
he looked sicker than ever.

'What noise?'

'I heard something in the night. I couldn't tell where it was
coming from, but it sounded like somebody hitting a pillow. You
know . . . the way you do when you can't sleep? Jesus, I've only
just realized—' He stopped speaking as imagery in his head told
him what it must have been.

'Don't think about it,' I told him. 'And then this guy turned up?'

He looked distraught. 'He said he'd killed Denys because he
refused to talk. Is that right – he's dead?'

I nodded. It was pointless hiding the truth and he had to know
how serious things were. I was still puzzled about who bullet-head
was and why he was here – and how he'd obviously known who I
was. I bent and searched his pockets. He had some cash, a cell
phone, a wallet with a couple of credit cards and a plastic ID card
which gave his name as Greb Voloshyn. A business card described
him as a private investigator and security guard with a company
called BJ Group based in Kiev.

In his inside jacket pocket I found two photos. One was of Edwin
Travis.

'Come on,' I said, and stuffed both photos in my pocket. I helped
Travis to his feet, taking care not to put any strain on his ribs. 'We
have to get out of here.'

As we moved towards the door, I glanced out of the window. In
the distance, two cars were approaching at speed with headlights
on. One had a red light flashing on the roof. The other was a military
jeep. It was just what we didn't need right now.

But what also worried me was the second photo I'd found in
Voloshyn's pocket.

It was of me.

THIRTY-THREE

B enson, Chapin, Cassler and Teller were once more in the secure library at Chapin, Wilde & Langstone. The atmosphere was brooding, following the news of growing tensions in Eastern Europe. This time they were served glasses of whisky with soda and spring water on the side. But none of them had added anything to the fine malt.

'I've been thinking,' said Benson, opening the meeting, 'that it would help us if the wheels were to come off this particular wagon.'

'What the hell does that mean?' Cassler was staring into the screen of a tablet showing a summary of the latest trading figures. To judge by his expression, the wheels had already come off his particular transport. As they all knew, the European markets had changed overnight and he'd lost heavily before he could take action. He looked far from pleased at the results and a bead of sweat was visible on his mottled skin. If there was one thing they all knew Cassler hated, it was losing money. Of all of them, he was probably the most exposed financially.

'It means this whole thing is moving too slowly and we have to force the issue.'

'Enlighten us, then.' Cassler looked irritated, as if his personal pain was being ignored.

'For our plans to work,' Benson announced, 'we need Congress and the White House to harden their stance on Travis's situation. The State Department's jumping up and down but Travis is just one man who happens to have his ass caught in a sling. As far as the White House is concerned, he'll be fine as long as everybody keeps talking.'

Chapin looked interested but wary. He hadn't touched his whisky and seemed tired, as if his reserves of energy had washed out of his system leaving him drawn and pale. 'What about the planned rescue operation? I thought that was under control.'

'I'm keeping close tabs on it. Travis was moved from his hotel, and the contractor managed to get him away from his escort. I don't know the details, but I gather he used force. Travis is now in a pipeline heading west, but I understand the contractor has run into some problems.'

'What sort of problems?' Chapin leaned forward. As a former intelligence officer, he knew what it was like to hear that an asset had been blown and was being hunted down. It was the kind of news that had haunted agent runners down the decades.

'His continued freedom is in doubt. In fact, if certain factions over there knew where he was right now, they'd pick him up and put him on display. Which would be a shame.' Benson gave a ghost of a smile that betrayed the sentiment for what it was. 'But that's a consequence of the games the CIA thinks it can indulge in.'

'A real shame,' said Chapin. 'Still, good plans fail all the time. But what will that mean to Travis? He's in this pipeline, isn't he?'

Benson hesitated. He'd been wondering how to broach the subject ever since making the phone call that had set things in motion. He still wasn't sure how the others would take it. He felt they weren't quite as . . . committed as him.

It came down to acceptable losses. Losing an unknown contractor was hardly a tragedy; it happened all the time in Afghanistan, Iraq and other places. But losing a member of the State Department was much closer to home. The ripples would be felt throughout Washington and would have even the most enthusiastic of apologists for Russian foreign policy demanding action against them and their agents. He wasn't sure how it would be received here among this small group of self-interested individuals, but he couldn't hold off for ever; time was getting short and he'd already set things in motion. It was now or never.

'He's in the pipeline, yes. But pipelines are fragile structures. They get breached from time to time. Sometimes with serious consequences.'

'What are you saying,' Teller queried. 'Pipelines? Breached?'

Benson threw him an angry look. He still hadn't forgiven Teller his lack of tact in front of Conkley. 'I'm saying we need a catalyst. A human one. Something that will harden attitudes.'

'Like?' Cassler prompted.

'What I'm thinking of would be a tragedy for Travis's family,' he said carefully, 'but every conflict has its casualties. The knowledge that a member of the US State Department was running around the country in the hands of people with questionable loyalties would raise questions all the way back to Moscow, I feel sure. They'd want to do something about it. Something that would give us an edge.' He sat back and waited. There. He'd got as far as he dared to voicing the unsayable.

Edwin Travis had to meet with an accident.

There was a long silence while they digested the full meaning of what he was suggesting. Even Cassler put down his tablet and looked around at the others. His expression was close to incredulity. But that might have been the onset of reality hitting home.

Benson caught the look and cursed beneath his breath. He'd been counting on the moneyman to seize any opportunity going to lead the financial charge. Once he was on board, he was certain the others would follow.

'What are you saying would happen,' Ambrose Teller asked in his convoluted way, 'if such a tragedy came about? Would Moscow really be so upset at finding he was on Ukrainian soil that they would use it? I assumed they must already know he's over there holding talks, as have many others.'

'Of course they know.' Benson bit back on his impatience. They were starting to get cold feet. 'But that's politics; better to have an appearance of openness than not. Even Putin recognizes that – up to a point. In any case, I'm sure Travis was being watched to make sure he didn't cause too much trouble. The Russians are clever; allowing a measure of foreign "discussion" is good for their image. Not that they're officially involved, anyway. Remember, they disclaim any control over these so-called separatists, so their hands are clean. They can stand by and watch it all without being tied to any nastiness that might happen. But given the chance, they'll make capital out of it just to deflect international disapproval from their own involvement.'

'Interesting scenario.' Chapin spoke softly, but there was uncertainty in his voice. He threw Benson a cool look. 'But you're talking about two men being wasted, Howard.'

'I'm suggesting what *could* happen.'

Chapin snorted at the other's careful choice of words. 'Jesus Christ, I always knew you were a ruthless bastard. I just never realized how far you were prepared to go. Are you serious?'

'I'll do what's necessary, Vernon – you know that.' The senator's voice was unemotional, his face calm. He looked at the three of them in turn. 'Are we agreed or not?'

Chapin said nothing for a moment. 'It might work,' he said finally.

'It might just work.' His eyes flicked briefly towards Teller and Cassler, although they all knew he wasn't really seeking their opinion. As long as it didn't threaten their investments, they would go with him and agree with whatever he decided was best. He looked back at Benson. 'Are you saying you can set it up?'

Benson waved a hand to disguise his feeling of relief. 'Consider it done.' As it already has been, he wanted to say, but he restrained himself. Time enough for self-congratulation later, when everything was neatly tied up. For now, he had to ensure they didn't suffer a change of heart.

'What will happen to him?' Cassler queried. As someone who had never been on the cold inside of intelligence or espionage work, he had no idea how these things were actioned, nor what the immediate consequences might be.

'Don't worry about it, Burman,' Benson assured him. 'It won't come back on you. People over there talk to the security authorities all the time. What's another call from a local source about a suspect foreigner allegedly travelling without a visa and making lengthy phone calls in the dead of night?'

'That doesn't answer my question, does it?' For a moment, Cassler looked annoyed by the deflection. 'What will happen?'

'He'll disappear, probably. Possibly. Everyone will shake their heads, deny all knowledge . . . and in time he'll be quietly forgotten.'

Cassler swallowed hard. 'And the man sent to get him back?'

'Forget him. He knew the risks. If it wasn't there, it would have been some other God-awful place the CIA liked sticking their collective nose.' It was brutal, but this had gone on long enough. He glanced at his watch. If the man he'd phoned a few hours ago had lived up to his word, Portman and Travis would shortly be scooped up. And the two addresses of the cut-outs he'd supplied would be raided and their residents singing their hearts and lungs out.

Cassler gave a nervous laugh. 'My God, Howard, you sound as if you've done this kind of thing before. Should I be worried?'

Benson didn't answer directly. Instead he said, 'I'm sure we'll all mourn Mr Travis's sacrifice on behalf of a grateful nation. But we'll benefit by it.' He smiled but it lacked warmth and left the other men looking faintly discomforted, as if they had suddenly found themselves party to something not quite palatable.

'How d'you figure that?' said Chapin, ever the realist.

'With Travis taken in and the inevitable media storm to follow, I think we'll find the White House suddenly revitalized in their energies against Moscow's heavy-handed approach, and the threat of sanctions should become a reality. And with it the release of export restrictions on energy supplies to Europe.'

Cassler gave a light chuckle and relaxed. It was in sharp contrast to his nervousness moments ago. 'Hell, in that case, how do I move sufficient stocks quickly enough to buy into the energy market?'

Back in his office, Benson found a voicemail waiting for him. It was from the man he knew as Two-One. He called him back using the secure cell phone.

'What have you got?'

'Citera, Lindsay Sofia.' Two-One sounded robotic, his usual way when delivering information, as if a lack of emotion would make it sound more matter-of-fact, like a military briefing. 'She has an interesting family background. Parents divorced, brother in the US army garrison in Mannheim, Germany, suspected of shipping in narcotics after a tour of duty in Afghanistan. She has a sister, younger than her, currently unemployed with a couple of misdemeanours for driving while drunk and some serious debt problems.'

'Is that all?' Benson was pretending not to be interested. In fact, his brain was already working on how he could use this information to his best advantage. For one, he wondered how Lindsay Citera had managed to clear the intense security vetting required by all CIA applicants with what seemed like such a dysfunctional family background. Surely she was a prime candidate for pressure to be applied by anyone seeking advantage over an officer with such inherent weaknesses. He made a mental note to add that to his list of complaints about the Agency's lack of oversight when it came to security vetting of employees.

'It's all I could find. That's usually the way with clean slates.'

'Is that supposed to be a joke?' Benson had never known this man to be anything less than carefully deferential. But his last remark was bordering on insolence.

'No. It means what it says: if it can't be found, could be it ain't there.'

Benson bit his tongue. For some reason the man was showing an uncharacteristic flippancy bordering on rudeness. He decided to let it ride. For now. 'Does she have contact with her family?'

'As far as I can make out, just the sister. But on rare occasions.'

'Financial?'

'Three times in the past six months. She made money transfers amounting to a total of three thousand dollars.'

'I think that will do nicely.' Benson felt the warm glow of a plan coming to fruition. Take a CIA officer of any level – but especially a trainee – with family members having money problems, and you had a situation ripe for exploitation. Add in another family member currently in prison for drug offences while serving in the US military, and the explanation was complete.

'I need a payment to be made. No trace-back.'

'Of course. To Lindsay Citera's account?'

'Yes. Can you handle it yourself? This is something I don't want other parties involved in.' He suspected that some of the tasks he asked of Two-One were completed by others. Normally that didn't bother him in the slightest, but when it came to financial and banking irregularities centred on a government employee, which could bring in the focus of the US Secret Service, it was a danger he didn't wish to court.

'Of course. How much?'

Benson thought it over. If Citera's sister was into her for three thousand at the very least – not counting any cash payments, which wouldn't be traceable but would be perfectly understandable between siblings – then any black payment turning up in her account had to at least match that figure or exceed it substantially. After all, if you were going to sell secret information, you would want to have some extra to put aside, wouldn't you? He smiled. It had to be a nice round figure, something which investigators would be unable to miss and Citera would find impossible to explain.

'Make it twenty thousand dollars.'

THIRTY-FOUR

Getting out of a hotel at speed without being noticed is no easy task. I had Travis by the arm to stop him falling over and to keep him moving, and I was ready in case Voloshyn had backup waiting. By my calculations we had about two minutes to get out of the building before Grey Suit and his cop friends had the area sealed off tight.

The woman cut-out must have been blown. It was the only logical explanation for the cops coming here like this. I felt sorry for her; she'd been in a no-win situation, and once the authorities had her home address she was done for. Just like 24d – aka Denys.

I urged Travis towards the rear stairs, ignoring the elevator. Elevators are rat-traps; once in, there's no way out. Forget about trapdoors in the ceiling; cops watch films, too, and know all the moves.

We passed the room maid on the way and I swore at the turn of luck. She'd seen me twice now, once in a room where a dead body was shortly going to be found and now dragging a traumatized and badly beaten man behind me. If she was making for the corridor upstairs, it didn't matter which room she got to first; the one with the late Denys or the one with the snoring and armed thug, Voloshyn. Either way she'd kick up a screaming fit and have a good fix on our faces.

I put on speed, half-carrying Travis, and we reached the rear lobby where two loaded baggage carts were sitting just inside the swing doors. A tour bus stood outside with a line of men being checked on board by a guy with a clipboard. They were all middle-aged in stiff suits and ties, and looked like a group of union leaders on a day out. It didn't look like they were having fun. But that soon changed.

In the background the wail of a police siren drifted closer. It caused a few heads in the line to turn, sensing that here at last was a bit of excitement to brighten up a dull morning.

Twenty seconds and counting, was my estimate. But my car was out front and across the road. Right in their line of sight. We'd be like two ducks in a fairground shooting gallery.

I grabbed one of the carts and pushed Travis towards the other.

'Head for the far side of the tour bus. Keep your head down and your face out of sight. Watch me and follow my lead.'

I didn't wait for him to agree, but pushed through the swing doors and headed outside, letting the baggage cart go first. Down a ramp, through a puddle and across the yard, the bogey wheels rattling and a suitcase balanced on the top of the pile threatening to take a dive at any second. I could hear Travis coming up fast behind me, his breathing louder than it should have been. I skirted the rear of the bus until I was out of sight of clipboard man and the line of passengers and let the cart go. I didn't stop or look back but continued walking, aware of Travis stumbling along behind.

We were now heading away from the rear of the hotel towards a development of small houses and a stretch of open parkland dotted with flower beds and bushes and a play area. A couple of women with small children were sitting on a bench while their kids played around a set of swings. They didn't seem to notice us, which was good, but I veered away so they couldn't see our faces. With each step we were getting away from the cops and Grey Suit.

I waited until I figured we were far enough from the hotel before turning and heading off on a circular route back towards the car. If we could reach it unseen and get going, we'd have a fighting chance of getting out of town before they shut the place down.

I checked Travis was OK. He was coughing and sounded like he'd just run a marathon, and I wondered at the internal effects of the beating he'd taken from Voloshyn in the hotel room. The guy had had fists like shovels and he hadn't looked the sort to make clinical value judgements about his target before laying into him.

By the time we reached the road we were three hundred yards from the hotel and I could see the police car and jeep coming to a stop outside the front entrance. The doors were thrown open and a couple of soldiers ran towards the tour bus, waving their guns and shouting at those who were already on board to get out.

We got to the Isuzu and piled on board, and I drove away at a sedate pace, with one eye on the rear-view mirror. By the time Grey Suit and his men had closed down and searched the hotel we should be away and clear.

I drove west, keeping to the speed limit until we were clear of the town before stepping up the pace. The Isuzu engine had been worked on by an expert, and in spite of the noisy muffler it had a lot of punch under the hood. I was hoping that would help us put some distance between Grey Suit and all the others following us until we could find another ride. I'd already hung on to this one for too long, and if Ivkanoy's reputation was what it seemed, he'd have a description out there by now.

Travis was very quiet, sitting hunched over in the passenger seat and clutching his ribs, eyes closed. His breathing was steady but I put that down to him nursing his ribs. I shook him gently by the shoulder to bring him round. The last thing I needed was for him to close down.

'You're familiar with weapons?' I had to keep him in touch; if he was hurting because of internal injuries his body, dulled by the pain, would begin to shut off and his mind would follow. Then he'd be a dead weight.

He coughed but opened his eyes and looked up. 'Weapons?' He probably thought I was about to ask him to start shooting at people. 'Of course. Why?'

'Look under your seat.' At the same time I reached down and pulled out the Grach semi-automatic I'd taken off the woman sniper.

He stared at the pistol, then did as I asked. When he pulled out the Ero and saw what it was, he looked stunned, as if he wanted to throw it out of the window. He may once have been in Military Intelligence but I guess he'd been behind a desk too long and this was all way too much on top of everything else that had happened.

'Who *are* you?' he demanded. 'More to the point, what are you? Do you even have a name?'

I ignored him. 'You were in the military, right?'

'Yes.'

'See any action?'

He shook his head. 'I don't remember.'

That meant no. If you see any, you never forget it. 'Doesn't matter. Check the load.' I handed him the Grach. 'This, too. Don't point them my way and try not to shoot yourself in the leg.'

I didn't tell him about the sniper rifle in the back. I figured that might send him over the edge. I'd leave it for later.

He shook his head in disbelief but checked both weapons, hesitating only momentarily over the Ero before disengaging the magazine and counting the shells, then doing the same with the Grach. As I'd hoped, having something specific and familiar to do was helping him forget his physical ills. Quite what it was doing to his mental state was something else altogether.

'Twenty-eight in the submachine gun and a spare magazine,' he reported. 'A full mag in the Grach and a spare.' He made sure both guns were safe before placing them on the floor of the foot well. 'Tell me you're not going to use them.'

'I don't plan to,' I told him. 'But you know how this country is right now. There are roadblocks popping up all over, not all of them official. We may not have a choice.' I didn't want to break his spirit by telling him just who we had on our tails, such as cops, unnamed security police, Ukrainian special forces, pro-Russian separatists and a gang leader with a sore head. As for which faction the man named Voloshyn belonged to, that was anybody's guess.

'The name's Portman,' I said. 'I was sent in to bring you out.' I reached in my pocket and took out a passport and a driver's licence, which I tossed on his lap. They weren't in Travis's real name but they were good enough, a present from Callahan and the CIA's document production centre. Forgery Central on the taxpayer's dollar.

He seemed to have trouble processing the information and stared uncomprehendingly at the documents. 'Portman. Is that it? You don't have a first name?'

'I do, but Portman is fine.' This was unfamiliar territory for me. I almost never met up with the principals I was shadowing from a distance, so names were never an issue. But the circumstances here were a little off-centre, and playing dumb on the name front wouldn't help Travis's state of mind or his confidence in me to get him out of here. For the time being we were a two-man team.

'Portman. OK. But these are false documents. Can't we just call the embassy?'

'Believe me, they wouldn't be in a rush to help, not now. Your presence here was known but that was before things got crazy. With everything that's happened since, it's gone too far and the diplomatic fall-out of you turning up at the embassy in Kiev would be uncontrollable. The separatists or whoever's controlling them would use you as an easy counter-propaganda target and accuse you of being here to stir up anti-Russian feelings. If I can keep you out of the limelight, they won't be able to do that. In any case, we have no idea who was behind you being taken in the first place, or who's following you right now.'

'It was the separatists, it had to be. You saw them. The Ukrainians wouldn't have anything to gain by it – and besides, they knew I was here trying to help.'

No mention of the Russians, I noted, the big wolf in the room. I wondered if it was simply government-think; deny the people in Moscow had any influence or involvement with what was happening on the ground here, and everybody could be happy.

'So who do you think controls the separatists?' I argued. 'The guy in the grey suit looked Russian to me, either GRU or FSB. And his men were too well-trained for separatist militia. I saw them in action. I'd lay odds they were Spetsnaz.'

He took that in, thinking it over, then turned and looked out the window. He wasn't playing dumb, simply coming face-to-face with reality. He would know all about Russian special forces and the extent of their involvement in influencing political events in the region; everybody in the State Department would have it on their reading list.

'I guess,' he said eventually. 'So where does that leave us?'

I took out the two photos I found on Voloshyn and glanced at them as I drove. The one of Travis could have been taken anywhere, but it looked like a file copy, posed and serious. Maybe even off a visa application.

But the one of me was more troubling. It took me a while to figure out where it might have been taken. It wasn't studio quality, but good enough for Voloshyn to have recognized me from it. It showed me passing through a glass doorway and walking towards the camera. It looked like a standard security set-up of the kind you get on most government and many commercial buildings. I couldn't make out enough of the backdrop to identify the location, so I concentrated on the clothes I'd been wearing instead. I had on a plain sport jacket and pants, and an open shirt. It was the kind of stuff I wore at home. Not that it mattered, because the location suddenly came to me. I pulled to a stop at the side of the road to make double sure I wasn't imagining it. I wasn't.

I put the photos away and pulled back on the road. If we could find somewhere quiet to stop, I had to ring Callahan and drop the bombshell on him.

Langley – or somewhere close to it – had sprung a serious leak.

THIRTY-FIVE

S enator Benson ordered his driver to take him to CIA headquarters. There was something urgent he had to do; something
that would be the first step on laying a trail to divert attention
away from himself if things got screwed up.

He had taken some serious risks by sending out the information
from the list he'd seen in Sewell's office. But that had been unavoid-
able. Putting a crimp in the Watchman mission had required drastic
measures and calling in outside influences was the only way he could
think of that would achieve the objective at short notice. He didn't
see it as disloyal or even treacherous betraying Travis to the Russians,
and neither did he give much thought to the danger the State
Department employee might run. He knew well how these things
went: there would undoubtedly be some protracted discussions and
a deal of posturing from both sides to satisfy national pride. But a
compromise would eventually be reached and Travis would be on
his way home soon enough, a shop-soiled but undoubted hero in the
eyes of the State Department and his loving family.

As for Portman, Benson wasn't remotely interested. Contractors,
or mercenaries as they used to be tagged, knew the risks they ran
when they took up their sordid trade; weeping tears over them when
they met their inevitable fate could be best left to soft-hearted liberals
and men like Callahan.

Thoughts of the CIA officer revisited a niggle of concern lingering
in the back of his mind. He was acutely aware that this whole business could come back to bite him if he didn't take great care. If
anything went wrong and the man with Russian connections didn't
get the job done, someone, somewhere – and he was betting on
Callahan – would set the tracker dogs sniffing along the audit trail
of anyone who had come remotely close to the mission. Although
he was certain that he would remain above any suspicion, given his
record and position in the Intelligence Community and Washington
generally, it paid not to ignore the possibility of fate playing a
deceitful hand.

Which was why, to avoid that possibility, he had decided to lay a false trail before it got that far. He could have simply sat back and allowed Two-One to arrange the payment to Lindsay Citera's bank account and for a phone call to encourage her fate to be sealed. Who was more likely to sell highly sensitive information than a young, impressionable but naïve trainee with a dysfunctional family and money problems?

But sitting back would be cheating. Where was the fun in not being in on the kill, if not specifically, then helping set it up?

On arrival at Langley he made his way through security to the Operations Centre, where he was greeted by Jason Sewell. The assistant director seemed puzzled by the request for the meeting until Benson casually mentioned the forthcoming Select Committee budget discussions.

'I need more beef on current operations, Jason,' Benson said easily. 'If they think things are quiet, they'll assume you don't need resources – which means they'll cut you back even further and give it to Homeland Security instead. I'm sure you wouldn't wish for that to happen.'

Sewell pulled a face. After many years of being in the senior echelons of the intelligence world, he knew all about the workings of these committees, and how there were some who were looking for any excuse to cut back on clandestine activities spending compared to other forms of intelligence gathering and security. If he had any thoughts about Benson's role in such areas, he hid it well. 'Of course, Senator. I can give you a rundown of what we've got on, certainly. But it's pretty much already on paper for them to see.'

'I know. And I sympathize, I really do. But don't you have some manpower issues I can feed them?'

'Such as?'

'Well, take this current Watchman situation. You told me Callahan had to pull a new recruit off the Clandestine Trainee Program to act as Watchman's communications support. That surely speaks of a lack of experienced personnel in key positions, doesn't it – of overstretch?'

Sewell lifted an eyebrow. 'Well, that particular person is not without some experience, it's true . . . but we could always do with more facilities. We're being asked to do more, with more targets to watch, so that's affecting our demands on current personnel. And with experienced operatives being attracted to the private market, and natural wastage through retirement and ill-health, it's an uphill struggle, I won't deny.'

'Good. Numbers are important, without a doubt. But it's the people situation that swings votes, Jason. Committees are swayed by the usual buzzwords of inclusivity and equality, and the bringing on of fresh talent across the board. Give them a sense that their budget-stripping is going to cut the feet out from under a new generation of, shall we say, gender-specific personnel, and they shy away from that potential fragmentation grenade.'

'I see. So what do you want from me?'

'As a percentage of intake, how many women have you got currently in training?'

'Right now?' Sewell had to think. 'I'd say with the current batch, probably thirty per cent. Why?'

'Because nobody, not even the bean counters in government, wants to be seen as responsible for killing the aspirations of young American women in the service of this great country. Especially not those prepared to engage in the dangerous fields of work like the Clandestine Service. It's even tougher with ethnic recruits, too; interfere with that and it's a vote-killer – but don't quote me on that.'

Sewell nodded. 'I see your point. So how can I help?'

'Let me have a chat with one or two of your trainees, find out what their aims and aspirations are. I think it's time to put some of these points before the right people, to flesh out the fact that these young patriots entering the service are not simply functionaries and bean counters but are actively involved in the war against terrorism and the protection of this country. What do you think?'

'Of course. I agree one hundred per cent. Tell me where you'd like to start.'

'Well, how about one of the live operations. Let's begin with the young woman working on the Watchman assignment, shall we? What was her name again – Linda?'

'Uh – Lindsay. Lindsay Citera. I don't see why not.' He picked up his phone. 'I'll get someone to take you downstairs.'

THIRTY-SIX

L indsay Citera was leaving the washroom in the Operations Centre when she heard a vaguely familiar voice drifting along the corridor. For a moment she couldn't place it, but she guessed it must be coming from close by her comms room. Callahan had arranged for a sit-in replacement for regular breaks, and she had left a fellow trainee named Matt to hold the phone while she was out for a comfort break. But if somebody was down here she needed to be back at her desk.

She smoothed her fingers across her eyes and picked up her pace. It had been a while since she'd last spoken to Watchman, and she'd been staring at the monitors ever since as if that alone would get him to call again with news. Not that she was hanging on his every word, but she could barely even guess at the stress he must be under. At least being able to exchange information with him, however insignificant it might be, was better than sitting here with nothing to do.

As she was learning fast, being comms support for a live operation wasn't the all-action, breathtaking activity she and most of her trainee colleagues had imagined. Forget everything you saw in films, with lots of shouting for more intel, location of target groups and calls for backup; most of it involved a great deal of waiting, with brief periods of feverish note-taking and background research work when the calls came in.

As she rounded the corner, the identity of the voice's owner suddenly came back to her, along with a tang of his cologne, and she felt a sense of panic. Benson. Why was he back here? Christ, she'd only been away from her desk five minutes, max.

She entered the room to find the senator leaning over Matt's shoulder while the younger man explained the workings of the various screens. One was a satellite display showing a detailed layout of the Ukraine countryside near Pavlohrad, with an overlay of local conditions such as traffic movements, weather and, recently added by a National Security Agency feed, a colour schematic of reported troop movements in the area, both government and separatist forces. On the next screen was a detailed log of Lindsay's last conversation with Watchman, with a timeline trace of his route from Donetsk and a computer-generated transcript of his report. This included the confrontation with the troops in Donetsk and his escape with Travis.

'Sir?' She stepped inside the room, easing past Benson's bulky form, and reached across to shut down the report screen. As she did so, she gripped Matt's shoulder angrily, digging her nails in, and threw him a murderous look as he looked up and took off his headset. She'd expressly told him to leave the screens in sleep mode, so that there was no danger of them being seen by anyone unauthorized.

'It's all right, young lady – Lindsay, isn't it?' Benson waved a casual hand and stepped away. 'I remember how conscientious you are. Nothing seen, nothing remembered. I have Assistant Director Sewell's authority to be down here.' He smiled in a self-important way, trailing his eyes over her chest before nodding at Matt. 'Your young colleague here didn't let anything slip, I promise. It was actually you I wanted to speak to.'

'Me?' Lindsay looked at him and felt the cold knot of apprehension in her stomach. What on earth could this man want to ask her? She glanced around hoping Brian Callahan would come to help her, but he was nowhere in sight.

Benson misinterpreted her reaction and gestured towards the corridor. 'Good idea. Perhaps we could find a seat somewhere quiet. I'm sure Matt, here, wouldn't mind staying on for a few minutes to hold the fort?' He glanced at Matt for confirmation, patting him on the shoulder like a favoured nephew.

'Of course, sir. No problem.' Matt flushed under the senator's touch and Lindsay was pleased to see that he looked ready to squirm. Serves him right for being such a suck-up, she thought.

'Good, good. I need your take on life here as a new recruit and trainee, Lindsay, and what your hopes and aspirations in the organization might be.' He led the way along the corridor to a room with a water cooler, and they took seats. He brushed at an imaginary speck on his sleeve and added, 'You'd be helping me enormously for a report I'm preparing for an upcoming Senate Select Committee.' He raised his eyebrows. 'It would be of great value, believe me.'

'Fine, sir. How can I help?'

'Well, first of all, why not tell me about your family. You have a sister, I believe? Karen, is it?'

'That's correct, sir.' Lindsay felt the knot loosen a fraction. Maybe this was nothing more than what he'd said: information for a report and background data about staff. Human resources stuff.

She looked down at her feet while gathering her thoughts. Talking about Karen wouldn't take long, and was easy to explain. She was a headstrong kid who'd got in with the wrong kind of people. But hopefully that was now heading the right way. She just hoped Benson wasn't going to ask about Tommy; that was something she preferred not to go into. It was all on her file, but Tommy had screwed up in so many ways it was hard to know where to start, especially telling it to a stranger. She felt disloyal at the very thought, but there was no hiding the fact that Tommy had brought most of it on himself and seemed not to care about the effects on the rest of the family.

She looked up and saw Benson was smiling almost patronisingly. At that moment it suddenly hit her that he knew Karen's name. But how could he? She felt the knot harden again. Did this mean he'd been given access to her personnel file?

'Yes,' he said. 'Tell me about Karen. What does she do for a living?'

THIRTY-SEVEN

We were back on the M04, which looked pretty much as it had the other side of Pavlohrad. It ran through predominantly flat farmland dotted with glints of water from rivers and lakes, and marked by the march of pylons disappearing over the horizon. We didn't have time to take the minor roads, the way I'd been forced to do after leaving Donetsk. Unless we ran into more trouble and had no choice but to find cover in the back country, I was sticking to the more direct route. The further west we could get, the safer we'd be.

I checked my phone for the map and considered what alternatives might be open to us if we were forced off-track. Moldova had been the exit route from the beginning, since heading east or north was pointless; sooner or later we'd run into the wrong people. Besides, neither direction offered a safe exit even if by some miracle we stayed out of trouble. Going south, on the other hand, would take us towards the Black Sea, but I didn't fancy our chances there, either.

That still left Moldova, a small country sitting on Ukraine's western border. I checked the app, which gave the distance as roughly 300 miles, give or take. It was a long way but do-able. If we made it and stayed clear of trouble, we stood a chance of being lifted out by Callahan's people. Before making that decision, however, and before calling Callahan, I had to make certain of some facts.

'Did Denys say what would happen after he handed you over at the Tipol?'

'No. I asked him but he said he didn't know. They operated on a strict cell structure. He knew the address and a phone number for the local cut-out in Pavlohrad but that was all. I think each cut-out had the same information. He stopped and made a call before we arrived in the town and was told to go to the hotel where you found me. We were waiting to hear from the local man to see where I was going next.'

'It was a woman.'

'Pardon me?'

'The cut-out was a woman.' I looked at him and held his gaze. I could have let it slide, allowing the fate of an unknown CIA asset to disappear unspoken into the history books of covert missions. But I needed him to know how serious this was. That people had got hurt and if he didn't do exactly as I said, he would go the same way. 'Her cover got blown and she was arrested by your pal in the grey suit.'

He looked stricken. 'I didn't know that – that she was a woman, I mean.'

'No reason why you should. At the request of the State Department, Langley activated a secure line of cut-outs to get you out of the country. You wouldn't have needed to know any of them beforehand, but it looks as if some or all of the addresses got out there. Starting with Denys.'

'How?'

I didn't tell him because I didn't know. I also didn't want to freak him out with an attack of departmental guilt over the fact that the State Department had sent the data unencrypted. He'd know soon enough when he got back – if he got back – that his bosses had been careless, even negligent, with sensitive data. That would be for him and them to live with. For now we had to focus on the next move.

'Did they say what they wanted you for?'

'Who?'

'The man in the grey suit.'

'At first he didn't say anything. He was fairly officious, even aggressive, but I put that down to being on edge with all the guns in the area. I got the impression he was taking me out of the hands of the separatists without their knowledge. Was that possible?'

'He certainly had the muscle for it.' I told him about the blanked-out trucks and the soldiers who looked anything but irregulars. 'I think he was going to ship you back east. If he'd left you with the separatists there's no saying what would have happened. But you don't need to feel grateful to him – he would have used you any way he and his bosses thought fit. What else did he say?'

'On the way to the place where Denys lived, he said he knew I was connected to western spies and traitors and he wanted all their names and addresses. I told him I didn't know but he wouldn't listen. He said he knew I'd had help while I was in the country, and if I gave him the names and addresses, he'd negotiate with the authorities and arrange for them to put me on a plane home. After you got me away and Denys took me to Pavlohrad, the other man showed up. I think he'd tracked Denys's car.'

'What did he want?'

'He asked pretty much the same questions, only not so nicely.' He winced at the memory. 'Was he Russian?'

'I believe so. Probably with connections to the separatists and on through to Moscow. I think he was there to take you back to Donetsk. Once back there you'd have been part of another trade. They're all looking for bargaining tools.'

'Those photos you were looking at,' he said after a while. 'The one of me is a State Department file copy. I recognized it.'

'If you say so.'

'How can that be possible? How does a file photo of me get into the hands of a thug like that?'

I didn't say anything. He was just thinking out loud and hoping against hope. A former member of Military Intelligence would know perfectly well how it was possible for information like that to get into the wrong hands without me having to tell him. The reasons for spying hadn't changed much over the years, but the various methods of acquisition and delivery had.

'And the one of you,' he continued. 'You know where it was taken, don't you? I saw it in your face.'

He was smart, in spite of his injuries, and perceptive.

'I know, yes.'

'Do you know who took it? Can you work it back from there?'

I knew the where, all right. The photo was a still taken from the security footage at the entrance to the CIA front office in New York where I'd first met Callahan. I could tell by the clothes I'd been wearing.

Who exactly had acquired the still was more of a puzzle. It was simple enough to do; you simply selected the section of footage and clipped the best frame you could find. From there you either copied the frame to a flash drive and walked out with it, or you emailed it from a secure, isolated workstation.

There was a third way, of course. Somebody with the right credentials could have accessed the hard drive remotely and simply taken what they wanted.

Somebody inside the CIA.

THIRTY-EIGHT

Walter Conkley had found himself an ally, albeit a slightly dubious one. Marcella Cready was one of the most feared journalists in Washington, and had long been a painful thorn in the sides of the establishment and the power brokers swirling around the Capitol, with few able to escape her scrutiny when in pursuit of a story. Winner of numerous awards for investigative journalism, Cready had focussed her work on exposing criminal activities in government agencies, the military and even the UN. Although now in her early fifties, she was as sleek as a fashion model and had lost none of her campaigning fight, and had the tenacity of a pit bull when she fastened on a story.

Conkley was well aware of the potential dangers to himself of approaching Cready. She was ruthless when it came to protecting her sources, but even she couldn't guarantee total secrecy in the city which never ever went off duty. She was too well known in official circles and anyone she met with was immediately considered to be providing her with information . . . or of being the next person on her hit list.

Surprisingly, she had agreed to an early meeting at a bar on 7th Street, where Conkley had been admitted by a security guard who had patted him down carefully before giving him the nod. Cready obviously carried some weight here, but he wasn't surprised. They probably owed her for past favours. Put a media hitter like Cready in any evening or lunch-time bar or restaurant with a known staffer close to government and the place would fill quickly with the kind of political observers who relished being in on the early stages of a media hatchet job. And Marcella Cready was known for following only the leads to the biggest of stories.

'I don't want every detail at this time,' she told him, gesturing for him to take a seat at a corner table. The rest of the room was deserted, the doors closed. Conkley sat down and wondered if the table was bugged.

Up close Cready was stunning, with slim legs, glossy hair, a full, curvy figure and flawless skin, save for a tiny hint of laughter lines around the eyes; only Conkley doubted they had anything to do with humour. She wore a suit that had probably cost what Conkley earned in a couple of months, and sat like a queen receiving a subject. But the good looks stopped short at the eyes, Conkley noted; they were almost dead, and ran across him without a flicker, assessing and probably dismissing him.

She made no offer of a drink, but that was fine. It didn't make him feel good, but he hadn't come here for a pep talk or a boost to his ego. The situation had gone beyond that.

He was accustomed to briefings, and gave her a summary of what he knew. She said little, occasionally making a brief note, which confirmed to him that there had to be a recording device nearby. The thought gave him a minor anxiety attack; he had never thought about his every word being recorded outside the confines of government before, yet here he was putting on record clear proof that he was involved with a group of men attempting to profit by using classified information that he had provided and been paid for.

When he finished speaking, she nodded once. 'Very well. It sounds like a possible story, but I'll have to run my own checks first. As soon as I've confirmed the viability of what you've told me we'll have another talk.'

Conkley was alarmed. 'You won't go near them, will you? I mean, Benson and the others. They'll know something's been said.'

She smiled knowingly, which should have made her look beautiful and helped light up those eyes. But it made her look even colder, as if the façade might crack. 'You mean everybody else will start asking questions about what I've got on such eminent gentlemen?'

'Something like that.'

'That won't happen unless I want it to. You think I only ever get seen by chance in this town?' The corner of her mouth dropped in an involuntary show of superiority, and Conkley decided he really didn't much like Marcella Cready.

But it was too late for that now. Needs must. He'd thrown the bait out, and it had been snapped up. All he had to wait for was to see if the bait was acceptable.

'Um . . . what about . . .?' He wanted to say payment, but he couldn't bring himself to utter the word. It seemed too . . . seedy.

Cready did it for him. 'I'll pay you ten thousand dollars in cash on confirmation that I'm happy to run with it, and a further fifteen on publication. I'll also require you to sign a contract confirming our agreement and the dates of all our meetings and exchanges, and an agreement to not divulge any information elsewhere.'

'What? Why?' The idea of his signature on a piece of paper alarmed him. What he wanted to do was talk the talk and fade quietly into the sunset and obscurity, not be on record for ever as some kind of paid betrayer.

'Because if I run with this, it will be my exclusive. I *never* share – you should know that by now. And when the lid comes off this – and believe me, if what you've outlined is true, Benson will *not* take the exposure lying down – I don't want any disagreements in court about who said what and when. Understood?'

He nodded. The interview was over. He stood up, feeling as if he was being dismissed from the principal's office, and was ushered out by the security guard, who smiled and wished him a nice day.

Marcella Cready watched Conkley go with mixed feelings. She had wanted to ignore him, to show her contempt for him and others in his position. A little man, like so many attached like grubby little pilot fish to the real power brokers in and around government, he was easy to despise. She wasn't even surprised by what he had outlined to her. Having never commanded real position, he had found himself drawn into a situation where he could exercise some kind of imagined power through the information he was able to sell, no doubt flattered by those who probably despised him just as much as she did.

But dismissing him simply as a weak little man with imagined fears would have been criminally negligent of her. She had realized that the moment he began talking; the moment he had mentioned Senator Howard J. Benson.

Benson was one of the big beasts of the Washington community; a charming, impressive, smooth operator with almost unlimited connections, he had ceased being a senator when he realized he could command greater power and influence in Washington by serving in other capacities. Capacities where she suspected – no, *knew* – he had crossed the line on more than one occasion, either by hiding facts that would prove unpalatable to the American public, or by accepting 'fees' that would in any other area of the administration have been regarded as bribery. Yet she had never managed to pin anything on him with the kind of absolute accuracy that was needed to bring him down. She had tried more than once, and come close. But Benson had friends, and those friends never spoke, mostly, she suspected, because he had something on them.

And he knew it. He knew it and revelled in his untouchability. She could tell by the way he barely bothered to conceal a smirk whenever they met on the various junkets and power meetings where the press was invited, and the comments he made within her hearing, as if challenging her to try again.

She had certainly tried, but nothing concrete had emerged and she had been forced to drop it, safe in the knowledge that one day somebody would talk and she would have her moment.

Now this. This was different. Conkley, for all his faults, had brought something real to the table. Something she could fasten on. Notes, dates, events. And recordings. It meant all the friends in the world wouldn't help Benson once the facts began to dribble out. Because one thing about friends like these was, they could quickly become enemies if the right pressure was applied and they saw the dangers to themselves of being associated with a man on the brink of disaster.

She gathered her things together and nodded to Sean, the security guard. He walked towards the back of the bar and opened the outside door for her, checking the street carefully before allowing her through. Leaving via the back entrance wasn't Cready's usual style, but in this town it paid to be unpredictable.

THIRTY-NINE

I stopped in a small town fifty miles west of Pavlohrad to get some supplies. It had been slow going, with several brief diversions off the road when I spotted military trucks or potential roadblocks. Travis wasn't looking great and I figured he was dehydrated and in need of something to eat. I also needed to call Callahan.

I'd seen signs of more military activity building behind us, to the east, with helicopters skidding about on the horizon and fighter jets trailing smoke across the skies. Trucks, too, had whipped past us the other way, carrying troops and supplies. Whatever was happening over towards Donetsk wasn't good and getting worse.

As we entered the suburbs I saw a roadside café with a couple of trucks and a handful of cars and, further along, a used-car lot. Mostly four-wheel drives, they ran the range of rough-country farming work-horses, with heavy-duty tyres and the kind of battered appearance that made them blend into the background.

I pulled up outside the café and told Travis to stay where he was and keep his head down. I could pass as a worker ant, but Travis looked too smart and groomed, as unwell as he was, to be anything other than someone with connections and money. He was also talking louder than he needed, even in the car, which I figured was a sign of fever from his injuries and the stress of the situation. An American voice out here would immediately stand out and be remembered.

The interior of the café was rough and ready, but busy enough so that nobody looked up when I walked in. Most of the customers and staff had one eye on the rolling news on a large screen behind the counter. It showed the countryside outside Donetsk, the sky blackened by palls of smoke rising from burned-out vehicles and makeshift barricades, and groups of soldiers and militia with a rag-tag of weapons standing around watching the skies for signs of incoming helicopters or fighters. The atmosphere in the room was subdued, and I guessed for most of them it was tough watching their country being slowly torn apart and not being able to do a thing about it.

I bought some bread, meat and fruit and three litre bottles of water, and took them back to the car. Travis barely noticed, so I left him to it and took a walk along the road to the used car lot.

The owner was sitting alone in a small hut, eyes fixed morosely on a tiny television screen. He had a bald head, bushy eyebrows and few teeth, and barely nodded when I signalled that I wanted to check out the models on display. Most were beyond their prime, and looked ready for the scrap yard. But a dark green Land Cruiser looked as if it had some mileage left in it and I asked the owner if he wanted to do a deal.

He shrugged; the sign of a man who'd thought he was going to make a sale too many times before now only to be disappointed when it didn't happen.

I told him to wait and went and got the Isuzu. When he saw it, he looked a little more interested and tore himself away from his television and came outside for a look. When I popped the hood and revealed the gleaming engine underneath, he looked suspicious.

'Why?' he said. 'It's a good car. Is it stolen?'

'Too noisy,' I replied, as if I didn't know you could repair broken mufflers. 'And my wife says it's too fast, that I'll upset the neighbours and kill myself and our unborn children.'

He shrugged, plainly not caring if the story was true or not. I stepped back while he did a tour of the car, kicking the tyres and checking the underneath, and hoped he didn't want to check the inside before agreeing a deal. I'd need to get the guns out unseen first otherwise he'd go back in his hut and slam the door.

He scrambled out from under the car with a toothy grin and nodding slowly. But the deal wasn't made yet.

'I have to call someone,' he said, and pulled a cell phone out of his pocket.

'A customer already?' I said.

'Of course a customer.' He sneaked a look at me from under his eyebrows. 'You think I'm calling the authorities to ask their permission?' He made a foul spitting sound and laughed. No doubt he'd already got a buyer lined up for such a vehicle and the authorities weren't going to know a thing about it. In the present climate of unrest I wasn't surprised. Under-the-counter sales were probably the best he was going to get and he wouldn't have to worry about paperwork on a rogue four-wheel drive that was going to disappear as soon as it left his yard.

He spoke rapidly for about two minutes, alternating between

cajoling and forceful and ending on a don't-care note. I didn't get anything from the one-sided conversation, save that the person on the other end was driving a hard bargain. In the end he nodded, said yes and snapped the phone shut.

When he turned back to me he was grinning widely, displaying a large amount of empty gums.

We agreed a straight swap, no questions asked, and shook on it. It was a great deal for him but I didn't have the leverage or interest to try holding out for more. If he was suspicious about why I was selling and who Travis and I might be, he didn't seem to care much.

I shook Travis awake and told him to keep his mouth shut while I transferred everything from the Isuzu, making sure the car lot owner wasn't looking when I moved the weapons. Travis looked shocked when he saw the OSV-96 with the sniper scope, but I ignored the questioning look and checked that there were no traces of us left behind.

I handed the keys to the owner and he gave me a spare set of keys to the Land Cruiser in return, which he'd left running to warm up.

'Where are you going?' he said, one hand on the door. 'Not east, I bet.'

'No. Not east. Why?'

He lifted his chin in the direction of the town centre. 'Don't go that way. Police and soldiers asking questions.' He pointed across the road to a narrow street. 'Go that way for a kilometre and you will see the road heading west out of here. Turn left and keep going.' He winked and disappeared inside his hut, and I wondered if the advice had been to keep us out of trouble or to stop any awkward questions from police coming back to this car lot.

It didn't matter; the advice was well-meant and I figured it was worth taking.

We snaked through the outer suburbs, following a series of quiet back streets, until I saw a line of lights heading west. I turned left and we soon left the town behind. After a few miles I saw a track running down beside a small lake and decided we'd come far enough. It was time to eat and rest up.

I made Travis drink at least half a bottle of water. Rehydration would clear his head a little and keep him going. We had a long way to go yet and I needed him as lively as possible.

Then I rang Langley.

FORTY

Lindsay picked up after two rings. 'Hi. We were getting worried.' I heard the rattle of keys and guessed she was checking my location by the signal. 'How's it going?'

'It's OK. We're heading west, currently static. Is Callahan in?'

She put me through. Callahan sounded calm but I knew he'd be chewing his teeth over the lack of hard information. We'd agreed from the start that I would only report in when and if it was necessary and safe to do. But I knew that was easier for me, the man in the field, than it was for him, stuck in an office and waiting for updates.

'I'm looking at your location on screen,' he said, no doubt referring to a map overlay on a satellite view of the countryside we were currently occupying. It was slightly unnerving to know that he was probably looking right down on the lake, although he wouldn't be able to see us, as the last satellite view would already be a few hours old. I just hoped there was nobody else with the same view, such as Grey Suit or any of the others currently tracking us, official or otherwise. 'Is Travis with you?'

I confirmed he was. 'He took a beating along the way but he's hanging in there.'

'Army or militia?'

'Neither. A third party named Voloshyn, a bruiser working for a private security company in Kiev. He killed the Donetsk cut-out after torturing him. He wanted to know where the next cut-out was, but I think Travis was the main prize. Somebody doesn't want Travis leaving the country.'

Callahan was silent while he digested that for a second. It was probably the kind of off-the-wall suggestion he didn't want to consider. 'What makes you say that?'

'Voloshyn knew exactly where to find Travis and the local cut-out. He could have only known that by having access to the list of addresses . . . or by having been given the location of the hotel where Travis was dropped off.' I didn't bother mentioning that 24d's car had been right out in the open for anybody to see, and that if

Voloshyn had been given the details, he'd have simply had to drive around until he saw it. The town wasn't that big and 24d wouldn't have been expecting company.

'I don't see how that's possible.' Callahan sounded doubtful, and in the main he had good reason. The CIA prides itself on its state-of-the-art security against leakages of this kind and the loyalty of its employees. But I had worse news for him yet.

'Thing is, Voloshyn also knew who to look for. He was carrying photos.'

'*What?*'

I explained about the snaps I'd found on Voloshyn. I'd already considered the possibility that Callahan himself had access and opportunity to acquire both photos, but dismissed the idea. If he'd wanted this mission to end badly, he could have arranged for a much earlier pick-up by security forces in Donetsk, not left it until now when we were more likely to get free and clear. In any case, I trusted him.

The fact remained that Voloshyn must have known the area Travis was heading for in the first place, so all he had to do was keep his eyes open. The rest had been down to simple grunt work and obser-vation. And as a PI, whatever his connections elsewhere, he'd have been equipped for both.

But it had needed somebody to feed him the information in the first place.

I gave Callahan the name of the security company Voloshyn worked for so he could check it out. Whoever had put Voloshyn on to Travis's location must have left an electronic trail somewhere, but I wasn't holding out too much hope of it being easy to find. But if Callahan could find a way to put pressure on Voloshyn's employers, it might give us a clue where the orders had originated, albeit probably not the actual source.

'I'll see what I can do,' he said. 'In the meantime we've issued a warning for all assets to take full security measures in case they've been compromised. It's going to shut down some of the networks for months to come. What's your plan from here on?'

'Unless you can beam us up, we'll continue west and cross the border into Moldova. I'm guessing the embassy in Kiev is off limits?'

'Absolutely. We had an update earlier and all arrivals and depar-tures are being filmed and checked, probably on orders from Moscow. Complaints have been delivered by the ambassador but the government in Kiev says the observers are nothing to do with them. The airport is also under virtual lockdown with restricted flights and long queues at passport control. Assuming you make it to Moldova, advise when and where and we'll arrange a pick-up.'

I asked him to put me back to Lindsay and he did. There was nothing for it now but to hit the road and get out of the country as fast as we could. But first I needed some extra information and was hoping Lindsay could step up to the plate.

'How can I help?' Lindsay didn't sound quite as upbeat as she had before, and I wondered if the situation was getting to her. It must have been tough sitting at a desk knowing what was going down but being unable to do anything to help.

I told her what I was planning on doing.

'Moldova? That's quite a road trip. Do you have a route?'

'Yes, I do, but it's subject to change. I need you to monitor all traffic along the way, including and especially military vehicles or roadblocks. All I can see is what comes up on the horizon; I need a regular overview of what's happening on the ground so I can avoid problems. Can you do that?'

'Sure can.' Her voice tone had lifted at the prospect of something to do and I could hear the click of the keyboard in the background. She was already checking out maps and data. 'Right, I have an overlay with satellite feeds and news reports of movements throughout the region. I'll keep an eye on your location and report in whenever I have something.' She hesitated. 'What about signals monitoring in the area? Won't increased contact make it more dangerous for you?'

'Not if you keep it short and sweet.' I figured that regular bursts of speech lasting less than ten seconds were unlikely to be picked up, since each burst would be too brief for monitoring stations to pin down our location effectively. And being on the move would help us stay off the radar. What it would do was give me eyes and ears on information that I currently didn't have.

'I can do that. Anything else?'

'No.'

'Good luck.'

FORTY-ONE

After signing off from Watchman, Lindsay sat for a few moments deep in thought. She felt oddly unsettled, her mood even a little flat out of concern for the two men out in the field and her own sense of helplessness, as if she should be doing more for them than simply sitting here in the safe cocoon of the CIA operations centre.

She'd been warned during training and by Callahan himself that such thoughts were entirely normal. Mission support staff wouldn't be human if they didn't have them, especially when their contact was limited to the close, almost intimate environment of a secluded room and a set of headphones, each word carrying such a wealth of meaning. And that closeness made it inevitable that the distance between them did not mean the support staff would be entirely removed from a real, tangible sense of the dangers the operatives might be facing.

But that was something she had quickly realized she would have to accept: that Watchman was doing his job, and she had to do hers, no matter what happened.

It was about this time that she came to realize that her particular job was attracting some attention from other personnel in the ops centre. On rare forays to the rest room area, which were mainly as a means of exercising her legs on the stairs, she was aware that she was a subject of discussion. Most of the personnel she saw were more senior in service, and she had the firm impression they knew the Watchman mission was something a little special and out of the ordinary.

That fact was even more noticeable since the imposition of red light rules. There were no actual lights, as one might see in a recording studio, but signs put up on the approaches to this section of the ops centre had undoubtedly changed the atmosphere, if anything intensifying the already muted air of calm purpose that permeated the building. She had also picked up a sense that if there was any scuttlebutt going on, it was centred around events in Ukraine. The others must have known she was a trainee, plucked off the program by Callahan, yet she detected no animosity, merely a curiosity and a shared understanding, even of approval as evinced by brief smiles and nods of recognition.

Without knowing it, she had become one of them.

What she hadn't found so easy to deal with was Senator Benson's questioning. She hadn't enjoyed being asked about Karen or Tommy, finding his manner too probing, too intrusive, especially since she had already given complete disclosure throughout the vetting procedure she'd undergone after applying to join the CIA.

But there was something else there, too; something she couldn't quite put her finger on. She'd had a feeling throughout the talk that there was something behind Benson's questions, an underlying purpose which had nothing to do with reports or an interest in the wellbeing of newcomers to the Agency. His attitude had been too secretive, almost insidious in nature, as if he were harbouring some ill-purpose which was going to come back and bite her and her family.

She was also dismayed by discovering that she had wanted to say something to Watchman about it. It would have been a gross infraction of protocol and hugely irresponsible of her to load that on him on top of everything else he was undergoing, and she was relieved she had come to her senses in time. Here was a man she didn't know, had never met, with indescribable pressures on him as he made his way through a war zone with the responsibility of bringing out another man to safety, and she'd very nearly blurted out her worries about being asked a few questions by an individual she found unpleasant.

She told herself to get a grip and turned to her keyboard. If she couldn't talk to Watchman and felt unable to discuss her concerns about Benson with Callahan, she could do the next best thing. She could put her thoughts in writing. At least that might alleviate the situation and her mood enough to allow her to get on with the job.

With a careful eye on the screens, she wrote down everything that had happened, listing as carefully as she could every question and comment he'd made, every nuanced suggestion and threat. It might not go anywhere, she knew that; she was after all a greenhorn at this game. But if something did happen following Benson's strange behaviour down here, she would have a dated record of her concerns.

That done, she busied herself linking up additional monitors to give her extra live feeds from the National Security Agency at Fort

Meade and the Defense Intelligence Agency's analysis centre at Bolling. Both were capable of giving coverage of activity on the ground over Ukraine, which she hoped would help Watchman through any trouble spots. Added to news reports and updates, she should be able to spot any build-up of activity before he ran into it.

However, it still left a small gap in up-to-the-minute data, and she wondered how to close that gap right down. What she needed was real-time coverage of the area Watchman was travelling through, an eyes-on view of what was really going on down there ahead of him. There was only one way she could think of, a method of intelligence-gathering that had been covered in some of the recent training lectures.

But to access the facility required a decision way above her pay grade.

She typed a brief note advising Callahan of her actions acquiring live data-feeds from the other agencies, and requested the one additional measure. He might say that it was impossible, that budgetary or policy reasons would get in the way. But if he approved it, she might be the first trainee ever to instigate the use of a camera-equipped UAV – an unmanned aerial vehicle or drone – to provide live backup for a hot mission.

FORTY-TWO

Brian Callahan was also deep in thought after his talk with Portman. He was astonished by what he'd just learned and what it meant for him and the Agency. The discovery of a photo ID of Travis in the hands of a Ukrainian private investigator was alarming enough, and following the plain-text message sent to Travis containing the address of the CIA cut-out in Donetsk, his suspicions were instinctively directed towards the State Department and their earlier carelessness. They had done it once – they could have easily repeated that mistake. But something told him that wasn't the answer. Something else was going on here. Because for the man to have had a photo of Marc Portman entering the CIA sub-office in New York showed a security breach of an unprecedented kind and could have come only from somebody on the inside.

Further, this wasn't the acquisition of documents or even archived files, which would have been serious enough. This was up-to-the-minute theft of security material and could have only come from somebody with current access to CIA storage systems – namely, hard disk drives.

He looked at a note he'd made while talking to Portman, and reached for the phone. He gave the details about Voloshyn to one of the team of researchers in the building. 'Find out everything you can on this man; where he lives, his history – including military service – and what this company BJ Group is all about.'

'Right away, sir.'

He put down the phone and went back to considering the issue of Portman's photo, and was mentally composing a security breach report for immediate circulation when Assistant Director Sewell walked in and dropped a folder on his desk with a slap.

'I'd like your comments on this, Brian.' Sewell sounded abrupt, even bad-tempered, which was out of character, and swung away to stare out of the window, his shoulders stiff.

Callahan reached out and opened the folder, wondering what was wrong. It was part of Lindsay Citera's personnel file, and contained a summary of the vetting reports and background analysis on her family, friends, contacts and lifestyle, which every applicant to the CIA had to go through. He skim-read it but could see nothing to indicate why Sewell should be so edgy or concerned.

'Sorry. What's the problem?'

Sewell turned back. 'It's been brought to my attention that Citera has family problems that might put her in a situation to become compromised. Were you aware of them?'

'You mean her brother being in a military lock-up? Of course. It's on file. So?'

'And her sister with serious debt problems?'

'That, too.'

'Did you also know that Citera has been sending her sister considerable amounts of money recently?'

Jesus, thought Callahan, where the hell is this going? 'Actually, I didn't know that, Jason. But so what? If we questioned the credibility of every employee who helped out their family with money, we'd have to clear out well over half our workforce, starting at the top. Hell, I send my daughter a cheque every month to help with her school expenses. That doesn't make me a security risk . . . unless, of course, someone thinks otherwise?'

'No, of course not.' Sewell blinked in surprise at the strength of Callahan's response. 'I'm simply checking something, that's all, and wanted to run it by you first.'

'I'm glad to hear it.' Callahan pushed the folder away, sensing it contained nothing relevant to Sewell's real reason for being down here. 'Do you mind telling me what this is really about? Are you unhappy with her performance as Watchman's comms support? Because if you are, I'd appreciate a heads-up on why – and how you came to that conclusion.'

Sewell's jaw tensed, and he sat down with a heavy sigh. He slid a sheet of paper across the desk. 'I'm sorry, Brian, but I've just had a call from one of our background investigators in the security section. They've uncovered evidence of an unidentified payment of twenty thousand dollars into Citera's account.'

Callahan felt like he'd been kicked in the gut. Instinct told him it was a mistake . . . except that the security section didn't make mistakes like that. He looked at the slip of paper, which was an internal memorandum of the kind he'd seen many times before, usually dealing with minor security lapses by personnel and intended to highlight possible action to be taken by their supervisors. 'It could be entirely innocent – or a banking error.'

'Not according to security. They do this all the time, checking out bank details and transactional movements. It's all very clear: the payment was made through an overnight hole-in-the-wall deposit vault at a downtown branch of Citera's bank. It was in cash, using a paying-in slip with a source name that leads nowhere. I've asked for a photo record of the deposit, but I'm not holding out much hope of getting anything.'

Callahan stared at him, amazed at the ease with which Sewell seemed to have picked up and accepted this particular bug. 'I see. And you don't think that maybe it's a little convenient? Even obvious? Lindsay wouldn't even know anything about this – she's been down here all the time.' He checked himself not to go too far; stranger things had happened in the intelligence world and against all his instincts he could be proven wrong. But he felt this was an important point to make his feelings known. 'In any case, may I ask since when did any assistant director check the background details of a trainee officer? We have a security section whose job it is to do that.'

Sewell's jaw clamped tight. 'Maybe so. That's why I'm giving you the chance to find out before I instigate an official security check into every aspect of her life going back to day one. You know what will happen if I do that.'

Callahan knew, and felt sick. Lindsay would be taken off the assignment and detained pending results of an enquiry. In the end she would be out of a job or consigned to whichever backwater dead-end post they could find for her. 'But we're right in the middle of—' He stopped, suddenly seeing visions of the photos Portman had talked about.

Christ, no. It wasn't possible.

'What?' Sewell had noticed. 'Brian?'

Callahan took a deep breath. 'I was about to come and see you, anyway, prior to making a security breach report.' He relayed what Portman had told him, and the likelihood that classified material had been leaked from within the CIA's own structure. 'No way would the State Department have had Portman's face on file, and certainly not from a security camera in the New York office. It has to be a leak.'

Sewell didn't look convinced, but Callahan wasn't surprised.

Sewell wouldn't have been the first senior officer of an intelligence organization to doubt the possibility of a mole on the inside passing on information. 'I hate to suggest this, Brian, but isn't it possible that Citera might be the leak – bearing in mind what I've been told?'

Callahan fought to keep his cool. This was in danger of turning into a witch-hunt. Sewell seemed ready to convict Lindsay at every turn, proof unseen. 'Seriously? I don't see how. She wouldn't have access to the camera hard drives, not unless she's a lot more IT-savvy than her record shows and managed to access systems that have all kinds of firewalls and security protocols to prevent that.'

'It's possible, though.'

But Callahan wasn't buying it. 'But why? For what purpose? She's not in the pay of a foreign government – I doubt she's ever given it a thought. Christ, Jason, she's *helping* Watchman, not trying to betray him! In any case, how did security know about this alleged unidentified payment? Something must have made them look. What was it?'

Sewell didn't even blink. 'You know I can't share that. All I can tell you is that a line of information was passed to them that indicated there might be a security problem with an employee, rendering her open to unacceptable external pressure.' He stood up. 'I think twenty thousand bucks amounts to quite a lot of pressure, don't you?'

Callahan stood too, his thigh slamming a desk drawer shut with a loud bang. 'Dammit, Jason, wait. This mission's at a critical point right now. Watchman's got Travis and they're making a run for the border with Moldova. That's a long drive through God knows what kind of obstacles in a country that's falling apart day by day. Watchman needs the eyes and ears and uninterrupted connection with a person he's come to trust. Take that connection away and we might as well kick his legs from under him. You know the effect it can have – you've been there yourself.'

Sewell didn't look convinced. 'People get replaced in mid-op all the time, Brian. You know that as well as I. Portman will cope.' He lifted an eyebrow. 'Didn't you say he's the best at this kind of work?'

'Sure I did. And he is. But this is a distraction he doesn't need. Don't forget, he's not on his own out there – he's got another man in tow. We owe them both all the guidance we can give them. You take that away and the consequences could be severe.' He stopped speaking, aware that he was sounding passionate and repeating himself, and in danger of overstepping the line. He wasn't so close to Sewell that he could get away with almost anything, and certainly not with telling him that this was all bullshit, which he was sorely tempted to do.

Sewell was chewing on his lip in thought. He eyed Callahan and slowly nodded his head. 'OK. I hear you. But from this minute on, you don't let Citera out of your sight. You ride right alongside her, monitor her calls, stop all visitors and make sure she doesn't have access to anything other than the equipment she needs for the job. Red light rules, got me?'

'I hear you.'

'In the meantime I'll have security hold fire on their investigation. Let's get Portman and Travis home first.'

'Fine.' Callahan nodded. He wanted to say more but knew he'd gone about as far as he could – for now.

Sewell stepped towards the door, then paused and turned back. He gave Callahan a bleak stare and said, 'One other thing, Brian. I appreciate and understand your loyalty to your staff. It's commendable. But let me remind you that if I wish to involve myself in internal security matters, it's well within my scope of responsibility to do so.'

With that, Sewell walked out leaving Callahan conscious that he'd come closer than he'd ever thought possible to bringing his career in the CIA to an abrupt end. But he didn't regret it. He might be wrong about Lindsay Citera, but only time would tell. For now, he had to keep this operation running. He'd deal with the fall-out later.

A ping announced an incoming internal mail message. He glanced at the screen and felt a twitch of disquiet. It was from Lindsay.

FORTY-THREE

Callahan opened the link. He read it through then printed off a copy before making his way along to the ops room where Lindsay was sitting. She made to stand up when he walked in, but he signalled for her to sit.

'At ease,' he murmured. 'How's it going?' He was desperately trying to figure out a way of broaching the subject of her sister, in the hopes that instinct and experience might answer some of the questions raised by Sewell's visit. But the walk so far hadn't given him any brilliant ideas. How do you tell an employee you trusted implicitly that you knew a lot of money had landed in her account from an unknown source without breaking that trust completely?

'Quiet, but about to go wild,' she said, and smiled as if excited by the prospect.

'Yeah, I think you're right.' He sat down in the spare chair. 'You prepared for that?'

'Yes, sir. Better than sitting here waiting.' She gestured at the extra screen which was carrying a split display. 'I hope it's not overstepping the mark, sir, but I brought in some live satellite and news feeds to give me more data for Watchman. I'll be keeping him updated as it comes in. I dropped you a note to that effect in the internal mail. I also made an additional request.'

'I saw it.' He waved the piece of paper holding the message. 'And I approve the request.' He took out a pen and signed it off for the record. It was a touch of rebellion on his part but Callahan was impressed with her thinking. The data she was referring to from NSA and DIA sources was available for anyone down here with the correct authorization, which Lindsay had by virtue of her assignment. But he was pleased she'd taken it on without having to ask for help, and even more pleased that she had thought of using a drone as overhead coverage for Watchman's exit strategy. It showed a logical and mature approach to her work and made him even more certain that she wasn't the cause of the leak.

'I'll have to speak to a couple of people to get it signed off, but this could be the one time we actually get the authorization to use it. Do you know where the drones are operated from?'

'Isn't it Ramstein Air Base in Germany?'

'Correct. This one will be a high-altitude camera-only, so it should go unnoticed. As soon as it's airborne you can advise Watchman. He won't see it but it'll be good for him to know it's there.' He gave a wry smile. 'Tell him we can't have it loaded with missiles, because that might cause problems.' He tried to imagine what it would be like for Portman and Travis, making their way across country to the border with Moldova. He hadn't been exaggerating in his description to Sewell; it was a long way and fraught with potential dangers. He just hoped nothing was going to come up that would place them in further jeopardy.

'Was there something else, sir?' Lindsay was looking at him and he realized he'd been frowning.

He shook his head, then decided to tackle the problem head-on.

'I've been instructed to put you on red light rules,' he told her.

'What's that?'

'It means that for the duration of this mission you and this room are off-limits to all personnel. I'll be here, too, in the office next door, to assist if you need it. It's placing you under more pressure, but I think it's necessary given the circumstances. Effectively it's cutting you off even more from the outside world. I hope it won't be for too long.'

Lindsay nodded. 'I'm fine with that, sir.' She hesitated. 'By all personnel, sir, who does that mean?'

'Everyone except Assistant Director Sewell. And the president. Although I think even he might find it tough getting past the security guards at the end of the corridor.' He tried a smile but was aware that it didn't quite come out right.

'Sir, are you unhappy with my work?'

'Why do you ask?'

'Because I can sense something, sir. It might not be my place, but I like to think I can read people. Did Senator Benson say something, sir?'

'Benson?' Callahan's eyebrows lifted in surprise. 'What does he have to do with anything?'

'Because he's been down here, sir, asking questions.'

'What sort of questions?'

'About my ambitions, hopes, what I think of the work. He said he was compiling a report for a senate intelligence committee on personnel and needed some background information.'

'Was that all he wanted to know?' Callahan was puzzled. Anything like this should have been steered through himself, although he guessed Assistant Director Sewell must have given Benson the OK to come down here asking his questions. But the timing was very odd. Why now? And why the focus on Lindsay?

'He asked about my family. My brother, Tommy, and my sister, Karen. I told him it was all on record, with the vetting procedure and so on, but he asked, anyway.'

She kept her expression blank, but it was obvious to Callahan that she wasn't happy at what she saw as an intrusion at a critical time, and he couldn't blame her.

He couldn't believe it. Was it Benson who'd raised concerns with Sewell about Lindsay's suitability for this job? Logic said that was impossible. Why would he bother? What would even instigate such concerns? As one of the most influential members of the Intelligence Community, Benson had the kind of background and status unequalled in Washington DC, giving him access to this and many other top-secret establishments around the city. The matter of personnel was surely so far down on his list of concerns as to be beyond thought.

'What did he want to know – about your sister?'

'He asked about her debt problems, sir. But as I told him, it's all on file.'

'Yes, it is. You've been very open about that. What else?'

She frowned. 'He said . . . I got the impression he knew that I sometimes help her out with money. I don't think that's on file, sir – but it's a personal issue, surely.'

'What did you tell him?' Callahan found he was holding his breath. Or maybe it was the closeness of this room. But he was beginning to see a picture emerging . . . and a possible motive. He was aware, like many of his colleagues, that Benson had expressed concerns about the way the CIA conducted itself many times in the past, sometimes with good reason. But behind it was often the rhetoric of a crusader who wanted change for change's sake.

She shrugged. 'I told him I do, sometimes, when she's really in a bad place. Karen, she's . . . she doesn't handle money well. I have to refuse her occasionally – but that's not your concern, I guess. Does he have a right to know that stuff?'

'No, he doesn't.' And in a virtual repeat of what he'd said to Sewell, he added, 'It's admirable that you help her, and I guess we all do what we can to help out family members.' He hesitated. 'This is none of my business, and you can tell me so if you wish, but I guess she probably doesn't pay you back, right?'

Lindsay shook her head with a wry smile. 'It would be nice if she did. But no, sir. Like I said, she's not good with that sort of stuff. What goes into one hand goes straight out the other.'

He nodded. 'I understand.' He desperately wanted to tell her about the deposit to her bank account, but couldn't. Learning that the security section had looked at her account might blow the trust that had grown between them at a critical time. Instead he was going to have to trust her to speak up about it later.

He made to stand up, then had a thought. It was one he didn't wish to entertain, but that particular horse had already left the starting gate. He asked, 'Has Senator Benson ever been in this room by himself?'

Lindsay answered with a slight hesitation. 'No, sir, never. I make sure it's never been left unattended.'

Callahan picked up on her hesitation. 'But? You had a second thought there.'

She coloured slightly, as if unsure of herself. 'Well, there was the time he came down with Assistant Director Sewell, not long after I started. You were overseeing another operation. Director Sewell was called away and Senator Benson stayed here, asking questions.'

'I remember. You told me he was asking about Watchman.'

'That's correct, sir.' She started to say something more, but paused.

Callahan noticed. 'Tell me.'

She told him, and he listened without interruption, feeling a cold fury growing inside him. This was way beyond anything that he'd ever experienced before, and hinted at betrayal of the most sinister and underhanded kind. Benson had used his position and name to bully a young trainee into giving him information to which he had no right. And, if confirmation was possible, he suspected that Benson had done so to compromise an operation and threaten the lives of two men in the process. Exactly why was a mystery, but that would come out in due course . . . unless Benson was able to use his influence to block any chance of an investigation.

'Anything else?'

'More recently I found him here with my stand-in while I was on a comfort break.'

'What was he doing?'

'He was asking about the monitors, getting a tour from my stand-in about the technical side of what goes on here, the maps, the overlays and stuff. I switched them off the moment I got back. That's why I thought he might have said something. Sir, I guess I might have been pretty blunt, I admit. I'm sorry, but he's got such a high clearance and AD Sewell brought him down here, so I thought—'

'What could he have seen?' Callahan felt bad about interrupting her, but he was getting a cold chill up his back at the thought of what this could mean.

She looked puzzled. 'Pretty much everything, sir. The maps, the routes for Watchman, the locations and coordinates . . . and a transcript of Watchman's latest report.'

'Specifically?'

'About the run-in with the soldiers in Donetsk, getting Travis out . . . and where he was headed next.'

There it was. Callahan had to work hard to contain his anger. He was thinking about the hard time he'd gotten from Sewell earlier, and the accusations levelled against Lindsay which could have terminated her career before it got going – and could do still if he wasn't careful. Yet the assistant director himself had allowed Benson to come down here unescorted and question personnel on vital information to which not even the president would have access.

It served to remind him of what Portman had said earlier about the man named Voloshyn who'd murdered the cut-out. *Voloshyn knew exactly where to find Travis and the local cut-out. He could . . . by having access to the list of addresses . . . or by having been given the location of the hotel where Travis was dropped off.*

He wondered how much Benson had seen and remembered from previous visits here . . . and what he might have talked about once he was out of the secretive atmosphere of this place. He had no idea whether the former senator possessed a better than average or even eidetic memory, but he'd never met a political in-fighter of Benson's experience yet who couldn't absorb details like a sponge when it suited them, and regurgitate them later when everyone else thought they'd been long forgotten.

What was certain was that Benson had contacts throughout the

Intelligence Community, and if he wanted something, he would have ways of getting it. Things like photos, for example.

As he left the room and headed for the elevator to the upper levels, he wondered idly how hard it would be to get a drone in the air armed with a Hellfire missile and to order a strike on the senator's home.

FORTY-FOUR

'Watchman, we're tracking a Mi-24 attack helicopter heading in your general direction from the east out of Sloviansk. The flight is not logged and the pilot is not responding to calls from Kiev air traffic control. Current distance from you is eighty miles, repeat eighty miles.'

'Copy that.' It was reassuring how with such ease we'd changed from normal speech to the rapid-fire truncated pattern normally found in battle conditions. Lindsay was telling me only what I needed to know, and I was confirming that I'd got the message.

What she'd told me didn't sound good, although just because the helicopter was heading this way and observing radio silence didn't make it a direct threat. 'What's at Sloviansk, anyway?'

'It's an air repair base, currently in the hands of separatist militias. They've also taken over the local government building, police and the local SBU office.'

The SBU is Ukraine's security service. If the militias had taken over to that extent, any forces in the area would have also been overrun.

'There's something else,' Lindsay continued. 'I ran a search of all information on the area. The separatists in Sloviansk recently shot down a military helicopter containing a dozen Ukrainian soldiers and a general from their National Guard. They also took over the repair base which is housing six Mi-24 attack helicopters from the Air Defense Regiment. Reports say those helicopters are currently being tested and made air ready, thought to be with the help of Russian ground crews.'

And one of them was heading this way. Damn. That certainly made it more relevant.

'Keep me posted.' I disconnected and concentrated on driving. Not that I was kidding myself that I could out-drive them. Eighty miles was nothing to a Mi-24. With a cruising speed of approximately 200 mph, it could be over us within twenty minutes without even trying.

'It's a coincidence, isn't it?' Travis asked. The way his voice rose at the end told me he already knew the answer to that. If Grey Suit had discovered our change of vehicles, and he had Russian connections, then calling up a rogue helicopter to stop us would have been easy meat. The separatists had a handful of them sitting on an airfield doing nothing; with a few sympathetic aircrew, which I was laying money on, then the problem was solved. Look for a car heading west with two men inside and that was their target.

'Don't worry about it,' I told him. 'Keep your eyes to the east. If you see movement, we'll have about two minutes to take evasive action.'

'Can't we get off the road now while we have a chance?'

I looked round at a flat terrain, with fields on either side of the road and no dead ground that I could see. The only building in sight was a broken-down barn a quarter of a mile off to our right. It might as well have had a giant target painted on the side. If the people in the helicopter couldn't see us, they'd reckon there was only one place we could be. It would give the gunner a great opportunity to try out his skills. Hell, it wasn't his ammunition, so what was the problem?

'Where do you suggest?' I said. 'We might as well be on the moon.'

He didn't reply and sat twisted round with his eyes glued to the rear.

Fifteen minutes later we received another info-burst from Lindsay.

'Watchman, the Mi-24 is currently five miles out, repeat five miles out to your rear and closing. It will be on your location very shortly. Kiev Military Command has been advised and will respond. In the meantime, you should take whatever evasive action you can.'

She sounded calm enough but there was an underlying tremor to her voice that I hadn't heard previously. A live developing scenario like this must have been mind-blowing for a trainee who'd never been in this kind of situation before. Nor could she have been fully prepared for the reality of what she was seeing and hearing. This was real-time action, not some classroom simulation, and I just hoped Callahan was there to support her if she needed it.

'Copy that,' I said, and continued checking out the flat landscape looking for cover but finding nothing to hide even a couple of men, never mind a Land Cruiser.

I put my foot down. There was hardly any traffic now, which meant I could hold the centre of the road to avoid the broken surface at the sides and keep our speed to the maximum. Not that the Land Cruiser had the same punch as the Isuzu, but it was game to try. I checked the petrol gauge; half full and plenty enough for now. If anything was going to happen it would be within the next few minutes and miles, and having a few extra litres of fuel on board wasn't going to make much difference.

'They're coming for us, aren't they?' Travis was looking at me, but quite calmly now. He still looked sick as a dog and was holding his ribs, but our predicament had taken hold of him in a positive way. He was expecting hell to turn up and it had hardened his resolve to the situation.

'We keep going for as long as possible. If we see a way out we take it, otherwise we hope Kiev send a plane that can kick an attack helicopter's ass.'

I picked the clatter of the blades beating the air before I spotted the craft. I turned my head for a quick look but the road here was too narrow for taking chances that would throw us into a ditch.

'Helicopter,' Travis said calmly. 'About a thousand yards at four o'clock and coming right in.'

I ignored it and checked the countryside again for cover. But I was flat out of ideas. There was nothing I could do but keep going, since sitting still and waiting to be blasted wasn't in my nature. If the helicopter was going to take us out, it would first have to take up an attack position, and that would be instantly recognizable. It would give us a few seconds to abandon ship, during which I'd unsling the OSV and see if I could inflict some damage first.

It was a limited hope because attack helicopters are built to take more than just the odd hit from incoming rifle fire, even one as heavy as the OSV. But maybe I'd get lucky and break something critical or put the pilot off his game.

The helicopter roared up alongside us, keeping station about a hundred yards out and fifty feet up. It was OK flying but I'd seen better. Attack craft by definition of their role require more than the average level of skilled pilots. They have to be able to throw their machines around on a dime because that's the kind of action they face. It's a dangerous role and requires absolute confidence and skill.

But I wasn't sure this pilot was among the best. If it was a scratch crew put together by the separatists, then their coordination wasn't going to be the smoothest. It takes months of training to get that right, and these guys would take a while to put their act together. Which might just be long enough to help us.

'*Watchman, a Ukrainian Sukhoi-27 fighter has been deployed by Kiev Military Command and is coming in from north-west of your position. ETA four minutes. Repeat, four minutes.*'

'Good news. Tell him he might like to put the hammer down and get here now.' Kiev must have spotted the Mi-24 coming east and had sent up an attack fighter to check it out. But four minutes when you're looking at being blasted off the face of the planet is way too long. It was going to seem like an age unless I could think of a way of playing for time.

Question: how the hell does one play for time with an attack helicopter in a bare landscape and nowhere to hide?

The noise from the helicopter was tremendous. The effects of the down-draught made the windows of the Land Cruiser vibrate and shook the vehicle hard, making the wheel tremble in my hands. I risked a glance to my right and saw a couple of faces checking us over from the open door in the side of the helicopter. They both wore flying helmets, but instead of the normal one-piece flight crew suits they had on mismatched combat jackets and pants.

I was right; it was a scratch crew, probably made up of ordinary flight crew members who happened to be available and wanted some action. The slight advantage that gave us was that their experience might be on different helicopters and not highly advanced attack craft like the Mi-24.

I know; when faced with a heavy storm, you look for any ray of sunshine you can find.

One of the figures leaned out and gave us an angry pointy-finger signal to stop. I ignored him. I wasn't going to make it easy for them unless I was forced to. He repeated the gesture, and this time showed us what we were up against by pointing at the barrel of a heavy machine gun mounted at one of the windows.

'Give them an OK sign,' I told Travis, 'but hold on to your seat.'

FORTY-FIVE

Travis looked at me as if I was nuts, but did what I asked and gave the helicopter a thumbs-up signal of compliance. It got a responding nod from the crewman, who lifted a hand to the comms connection of his helmet and said something.

The target is stopping.

Like hell I was. I reduced speed slightly as if I was looking for a suitable place to pull over. It had the effect of making the helicopter drift slightly ahead of us. The pilot began to slow down to match our speed and position, so I stamped hard on the brakes for two seconds, slowing almost to a stop. It caught the pilot by surprise; midway between adjusting his speed and angle of flight, he suddenly lost sight of us. His dilemma wouldn't have been helped much by the crewman in the doorway; I could see him yelling animatedly in his intercom. For a pilot with a strange machine, it would have been chaotic and unsettling, which was what I was counting on.

There was now no chance he could turn and attack us quickly, and I was betting the side gunner wasn't good enough to take us out from the angle he was now facing. The pilot managed to correct and began to drift back alongside, turning the machine face-on, so I put on speed again. This made him correct again, the tail jigging around alarmingly as he over-compensated to adjust his height and position and to give the side-gunner a clear field of fire. It was a lot to think about in a very short space of time.

'Two minutes, Watchman. ETA two minutes.'

It was now obvious to the crewman that I wasn't going to comply. He turned and nodded to someone on the inside. No words this time, just a nod.

'Get ready!'

A long burst of gunfire hammered out, churning up the ground a hundred yards ahead of us and throwing dirt and stones into the air. I hit the brakes as the roof was pounded by falling debris, wary of losing the windshield and running blind into a hole and busting the suspension.

The firing stopped and the Mi-24 came back in, closer this time and more controlled. The pilot was getting his coordination sorted out, which reduced our chances of getting away by trying to fool him. The man in the doorway looked as if he wanted to jump out on top of us and stamp on the roof, and repeated his signal to stop. This time he followed it with a no-mistaking flat-hand gesture across his throat.

We'd had all the chances we were going to get. If we didn't stop we'd be obliterated. It was a convincing threat and he had all the aces.

I didn't respond. I'd had my eyes on a small clump of trees half a mile away. It was almost useless as cover, but I'd figured that if we could get the helicopter to land and drop men on the ground, we stood a better chance of fighting back against them than against an armoured and heavily armed military machine.

'Watchman, the fighter is coming in on your position and the pilot has orders not to open fire unless attacked. What is the situation?'

Damn. Kiev were playing careful. The pilot would have to make a pass to assess the situation before making a decision – and then only join the dance if he saw what was happening. Too long and too late.

'Copy that,' I replied. 'We've received warning shots and he's not going to tell us again. Firing is imminent.' I began to slow down, this time waving my hand out the window. I was hoping the pilot had orders to take us captive if possible, but only to use his guns as a last resort.

Twenty long seconds and Callahan came on. *'Watchman, we're picking up voice from the Mi-24. He has orders to engage target. Repeat, orders to engage.'*

He didn't say anything else. I figured there was nothing else he could say.

The fighter wasn't going to make it in time.

FORTY-SIX

There was nothing for it. It was no good running. I slammed on the brakes and this time we stopped dead. I threw my door open and Travis did the same.

'Out and go!' I shouted, and saw Travis respond and bale out, hitting the ground in a roll. It must have hurt like hell but it was better than staying to be used for target practice.

I paused long enough to lean into the back, then ran round and hauled Travis to his feet and dragged him away from the car. I was keeping low so the men in the helicopter didn't see the OSV.

If I was going to have to fight, I wanted to fight back with something they'd know about.

When I glanced back the Mi-24 was hovering two hundred yards out, the pilot looking right down at us through the upper windshield. I wondered why he wasn't using his guns. Maybe they were simply puzzled by our actions . . . or maybe they thought we were truly delusional and were going to try to out-run them.

I caught a glimpse of the crewman in the side door; he was leaning out to get a better view of us and shouting something into his intercom. He looked really pissed about something, and I suddenly realized what his problem was.

They hadn't got a full complement of weapons. There were no rocket pods under the stubby wings and I was guessing they only had the side-mounted machine gun. They'd grabbed the only machine that was airworthy but it wasn't fully equipped. To do anything to us they'd have to turn sideways on, and the pilot's lack of experience with the machine wasn't helping.

Then the pilot flicked side-on to us, and the man in the doorway grinned and punched the air with his fist. Damn.

I pushed Travis away. 'Split and stay down!'

He rolled away and scrambled into a shallow depression in the ground, and I found my own a couple of seconds later. Neither spot was going to help one bit if the gunner opened fire, but if he was as inexperienced as the pilot, we might just get a few seconds' grace.

I checked the OSV and slung it into my shoulder, and the pilot's face jumped into the lens of the optical gun-sight. He was fighting with the controls to keep the machine steady and I figured having the crewman screaming orders at him wasn't helping his coordination any.

I swung right and saw the barrel of the machine gun coming towards us, and to one side, the crewman waving his arms and giving instructions.

From what I recalled of the Mi-24's characteristics, the 12.7mm rounds from the OSV, as heavy as they were compared to normal rifles, would probably bounce off the fuselage and the glass of the twin bubbles. The aircraft had been designed to withstand a lot of punishment and was all but invulnerable to normal weapons.

But I was hoping the pilot didn't know that.

I got a bead on the pilot's cockpit and squeezed the trigger.

Even with the helicopter's twin engines pounding the airwaves, the sound of the shot was loud. The gun kicked hard against my shoulder and jumped a little sideways, and I pulled it back ready to sight on the gunner's window. But I didn't get a chance to fire. There was a split second of nothing, then the helicopter tipped sideways as if it had been hit by a battering ram and veered away. I followed it, watching the pilot's upper body moving frantically to bring it under control. The crewman was hanging from the doorway by his safety harness and trying to grab hold of anything to hand.

It took maybe ten seconds for the pilot to get his act together and for the machine to become stable, by which time they had moved a couple of hundred yards away. But even at this distance I could tell the impact of the round on the window near his head must have scared the pilot and made him even more jumpy than ever. He was looking towards us, his mouth open, and I could see what looked like a star-shaped crack in the glass.

'Watchman, we have new information. Incoming fighter is arming, ready to attack. Suggest you get off the road now.'

I sighted on the side rear window where the machine gun was mounted, and fired again. Then I immediately swung a fraction to the rear and fired into the open doorway, where the crewman was scrambling to get back inside. I had no idea what the shots did inside the cabin, but in such a confined space, it might serve to give the crew a taste of what the pilot had just suffered.

If the pilot hadn't been busy fighting to stay in the air, or blowing a Land Cruiser and its passengers to pieces, he should have picked up the warning blare from his instrument panel of an incoming fighter on an attack run. But maybe he could be forgiven the lack of focus. One moment they were kings of the sky, rulers of everything below them; next moment there was a thunderous roar and the ground beyond them was blown apart by a volley of shells, followed by the shape of a fighter plane going by close overhead and curving round in a tight turn.

It had been a warning pass. The next one wouldn't be.

The helicopter pilot instantly got the message, and veered away. But his gunner didn't receive the memo. He was now facing the departing fighter, and let loose a long burst of machine gun fire for the sheer hell of it. Or maybe he was too scared to know better.

When the fighter came in on its second run, the pilot was no longer kidding around. He must have picked up on the fact that he'd been fired on.

The plane came in low, streaking across the landscape, the twin upright tail fins flashing in the light, a deadly arrow on-target for a kill. The sound of the engines wasn't yet reaching us, but a slight buzz was building in the atmosphere.

Then the pilot opened fire and the Mi-24 disintegrated.

Travis and I hit the ground and covered our heads. I heard him yelling something but I couldn't tell what it was; the air was being ripped apart by the noise of the helicopter exploding and the shattering roar of the Su-27 going over and disappearing into the sky. It left behind the smell of kerosene, explosives and burning metal, and a shower of wreckage coming down around us like heavy rain.

Travis began to get to his feet, wide-eyed with terror, and I reached out and grabbed him, pulling him back down. There was nothing we could do but stay down and wait for it to end. If anything bigger than a dinner plate came down on us, we wouldn't know much about it, anyway.

When I judged it was clear, I looked up and got to my feet. The majority of the wreckage had fallen pretty much where the helicopter had taken the hit. But we were lying in a sea of fragments, of glass, of metal, of plastic and unidentifiable shards of blackened metal. A scrap of paper fluttered down and fastened itself to my chest. I took it off.

It was a warning label about the dangers of live ammunition.

I shook my head to clear my hearing, temporarily dulled by the noise, and dragged Travis back towards the Land Cruiser which, other than being sprinkled with tiny bits of wreckage, had survived intact. As we approached it, a pickup truck appeared from the west and stopped a hundred yards away. An old man climbed out to inspect the damage, then looked at me as I opened the door of the car, noting with a look of awe the sniper's rifle and drawing the wrong conclusion.

I nodded politely and we got in and drove away, leaving him to rationalize what he had seen and tell his grandchildren when he got home. They would probably never believe him.

'Watchman, report. Come in, Watchman.' It was Callahan again.

'We're good and mobile,' I reassured him. 'You might like to pass on our thanks to Kiev for the help.'

'Wish I could.' There was a smile of relief in his voice. 'But all we did was pass them the coordinates and told them it was on an attack run.'

'Just in time. We were lined up for the kill.'

'It might not be over yet. Two Mi-8 transports have just left Dnipropetrovsk airborne brigade base heading south towards your location. Estimated convergence in eighteen minutes. No indications of target, but comms analysis between them and their base shows it to be a scheduled flight. But be aware they might be diverted to recce the site.'

'Got that. We won't be here.'

I disconnected and settled down to drive. My nerve endings were sky high and taking a while to settle, but I'd been in situations like this before. I knew it would be a long while before Travis regained any equilibrium. I left him to it; it was best if he got to grips with what had happened without me trying to force it. Some people took longer than others to get over a near-death experience of military action, others never truly did.

I kept a weather eye on the sky to the north. I wasn't particularly concerned by the two transport helicopters heading this way; if what Callahan had surmised was correct, they would circle and examine, but wouldn't stop unless they had good reason. In all likelihood they'd arrange for a ground team to come out and examine the site of the wreckage and clear it off the road, but in the current climate, that would be the extent of their concern.

We encountered no traffic coming towards us to speak of, save for three delivery trucks from a small haulage company, no doubt desperate to keep going in spite of the unrest, and a handful of farm-type vehicles, off-roaders and pickups, mostly bashed and smashed and carrying bales of hay or animals. The Land Cruiser fitted right in, and I kept my fingers crossed that it would stay that way. I knew I could probably talk my way past any normal patrol, but I wasn't so sure about Travis. He was too obviously foreign, clearly not well and jumpy as hell. If they were looking for a guilty man, he was right out of the police training manual suspects page.

He'd fallen asleep and was mumbling vaguely with the onset of a temperature and the influence of a couple more painkillers I'd given him. But he came sharply awake when one of the trucks blared a horn in a friendly salute and the Land Cruiser rocked under the side-draft of its passing.

'What was that?' He looked around, eyes struggling to stay open, and relaxed when he spotted the trucks disappearing behind us. He reached down at his feet and gulped some water from a plastic bottle. 'Sorry. Gave me a surprise.' He dropped the window and spat out to clear his mouth. 'The woman earlier,' he said. 'She sounded young. What is she – CIA?'

'Yes. But you didn't hear that from me. She's our eyes and ears in the sky.' I stared hard at him to gauge if he was fully awake enough to absorb some instructions. It was time to get a few facts straight between us. 'I'm heading for the border with Moldova. It's about the best way out of here. It'll take several hours, even longer if we have to use secondary roads or tracks for any reason, which is possible. I don't know what we're going to run into up ahead, but if anything happens to me, listen to Lindsay and do exactly as she says. She will guide you out of here.' I tapped the cell phone which lay on the seat beside me. 'This is a direct encrypted link, so you'll get through to her every time. But it's only to be used in short bursts. And don't use it to call home.' I pointed at the sky. 'You know who might be listening.'

'I understand.' Travis looked sombre at the reminder of home. It was tough on him, having the means to call them so close at hand; but doing an E.T. was out of the question. 'Are you expecting something to happen to you?'

'Not if I can avoid it. But it pays to be ready. You OK with that?'

He nodded carefully, as if he knew it made sense but was struggling to accept the fact. Rules were easy if you could follow them without question. But sometimes it went against the grain of emotion and logic to take it on board. 'Yeah, I got it.' He turned and stared out the window, and I let him do it. He needed to get back in the frame and focus on not doing anything that might stop us getting out of here in one piece; otherwise calling his family would be the last thing he'd ever accomplish.

I checked in the mirrors for signs of movement, but the horizon behind us was clear save for a wisp of dark smoke hovering over the crash site. So far so good.

'Christ, Portman,' he said suddenly, his voice soft, 'how do you do this work? Do they seriously pay you enough to make it worthwhile?'

'Enough? Probably not. But nobody forces me to take it on.'

I steered round a long right-hand curve and overtook two small trucks carrying vegetables, and peered past Travis to watch the skies to the north. A couple of large transport helicopters travelling together on the same heading should be easy enough to spot, and I hoped would ignore us and keep on going.

FORTY-SEVEN

'**H**ave you always done this work?'
'No. Not always.'
'So what got you into it?'

Now Travis was more or less fully awake he was nervy and desperate to talk, and I had no reason to shut him up. If we were to get out of this, I needed him alert and ready to react to anything, not dulled by sleep and painkillers. Talking seemed a good way to go. In any case, I doubted he'd remember much of what I said when we got out of this. Just to be sure, I gave him the short version.

'I was in the military for a while. Got shot at, missed a couple of IEDs, the usual stuff. Then I figured if I was going to risk my life I might as well do it properly, so I applied for special training.'

'Delta?'

'Not Delta. That kind of area, though.'

'Iraq?'

'Among others.' We got moved around a lot, wherever we were needed.' The moving had included liaison spells in counter-terrorism, in anti-drug operations in Latin America, reconnaissance missions in Africa and southern Europe on attachment with combined units of French Foreign Legion, Spanish Legion and the Italian 4th Surveillance group.

'So how did you end up doing this?'

'I wanted to choose my own assignments. I'd done a lot of close protection details and a colleague gave me the heads-up about a couple of private high-paying contracts for experienced personnel. It seemed the obvious way to go.' I'd also discovered a dislike of operating in military units and being responsible for others, often in impossible situations. For the most part it was fine, but losing colleagues was something you never truly got over.

'What happened?' Travis was fully awake now, and sharp.

'What do you mean?'

'Something bad happened. I can see it in your face.'

'There were plenty of bad times.' One was worse than most, but it was something I wasn't prepared to talk about in detail – not to a man who was relying on me to get him home safely.

'I'm listening.'

'Short story, we had to leave a colleague behind on an anti-insurgent snatch op in Djibouti. He got separated in a sandstorm and lost contact.'

'American?'

'French. Our unit was on attachment to the Legion. We were about to go back and shut the area down to look for him, but the situation went hot and the politicians ordered us out. It was a lousy deal but we had no choice. Not then, anyway.'

'What happened?'

'We found him but it was too late.' That was all I wanted to say. It had taken us three days to convince the local command to allow us back in to mount a search. When we got the green light we went in and located him, but he was dead. The insurgents had tied him to a tree as a warning message. What was left of him. 'One of the Legionnaires was a skilled bush tracker, so we made a group decision to shut down our communications and go after the people who'd killed him. It took us five days.'

'What happened?'

'We found them, too.' It was about that time that I'd decided I didn't want to answer to politicians anymore; that going on operations on the say-so of people who'd never done it themselves, was no longer a career choice. I wanted to make my own decisions. That way if it all went bad I'd only have myself to blame.

It was also the time that I decided I'd never leave anybody behind again.

Travis said nothing for a while, then: 'I don't get it. Isn't this the same kind of thing – being responsible for others? Worse, even – we're people you don't even know.'

'It's not the same at all.' I couldn't explain it to him, but operating remotely, or even up as close as this, as I'd been forced to do with Travis, allowed a level of disconnection. He wasn't a colleague or friend, he wasn't going to throw himself into a lethal situation; he was relying totally on me to get him out, to protect him. That meant I had the call on everything he did, when he did it and how fast.

It wasn't the same.

I was about to explain this when I saw movement out of the corner of my eye.

Helicopters.

I dropped the window for a better look. Two bulky transporters, the Mi-8s, lumbering along at five-hundred feet. They came over the brow of a hill three miles away and headed towards us. Low to the ground, heavy metal dragons, the throb of the engines already stirring the atmosphere around us.

'Hold tight.' I'd been keeping an eye out along the way for suitable tracks or side roads where I could make a rapid diversion if necessary. It didn't have to be long-term, but enough to avoid a traffic jam or a potential threat. We'd passed a pull-in about a mile back, but it was too open and now too far off to turn back.

I saw a turning up ahead, little more than a gap in the verge and a grass-covered track leading into a small copse of trees. It would do. I hit the brakes and turned off, feeling the wheels beginning to slide as we hit the grassy surface and the moisture turned slick under the tyres. There was a crash as we hit a bump and everything in the car jumped, and Travis yelped. But we were OK. We slid behind the cover of the trees and I stopped.

Two minutes later the air around us throbbed and the trees were buffeted violently as the shapes of the helicopters passed overhead.

We watched them go, trailing swirling plumes of exhaust smoke behind them, and I let them disappear over the horizon before getting ready to move.

'Watchman, report. You OK?' Lindsay again, checking our progress. She'd been timing the situation and was checking we hadn't been drilled into the ground.

I killed the engine. 'We're good. How's it looking?'

'Quiet for now, but our cameras show static heat signals ten miles ahead of your location either side of the road. It's most likely a collection of large vehicles parked up. Probably trucks. We'll get pictures if we can.'

'Do you think it's military or a roadblock?'

'We're waiting on another camera pass, but I'd suggest a military convoy on a temporary stop. I haven't seen a build-up of haulage trucks for some time now, and we have no reports of police or official roadblocks in operation anywhere near you.'

'Copy that. Out.'

Cameras. Lindsay must be using an overhead spotter; most likely a drone. It would be telling what was happening in real-time, relaying pictures back to its controller, who would be feeding them through to Langley. Allowing for a slight time delay, she would be seeing us as we moved. I couldn't even make a guess at how tough it had been getting authorization to call in a drone over a sovereign territory in this neck of the woods, but it was a clever move.

I debated on what to do next. If the vehicles up ahead were part of a military convoy they would have sentries posted with orders to watch out for any other traffic movement too late in the day. It meant that our getting past them without being stopped was unlikely.

I checked the map. There was a small town off to our left, but heading away from where we wanted to go. It was risky but so was heading off along some other track in the dark into open country. A breakdown would leave us stranded with no way out. And if Lindsay's cameras could pick out heat signals, then so could Grey Suit if he had access to the same technology – and if he was still alive.

I made sure we were as concealed as we could be and checked the Grach, then called Lindsay and told her we were going to be static for a while.

'Copy that, Watchman.'

'What are we doing?' Travis looked tired, and his words were indistinct, as if he really couldn't connect the dots. Exhaustion was hitting him hard on top of everything else and he wasn't coping too well.

'We're stopping here.' I handed him a bottle of water. 'We need to rest. Drink as much of that as you can take and eat something. Then get some sleep. I'll keep watch.'

He protested but his heart and mind weren't in it. I took off before he could argue further and walked back to the road, checking in both directions for incoming traffic. I hadn't seen another vehicle for a while and figured most sensible people were staying off the roads until daylight. I walked back away from the trees and checked the layout from the road. We were concealed from the road, especially with the falling darkness, and it looked just like a bunch of trees, not an obvious stopping place.

I walked back to the car and took a drink. Travis was snoring, which was fine by me. He had asked enough questions for the day and needed as much rest as he could get. We still weren't out of the hot stuff and I had no idea what lay ahead. All I knew was we'd have to be prepared to face anything that came our way.

After a while I felt my head going down. It was a bad sign and I shook myself awake. I could get by on little sleep, but I couldn't risk Travis by letting myself go. I checked my watch and was surprised to find we'd been there nearly two hours.

I walked back to the road to stretch my legs and get some blood into my veins and brush off the tiredness. Checking your surroundings in a hostile area is always a good way of staying awake. But you have to be wary of seeing shadows where there are none, which is a product of general lack of sleep and battle fatigue. Shooting holes in the darkness might be good for a couple of seconds, but it's no way to scare off the bogeys.

I got to the road and looked both ways. Nothing. In fact, less than nothing. Total blackness, which suited me fine. This was big country with zero lights and no stars to guide us or light the way. But just for a few moments all that dark was relaxing in a way that daylight would never have been.

It was a reminder that it had been a long time since I'd stood and listened to the dark without wondering if someone was out there coming for me. Smelling the coffee was a modern cliché, but it was easy to lose sight of the fact that there was a world going on around you, and sometimes you had to kick back and look at it.

Then I heard something. Or maybe it was simply an animal thing, of being in the night and using usually dormant instincts. I turned and looked back along the road towards Pavlohrad. Nothing out there that I could see. A long stretch of empty road swallowed by the night.

Then I saw a light.

FORTY-EIGHT

I t was just a flicker, there then gone. Like somebody opening a car door. I waited for five long minutes but didn't see it again. If it had been a vehicle, it was static, and if my judgement was right, it was approximately at the point where I'd seen the pull-in earlier. Whoever they were they must have decided to stop for the night for the same reason we had: to avoid running into trouble.

Or to make sure they didn't miss us in the dark.

I gave it five minutes to make sure my eyes weren't deceiving me, then set off along the road, ready to dive into cover. It was easy going on the metalled surface, but with no lights to guide me also easy enough to wander off course and stumble over the rough grass verge.

I stopped periodically to check my bearings. The trees where I'd left Travis were now invisible, as if they'd never existed, and I was in the dark in more ways than one. But at least I had the road to follow as a guide in both directions.

I hoped nobody else had the same idea.

The first indication I got of other humans present was the smell of cigarette smoke. It was faint, but unmistakable. Then came a short burst of laughter. It was probably no more than a hundred yards away and whoever they were they clearly weren't expecting company.

I stopped and hunkered down, closing my eyes and slowly absorbing the night sounds and atmosphere and the area around me. If this was Grey Suit and his men they would almost certainly have someone on watch. And the easiest and most logical place to do that was by the side of the road.

I stepped across the grass verge, feeling my way across a shallow ditch on to more solid ground the other side. Then I started walking in a parallel line with where I judged the road to be. It was unscientific and entirely by guesswork, but the only way I could do it.

The best scenario would be to find that I'd stumbled on a lone traveller or a family that had stopped for the night. The alternatives were pretty obvious.

There was a dry clicking sound a few feet away, and it took me a moment before I recognized the noise as a cigarette lighter being used. Then I saw sparks flying off into the dark before the flame caught. I closed my eyes instinctively and froze. But even with the initial spark of light I had an image printed on my retinae of a square block of a vehicle standing nearby, its utilitarian outline instantly recognizable and confirmed by the powerful tang of diesel.

A military UAZ jeep.

I ducked my head and waited for the lighter to go out. I'd seen enough. If it was the same UAZ from before, and I guessed it was, then Grey Suit was here, too, or not far behind. By now he'd have realized the helicopter wasn't going to work, so he'd closed in as far as he dared and was waiting for daylight to continue the chase.

Just to be sure, I made a wide sweep of the area, keeping the sound of voices within my hearing and stopping when talk ceased in case they heard me moving. By a process of elimination I picked up three different voices. Occasionally I saw the flare of a flashlight and a face would be lit up, then I heard the sound of paper being torn. I guessed they were eating some kind of field rations. The absence of a fire or more obvious lighting meant they were keeping their presence low-profile, which indicated that these men, whoever they were, were not comfortable being this far west.

I backed off and turned to go. I'd already spent enough time out here. Time to get back and check on Travis. But I hadn't gone more than three paces when I sensed somebody else very close by. A smell of stale sweat and tobacco washed over me, and I started to move to one side, but realized just in time that the man was stepping out from behind a tree to my side and was probably as surprised as me.

I reacted instinctively. There was no use pretending I wasn't there; it was too late for that. But turning and running wasn't an option. I'd also picked up on another smell coming off the man, one that I recognized all too well from years of handling weapons.

Gun oil.

I was holding the Grach with the safety on. I saw just a faint hint of movement in front of me, so close I could have touched him. There was a sharp intake of breath as he opened his mouth to yell, so I swept the Grach up and across, and felt the heavy metal connect with the side of his head. He went over without a sound, and I managed to catch him and ease him to the ground gently.

Then I stepped away and retreated. I was a hundred yards away and walking along the roadside towards the trees when I heard someone calling out in the dark. I picked up my pace to a jog. It was time to go.

Travis was awake when I got back, and looked jumpy.

'Where did you go?' he asked. 'I could have sworn I heard voices.'

'You did. But don't worry about it. You ready to go?'

'Anytime. Was it them?'

'Yes.'

I climbed aboard and turned the ignition. Travis said he'd heard the sound of voices, but I was hoping the drone of our engine would be more difficult for the men in the UAZ to pinpoint. I couldn't use the lights or the brakes until I was certain we were in dead ground, so I had to drop the window and drive slowly until I heard the faint whine of rubber on solid road. It was risky moving anyway, but we had no choice. If we stayed where we were, come morning I was pretty sure the men in the UAZ would see us as they drove by.

Then we'd be dead meat.

Once we were clear of the area I switched on the cell phone and dialled Lindsay.

'Hey, big eyes, are you listening?'

She must have been alert and watching her screens because she barely missed a beat. 'I'm here. Are you mobile?'

'That we are. What's the situation on the ground?'

'No local activity anywhere close on the last camera pass. The next one is due in ten minutes. What's your situation?'

'We're bugging out from the current location. We had company.'

'Hostile?'

'Definitely. If not then, certainly now. Can we get past the convoy?'

'That's a yes. We last picked up their signature moving due east from that position on what we believe is a military access road. Your route now looks clear but be aware.'

'Copy that.'

I switched off and focussed on driving and watching the road for signs of life. Running into a patrol was a possibility, but I was hoping we'd get some warning before we hit trouble.

The road was clear and easy to follow once I could use the lights, and it was almost easy to forget that we were in hostile territory and making our way out.

'Do you have family?' Travis asked after we'd been travelling a while.

Jesus. More questions. And it was stuff I didn't want to discuss. I debated ignoring him, but that wouldn't help either of us. And I needed him to be with me whatever I did, one hundred per cent. The best way to do that was to play along for a while.

'A sister. Why?'

'I'm trying to understand you, that's all. I've got two sisters and a brother. All accounting professionals, would you believe that?'

Somehow I would, but I didn't want to offend him. 'Not really. What made you join the State Department?'

He deflected the question by saying, 'Actually, I'd rather talk about you.'

'Of course you would. But I'm a closed book. You first.'

He nodded. 'OK. I guess I took the easy route all along; through school, then college, then the military, and when I'd had enough of that, I applied to the State Department. I figured four accountants in the family was way too many.'

'What about your family?'

'I told you about them.'

'I mean your own family – your wife and kids. You have two, right?'

It was a brutal reminder, but I figured he couldn't not think about them for long. And talking about them might help, too.

He was quiet for a while, then started talking. It was slow going at first, but he picked up enthusiasm and speed, and even started to smile a lot more. After a while he stopped and looked at me and said, 'You're a sneaky bastard, you know that? But thank you. It was good using their names out loud. Kind of made a connection, you know?'

'I know.'

A little later he said, 'Do you have a girlfriend? I'm guessing you aren't married.'

'No, I don't have a girlfriend, and no, I'm not married. Never found the time or the right person.'

'Don't you have aspirations for something different?'

'Like what?'

'Like marriage, kids – that kind of thing.'

'No. Maybe one day I'll hit the wall and do it, but not yet.'

'The wall?'

'The point at which I find that there's something else I want to do, that life will throw me a random card and use up whatever chances I might have been given.'

'Random? Is that another way of saying fate?'

'You can call it that if you wish. Life is random; it's not predictable like a lot of people think. If it was, the biggest growth industry on the planet wouldn't be technology or social media or alternative energy; it would be soothsayers and palm readers. Look at Denys: he thought he was out of it and clear. Then random came along in the shape of Voloshyn.'

'I guess. I hadn't really thought of it that way before.' He was silent for a while and I let him be, allowing the rumble of the engine and the tyres on the road do their stuff. It was soothing, being out there in the middle of the dark, especially after what we'd been through. There was no intrusion from outside, no phones, no traffic, no lights.

'That helicopter back there,' he said eventually. 'That was pretty random, wasn't it?'

'Actually, that was fairly predictable because we knew it was coming. But the helicopter crew, now they'd have said the fighter was random.'

He chuckled, which was a good sign. 'You think you'll hit your wall one day, Portman?'

'I guess I will. Until then I'm doing a job. Like you.'

'You're nothing like me.' He stopped. 'Sorry. I don't mean that to be offensive. We're just very different people, you and I.'

'You're right. And that's a good thing.'

He didn't say anything after that, but his words left me thinking about my own life and how long it could go on. We all make choices and I'd never seen mine as any different to a thousand others. I knew other guys in the same line of work, most of them on the surface no different to Travis; they had family and hobbies and ambitions, they played ball with their kids and to everyone else they looked normal on the outside. Then one day they hit the wall. It could be brought on by seeing too much bad stuff happen and having too many near misses. Who knows? Some deliberately shrugged it off, but others decided to do something else with the time they had left.

I wasn't shrugging off anything; I just hadn't yet reached that point.

Two hours later, as a thin dawn began to push back the night, I discovered we had a more immediate problem than fate to deal with. A vehicle was coming up fast from the rear. It was the first one I'd seen since last night. It approached to within half a mile or so behind us, then held station for a while before dropping back and disappearing. The light wasn't good enough to make out the type of car, but it looked to me like the profile of a sedan. It might have been a fellow traveller looking for some morale-boosting company on a lonely road, before having a change of heart.

But I had my doubts.

FORTY-NINE

After a lifetime of almost unqualified success and achievement, where the tang of anything approaching disappointment had been limited to political ups and downs, Senator Howard Benson was undergoing an emotion he had not experienced before: a feeling of dread. Twenty minutes ago he'd had a call from the number calling himself Two-One. The news was about as bad as it could get.

Walter Conkley had turned into considerably more than just a minor irritant.

'The subject has had two meetings with a white female identified as Marcella Cready,' Two-One informed him, his voice flat with the tone of a minor news briefing. 'She's a well-known investigative hack around town.'

'I know damn well who she is,' Benson growled. He'd crossed swords with Cready on more than one occasion. She had twice tried to tie his name to unauthorized payments made to opposition campaign staff in what was effectively vote-rigging, and had mentioned him in connection with the suppression of secret transcripts related to extraordinary rendition flights out of Iraq and Afghanistan. 'You said two meetings?'

'I did.'

'Why didn't you tell me after the first one? This is disastrous.'

'Because the first one was a sniffing exercise; each was seeing what the other had before they committed. I knew pretty quickly that they were lining up for another so I figured it would be better to wait until I had something more concrete to tell you.'

Benson bit down on his anger, knowing the other man would see it as fear. He took a deep breath to calm his voice. 'What were they talking about?'

'You. And the Dupont Circle Group. Names, dates and details – and some digital media. Cell phone recordings.'

'What?' Benson swore long and loud. *The little bastard had been recording them?*

'I'm pretty certain you don't want me to read them out here and now,' Two-One continued, 'so I'm sending the material across to you by special messenger. Should be with you any minute.'

That had been twenty minutes ago, and now Benson had heard the first ten minutes of the second meeting his gut was killing him. The sound quality of the recording was too clear to leave any misunderstanding, and he could picture Cready in living detail as she gently prised the story out of Conkley with all the expertise of the interrogator that she was. She was good. Very good.

And the biggest danger was that everybody knew it and fed on it. Such was her record in exposing the underbelly of administrative failure and corruption, when she turned her attention on something – or more often than not, someone – the associated target was already deemed by news watchers as probably guilty anyway, otherwise why else would Cready bother looking?

All the eager readers had to do was simply wait for her to bring the story home and prove it in her usual way – with pictures, transcripts, witness evidence and, more often than not, sworn affidavits to back up her claims.

The recording was painful listening. According to Two-One's surveillance notes, the weasel Conkley had met with her twice in a six-hour period; once at a bar on 7th Street, the second time at an apartment she leased as a place of work while in Washington. Two-One had made a notation with the recording that he had been able to get inside and place a recording device when he'd heard her giving Conkley the address and arranging the time of the second meeting.

'Bitch,' Benson swore. He didn't ask Two-One how he'd managed to record Cready, nor did he want to know. The man was an expert in surveillance and covert operations, and had clearly been trained by the best. He'd been using his services for some time now and the man had never failed him yet. The fact that Benson still didn't know his true identity was a matter of choice; it was better to keep his distance and his hands clean where this kind of dirty work was involved.

He stared out of his office window, the famous landmarks of Washington glinting in the sun as he chewed over the bitter facts. He should have foreseen Conkley going to a hack like Marcella Cready; she'd have gone on heat the moment she'd been approached by him. Known White House staffers like Conkley did not talk to gutter journalists like her unless they had something official they wanted broadcast . . . or they wanted to speak strictly off the record. Either way it would have told her that there was a story in the air – a possible scoop. She had clearly decided against meeting with Conkley where she might be known, especially by other journalists. Opportunities like Conkley didn't come along every day and she wasn't going to share him with anyone else or allow herself to be outbid by a rival hack.

His gut churned at the thought that even as he was sitting here she would be verifying facts and details, timings and dates, prior to writing a summary proposal for an anxious editor.

The shit, Benson decided, was going to hit the fan long and loud, and there was only one thing to do about it. He swore again. From that first moment when Teller had exposed his venal nature at the possibilities coming from the social upheavals in Eastern Europe, he'd sensed Conkley was a problem. Benson had gone against his own instincts and allowed the matter to drop, trusting in Conkley's greed and his instincts for self-preservation in the face of exposure to keep him from talking. But it hadn't been enough.

Now the situation had undergone a seismic change and he had to do something about it. He took out his cell phone and dialled a number. It rang twice.

'Two-One.'

'Thank you for the material. It's good work. Very good.'

'Thank you. Anything else?'

Benson had been chewing over what he knew he had to do. He'd known it would come to this, but had been putting it off in the hope it would simply go away. Now that hope was right off the board.

'Yes. I want you to arrange an accident. Effective immediately.'

'As you wish. It will cost you.'

'Of course. Just do it.'

'Very well. I'll be in touch.'

'Wait.' Benson hadn't finished. His mind was leaping ahead, contemplating the enormity of what he'd just arranged . . . and thinking that maybe, just maybe it wouldn't be enough. After all, there would still be another source of information out there. 'Make it two.'

There was a short silence. 'Are you serious?' The voice was utterly calm, simply posing a question. But the words and tone carried a hint of censure, even of faint disbelief.

And if there was anything Benson hated more it was censure of any kind, especially of his own actions or decisions.

'Do you have a problem with that?' he snarled. 'Or should I go elsewhere?'

'No. But it increases the element of risk.'

'Christ. OK – how much?'

Two-One gave him a figure, and Benson's instinct was to refuse. But he realized that the fee for getting rid of both people would be chicken feed compared with what he and the others would make on the energy markets if everything worked out and their plans weren't ruined at the last minute.

'Very well.' He closed his eyes and felt a moment of almost sexual excitement go through him. His instinct had been to deal with Conkley, to stop him talking further and to teach the gutless little creep a lesson. But there was a survival aspect to this, too. Take out the disaffected and treacherous civil servant and there would be no case, no matter how persuasive Cready might be. Allegations were just that and without living proof the story would wither and die. But there would always be lingering suspicions in the minds of some in this city, where seeking advantage through rumour was almost an Olympic sport. And he had too much to lose to risk coming under the microscope that was insider talk.

'Are you certain?' Two-One's voice again, probing and soft, wanting confirmation.

'I'm certain.' And indeed he was. Why not wipe the board completely clean? Dealing with Marcella Cready would be payback for all the grief she had caused him and others in the past by her allegations and suggestions. More than one person in the administration had dismissed her at their cost, and he knew her passing would be met with quiet smiles and raised glasses all over town. Elegant. Clinical. Final.

'Both,' he confirmed. 'And wipe out any records.'

'Of course. I'll be in touch. Keep your eye on Fox News.'

FIFTY

'**W**atchman, you have two unidentified vehicles just over seven miles to your rear and moving up fast. We suspect militia.'

I could guess who it might be but I needed confirmation. I hit the amplify button. 'Copy that. Can you describe?'

'One is a Mitsubishi Lancer sedan. No visible markings but it looks like it has a strobe roof light. The other is a light utility vehicle thought to be a UAZ model 469, colour green.'

Damn. Grey Suit. It had to be. And the Lancer could be the sedan that had showed up a while back before dropping out again.

The same two cars that had turned up at the Hotel Tipol.

I had no way of knowing who Grey Suit was working for, but it really didn't matter right now. He was probably employed by the Ukrainian Ministry of Internal Affairs, but since that organization was thought to have been infiltrated by officers affiliated to the Russian GRU or FSB, his real bosses were most likely sitting in Moscow.

It would certainly explain how he was able to bulldoze his way around the country and why he was so determined to get hold of Ed Travis again. If push came to shove, having a US State Department employee in their hands would count as good leverage in any war of words over Moscow's involvement in Ukraine and the Crimea.

Seven kilometres. Less than five miles. It wasn't a big enough gap; the Land Cruiser was solid enough but way past its prime when it came to speed. The Lancer could overhaul us easily within minutes and the UAZ wouldn't be far behind.

Travis got the message quickly. 'It's them, isn't it? How did they find us?' He turned and studied the road behind us but it was clear for maybe half a mile before dropping off the horizon.

'They figured out which way we were headed from Pavlohrad and covered the ground. It's not as though we had too many options.' The amount of traffic had dropped dramatically in the past few hours as tension spread across the country, so any vehicles with two men in would have been easy to spot. My guess was the man at the used car lot had been too eager to shift the Isuzu and it had somehow come up on the radar. He wouldn't have resisted more than two minutes when faced with questions about where he'd got it, and the next stage of the hunt would have been to track down the Land Cruiser we'd taken in exchange.

I said to Lindsay, 'I need a way off this road. What have you got?'

A few moments of static, then, 'Two miles ahead of your location there's a small lake with an access track and what looks like dead ground behind it. Apart from that we're talking maybe fifteen miles of open country and zero cover.'

'Copy that.' I checked the odometer and noted the figures, then put my foot down. Any way off this road was worth a try. It would give me some control over the situation and was better than staying in their line of sight when they could take us out any time they felt like it.

'Check our firepower's ready,' I said to Travis.

He didn't need telling twice. He hit the button to throw the seat back down, then slid into the rear and got busy. I heard him ejecting magazines and re-loading, and when he was finished he caught my eye in the mirror. 'You never said where these came from.'

'You never asked. I did some foraging. I like to improvize.'

He slid back into the front seat, grunting with pain and clasping his ribs. Now he had nothing to focus on, the discomfort was making itself obvious. I handed him a blister pack of painkillers and told him to take two, and watched while he did it. If things got scary I was going to need him ready for action, not rolling around unable to move.

The turning came up on the button. It was little more than a break in the grass verge, almost invisible at speed. I was counting on it staying that way to the two cars behind us. We bumped over some ruts before hitting a section of long grass, which made a hoarse swishing noise as we went down a long slope. At the bottom lay a lake, mirror-still and dark as night, surrounded by reeds and some scrappy bushes. I was praying nobody had decided to come fishing today; they'd be in for a surprise.

I drove round the other side and up a short slope to higher ground. After four hundred yards the ground dipped again past a granite outcrop. It was a dead end. I pulled to a stop and jumped out.

We were in a good position for now, screened from the road, and all we could do was wait it out. I walked back to the brow of the slope and lay down with the binoculars, where I had a good view of the road going back at least a mile, maybe more. It was empty.

'Are we safe here? Those marks in the grass look pretty obvious.'

He was right. I checked the ground where we'd come off the road. The verge looked fine, where the grass was scrubby and compacted. But where we'd hit the longer growth it was easy to see where the wheels had left twin tracks behind, a clear signature to anybody using their eyes. I couldn't tell if they looked as obvious from the road, but there was only one way to find out.

I had about fifteen minutes, maybe a little longer. Any more and we'd be in trouble.

I handed Travis the binoculars. 'Stay here and keep watch. I'm going back to wipe out the tracks.'

'There's no time. You heard Lindsay. They're right behind us.'

'That's why I need you to stay here. Keep an eye on the road and whistle if you see them coming.'

I didn't waste time arguing, but went back to the Land Cruiser and took out the Ero. If I had to risk facing the opposition I'd be better off with some close-up heavy metal.

I ran back round the lake, scaring up a trio of wild ducks from the reeds. They curved away in perfect formation, protesting loudly, and headed west, which I took as a good omen. At any other time it would have been a nice place to stop for a while and admire the scenery. But right now that was a luxury I couldn't afford.

I stopped before heading up the final slope to break off a branch from a bush by the water's edge, then ran up to the road. My thighs began burning as I reached the top and I reflected that if I hadn't been getting enough exercise lately, that was probably about to change.

Nothing in sight. I checked the verge and spotted a couple of marks in the stubby grass where we'd come off the metalled surface, so I brushed them with the branch until the stems sprang more or less upright. It wasn't perfect but it was the best I could do.

I worked my way backwards down the slope, stroking the longer grass back into place, and had just reached the bottom when I heard a long warning whistle from Travis.

I was out of time.

FIFTY-ONE

B rian Callahan's attention was torn away from the screen showing Watchman's location and the two vehicles tracking him by the arrival of an internal messenger. The man was holding a sealed envelope. He handed it over, got a signature and disappeared back the way he had come.

Callahan opened the envelope, one eye on the screen. A single sheet of paper inside detailed the results of research into the private investigator, Greb Voloshyn. It gave his home address, workplace and some facts about BJ Group, his employers. Callahan was about to put it to one side for reading later when he noticed a familiar acronym further down the page.

FSO.

He felt a jolt go through him. The FSO was the Russian Federal Protective Service, responsible among other things for the security of the Russian president and other high-ranking ministers. They were bodyguards of the highest order, similar to the US president's Secret Service detail. To most western observers, the FSO was simply another branch of the once all-powerful KGB, now the FSB.

And Greb Voloshyn was listed as a former officer of that organization.

'Can you handle this?' he said to Lindsay. 'Something's come up.' He held up his pager. 'Call me if anything happens – I won't be far away.'

'Yes, sir. Of course.'

Callahan hated leaving her at such an important juncture, but there was something he had to deal with that couldn't wait. He hurried along the corridor and took the elevator to the research section where the report on Voloshyn had been compiled. He checked the researcher's name listed at the bottom of the form, followed by a signature. David Andrews. He was one of the team of IT and intelligence geeks who trawled the internet's darkest corners and instigated investigations into whatever officers like Callahan required. It was an intensive job and demanded absolute focus and accuracy.

Andrews's particular strength was his knowledge of the current Russian security and intelligence apparatus and its history.

He found Andrews and took him to one side. 'I don't have to ask if you're sure of your facts,' he said, 'but do we have any way of telling if Voloshyn is still connected to the FSO?'

Andrews gave a knowing smile. He was short and chunky in build with a wispy moustache and the complexion of a man who spent too much time below ground out of the sunlight. Like a groundhog, Callahan thought not unkindly. Only a particularly smart one.

'They're always connected, sir. Guys like him might leave the service, same as the FSB and the SBP – the Presidential Security Service – but there's more than just an *esprit de corps* involved; they have a duty to remain in touch at all times. Like auxiliaries, I guess. As we're beginning to learn with the events in Ukraine at the moment and South Ossetia before, some of these people were farmed out with a deliberate mission in mind.'

'To do what?'

'To infiltrate government departments in the former satellite states of the old Russian Federation. We know the Ukrainian Ministry of Affairs and their intel and security services have got former FSB and GRU members in their ranks, as have a few government offices. It's the way they do things: infiltrate and take over. By the time anybody finds out what's going on, it's usually too late.' He grinned and made rabbit's ears signs with his fingers. 'Like the Borg Collective.'

'The what?' Callahan scowled. He was never entirely sure with some of the geeky types down here if they were having a quiet joke at his expense or not.

'*Star Trek*, sir. The Borg Collective was an alien race who—' Andrews stopped, sensing he'd lost his listener with the first two words. He was right.

'But Voloshyn's with a private security company based in Kiev.'

'Same thing, different uniform. During my research on Voloshyn I found references to BJ Security working in Russia, on contracts issued by government departments and under direct orders of Russian military and security personnel. But they've also got connections with Russian organized crime. In fact one of their directors recently finished a five-year term for robbery. They're a pretty diverse organization and a lot bigger than their public face indicates. In fact,' he added, 'I recently circulated a report advising that BJ Group has established a representative office here in Washington DC.'

'*What?*'

'Yes, sir. I believe there's been a watch placed on it since then, but there's nothing on the file yet. I checked.'

'What, they're just watching it?'

'Yes, sir. The FBI and Homeland are arguing over whether to leave them be until they make a mistake, or close them down. Trouble is if they do that the guy could go underground and they wouldn't know where he was.'

It made sense, Callahan thought. Keep your suspects where you can see them. 'You said guy. One man?'

'Yes, sir. Name of Gus Boranov. Looks, dresses and sounds all-American, but my guess is his heart is pure Kremlin. He has a nice office downtown and does a lot of entertaining.' He grinned cynically. 'I guess they don't believe in travelling economy.'

Callahan felt as if he'd been living in a bubble. On the other hand, that was why the CIA employed people like Andrews: to keep a weather eye on what else was going on out there. This news altered his whole line of thinking. 'Right. So what's the bottom line with this Greb Voloshyn?'

'Bottom line?' Andrews shrugged. 'Bottom line is, I don't have definitive proof right now, but I'm prepared to bet my girlfriend's car, which is a very nice 1978 Mustang, that Voloshyn is still a serving FSB or FSO officer.' He smiled with the supreme confidence of a man who knew his job. 'And you can take that to the bank. Sir.'

FIFTY-TWO

I threw the branch away and ran back round the lake. I was heading up the slope when I heard three short whistles and looked up to see Travis beating his arm downwards in a frantic 'hit the deck' signal, before he dropped out of sight.

Even travelling at high speed the Lancer's tuned engine hadn't carried far, and was almost on me before I knew it. I dropped to the ground and heard the buzz on the road as it went by. Then I heard the harsher sound of the UAZ coming. I stayed where I was and cocked the Ero. The Lancer would have been going too fast to see any detail at ground level, but the UAZ was making heavy weather and the men inside would have more time to study the surrounding countryside.

I waited as the high-pitched whine of the tyres went by and counted to ten. No slowing down, no change of engine note. Gone.

I gave it another count of ten to be sure then jacked myself to my feet and started running.

I was almost at the top of the slope when I heard the squeal of brakes behind me. I turned to see the UAZ doing a virtual ninety-degree turn off the road, its tyres stuttering as they lost traction on the surface. It barrelled across the verge and started on down the slope, and a soldier in the back stuck a rifle out the window and began firing.

He was good. I guessed he'd been trained to shoot while mobile, and was probably a member of a Russian raider force. I heard the snap of rounds going past me and saw grass being kicked up in vicious clumps, the shots following me up the slope like angry hornets. Something plucked at my sleeve and I knew I was running out of luck. I dived off the slope and rolled behind cover.

The UAZ was still coming, following the same path round the lake that we'd just taken, the engine howling as the driver pushed it as hard as he could.

I looked out and levelled the Ero, waiting for the right moment. Where I was lying I was in dead ground. If the UAZ appeared, I'd have maybe two seconds to open fire and take them out of the game.

The engine started grinding as it hit the slope and I got ready to go for it, following the sound as it came nearer.

Then I heard the flat bark of a semi-automatic, firing evenly spaced rounds.

Travis?

I looked up. He was on the rise above me, using a two-handed grip, feet planted wide and shooting down the slope at the oncoming vehicle. He was right out in the open, and looked pale and unsteady, but determined, and had evidently remembered enough from live firing exercises to know what to do.

The UAZ's engine note changed and went up the scale for a few seconds, rising to a screech, then it fell silent and Travis stopped firing. *'Portman, come on!'*

I scrambled up the slope and looked behind me. The UAZ was nose-down in the lake, muddy water washing around the base of the windshield and steam brushing across the windshield and roof. I could see the driver slumped over the wheel, but two soldiers had already scrambled out of the back and were rolling desperately into the reeds to find cover. One of them turned and fired off a couple of wild shots with his rifle before disappearing.

I fired a return burst with the Ero, peppering the reeds and digging holes in the side panels and windows of the UAZ.

Silence.

'Good work,' I told Travis. 'Get the car and I'll check them out.'

I jogged back down to the UAZ. The driver was out of it, slumped over the wheel with blood on his face. I walked over to where I'd seen the two soldiers dive into cover, ready to return fire if they came up shooting. But it wasn't necessary. The first one had lost his weapon and was clutching at a bloody wound in his leg. When he saw me he forgot about the wound and shook his head, throwing up his empty hands. I motioned for him to stay where he was and went looking for his pal. He was half in the water, but buoyed up by the reeds and holding his arms out wide. He looked dazed and wet, all the fight gone out of him.

I dragged both men out on to solid ground and told them to lie down back to back, then stripped out their bootlaces and tied their thumbs together. It would be uncomfortable but bearable. And at least they were alive to tell the tale. I checked the wounded man's leg but it wasn't a killer. The driver was coming round so I left him where he was.

Travis drove up in the Land Cruiser and I climbed in. He took us back round the lake and up the other side, and we got back on the road heading west.

The Lancer was coming towards us, kicking up dust.

'Keep going,' I told Travis, and took the Grach. The Ero was virtually empty and I didn't want to have to change weapons in mid-fight if it came to it.

It did.

The Lancer saw us and slowed, then swung across the road to block us. Nobody got out, and I figured they were ready to move if we tried to squeeze by them. All it would take was a nudge and we'd be off the road and helpless.

We got to within a hundred yards when I said, 'Stop.'

This kind of stuff could go on all day long if I didn't neutralize them. For all I knew they had reinforcements on the way here or others ahead of us ready to block the road. It was time to call a halt.

Travis stamped hard on the pedal and the Land Cruiser slewed sideways as the brakes bit unevenly. I was out of the car before it stopped moving and walking towards the Lancer. I could see Grey Suit sitting there watching me, mouth open, and the driver frantically moving the gear shift to go.

This was something they hadn't expected. In their world fugitives simply don't get out of their cars and walk towards trouble.

Well, this one does.

I fired twice into the nearside tyres as I approached the car, and twice more into the engine block, killing it dead. Or maybe the driver stalled it in his haste to move. Just for effect I put another round through the rear window. I've been in a car taking incoming shots and the noise of impact damage is considerable. No matter how experienced you are, when a window goes bang it's enough to scramble the brain and delay a reaction.

The two men sat very still.

I signalled for them to get out of the car and told them to sit on the ground at the side of the road. The driver was in standard police uniform, but he didn't have the look of a real cop to me, and was shaking with nerves. Grey Suit was a different animal altogether; he looked mad enough to spit but kept his mouth shut. Wise man.

I motioned Travis to drive by. It was a squeeze but he made it. Then I leaned into the Lancer and disabled the car radio, and tossed a cell phone I found into the ditch at the side of the road.

FIFTY-THREE

Walter Conkley was feeling relaxed for the first time in days. After a second meeting with Marcella Cready, this one at her apartment and going into far greater detail about his meetings with the Dupont Group, of dates, times, topics under discussion and even some recording of recent talks, he'd experienced a sense of enormous relief at what she had agreed to. His own position as a newfound 'Deep Throat' would be protected at all costs, and Cready had claimed the discovery of enough information on Benson and his friends in the Dupont Circle Group to confirm that she would be going after them with everything that she had.

He took a deep breath and chuckled with an almost childish sense of excitement. An enormous weight had been lifted from his shoulders and he felt like a new man. Cready's reputation in Washington DC was awesome. She was the pit bull of investigative news-hounds, and once she began looking into a case, the end was already in sight. All she had to do was drop the investigative package on a news editor's desk and the fallout was both guaranteed and earth-shattering.

He decided to walk while mulling over his next move. Staying on in the White House might prove less than comfortable after the story broke, and he'd already made a few enquiries into property in the Catskills in New York State. He had lots of stories to tell, and there was always a demand for memoirs and nuggets of gossip from people in the know, like himself. He could already imagine an 'insider' column syndicated in various newspapers, and who knew – maybe a book deal?

He headed northwest to Connecticut Avenue, then drifted along, needing the exercise, his mind in a whirl as he considered the possibilities open to a single man with enough money to keep himself comfortable in a world that wouldn't ask too many questions. Time to forget his lack of discretion and the way he'd allowed himself to be sucked in by others; time to kick back and let others listen to the daily fights and squabbles among the movers and shakers of home and foreign policy in the bear-pit that was Washington.

He found himself close to the Parrotts Woods area and wondered how he'd managed to walk so far without noticing. He smiled to himself. Maybe this was an indication of a newfound interest in life; being free and able to do whatever the hell he wanted, when he wanted.

He decided to eat somewhere special for dinner, and took out his cell phone. A little early to celebrate perhaps, but he felt he owed himself at least a little something nice. A French menu, perhaps. And a nice Burgundy – a Brouilly. He could already taste it along with the sense of victory.

He checked the street and turned to cross when he saw no traffic.

The phone screen flickered brightly as his thumb accidentally brushed the keys, and he glanced down automatically, eyes off the road. It was enough. His mind filled with thoughts of pleasures to come, while slowly registering the unchanged home screen and no incoming messages. Simultaneously, his auditory senses became aware of the roar of a powerful vehicle engine approaching very fast.

His final thought was that it was too fast for these streets.

When he looked up, it was too late.

FIFTY-FOUR

Marcella Cready sat and stared at her laptop screen, where she had been thrashing out the main details of what she had learned from Walter Conkley. She was too experienced to be thrilled by what she now knew, too hardened to feel anything but quiet satisfaction at the promise of what lay ahead. She had uncovered other men and women involved in corruption, double-dealing and outright criminality on a vast scale; but the members of the group Conkley had called the Dupont Circle Group were something else. Benson, especially.

She had only a vague knowledge of Chapin, Teller and Cassler – a man she'd thought was long dead – but the former senator from Virginia was the big beast who would occupy the very heart of the story, providing it with the meat that would make it fly. Financial investors, bankers, lawyers – even former members of the Intelligence Community going back to the Cold War era – were big game, but Benson would be the biggest kill of all. The reverberations caused by Conkley's testimony would echo around Washington DC and the rest of the country for years to come.

She decided to celebrate with a drink at the thought of Benson's upcoming fall from grace. She walked round the room first, straightening cushions, adjusting pieces here and there. She regretted inviting Conkley to her apartment, which she habitually kept as her private space, a retreat from the daily grind of interviews and reports. But with what Conkley had promised to reveal in detail, she hadn't trusted anywhere else to be private enough. And she needed absolute trust in her surroundings to put the facts down that would effectively nail the Dupont Circle Group to the wall.

As she lifted the whisky decanter, she heard the buzz of the entry phone. She walked over and pressed the button.

'Yes?'

'It's Walter Conkley. I have something else—' The voice was indistinct and the rest of his words were lost in the clatter of a delivery truck roller going down. Maybe he had more juicy details he'd forgotten about. Jesus, like what – that Benson was in bed with the North Korean president? Or had he simply developed cold feet and wanted to retract his story?

No chance, not now. This was going global. She pressed the button.

'Come on up.'

Two minutes later the doorbell buzzed and she walked down the corridor, whisky in hand and already experiencing a light heady feeling. She needed food to counter the alcohol. She hadn't eaten a bite all day. But that could wait. Maybe she'd send out for a pizza and get this thing done and dusted.

She opened the door and a man she'd never met before stepped into view. He was smartly dressed, young and even handsome if you liked men with Clark Kent glasses and wide, brown eyes. A mid-level government employee, perhaps, or a corporate middle-manager on the way up the ladder.

'Who are you?' she asked, and leaned forward to look past him, expecting to see Walter Conkley lurking in the background. 'You shouldn't be up—'

The man stepped towards her before she could move away, and she felt his breath on her cheek. At the same moment she felt a sharp pain in her side, shocking and icy-cold. Just for a brief moment she was overcome by a sense of weightlessness, and felt the whisky glass being taken out of her hand. Then her legs gave way and she began to fall down a long, darkening tunnel.

FIFTY-FIVE

'It's done.'

Benson heard the words on his cell phone as he drove through the Washington DC suburbs, and experienced a mixture of relief and apprehension. Relief because he'd had no other choice but to take care of Conkley for good. The little man was a cancer that had to be excised. As for Cready, that was different; that was payback and worth every cent of the fee demanded.

The apprehension was something else. Drastic action always carried risk, no matter how cautious you tried to be. He had no reason to distrust the man he knew as Two-One, the one he'd ordered to arrange the hit on Conkley and Cready. He knew enough about him – not everything, but enough – to ensure his silence on the matter. But as he'd learned in over forty years in politics, nothing was ever one-hundred-per-cent certain. And people had a way of surprising you all the time.

He shook off the doubts and dismissed the subject as closed. 'Good. Thank you.'

'I'll look forward to payment as usual.'

'You'll get it, don't worry.'

Benson disconnected the call. But the apprehension stayed with him. Even after he'd arranged another meeting of the Dupont Group, there was a niggle that simply wouldn't go away.

He wondered if it was the way Two-One had asked for his payment that had got to him. The man usually did the jobs he was asked to do, no questions asked. And Benson arranged payment within twenty-four hours of completion. It was the way they worked, each dependant on the other, a disconnected but satisfactory arrangement.

He wondered if it was time to review his arrangement with Two-One. Perhaps the man was getting greedy. Greed, as he knew well, had a way of cutting ties and breaching any feelings of loyalty. If that were the case, so be it – in this city there was always somebody else who could handle the same kind of work.

He rang Jason Sewell for an update on the Watchman situation.

Having kept a close eye on it thus far, it might seem odd if he were to suddenly lose interest.

'I'm sorry, Senator, but I'm not able to discuss the matter.' The unmistakeable tone of finality to Sewell's response came as a surprise. He was accustomed to having his questions answered instantly and saw this as a personal affront.

'What do you mean, you can't discuss it? Do I need to remind you that bringing down the shutters on this operation might be perceived in some quarters as a form of stonewalling? You of all people should be aware that there has already been quite enough of that in Langley.'

'I'm aware of the views expressed about us, Senator. But we have our procedures. Part of our mandate is to ensure that live operations are not compromised in any way. There are times when circumstances mean we have to raise our security level, and this is one of them. The section of our facility dealing with the Watchman operation is now closed to non-essential personnel.'

'What the hell are you saying, Sewell?' Benson snarled, momentarily forgetting himself. 'I'm not some two-bit politician in town on a social junket, and I shouldn't have to remind you of my position in the Intelligence Community in relation to the approval of special activities, especially of your organization.'

'I'm mindful of that, Senator.' For a man who had always shown appropriate deference, Sewell sounded surprisingly unperturbed by Benson's bluster. 'Now, if you'll excuse me, I have to brief the White House.'

There was a click and he was gone.

FIFTY-SIX

'I hear Walter Conkley got hit by a car.' Chapin was staring at the library ceiling, his expression thoughtful. He didn't seem too distressed by the news, but was clearly intent on making a point. 'Did you hear that, Howard?'

'I heard something about it.' Benson was checking his phone messages, stabbing at the buttons and scowling at the lack of response. 'A pity. He was useful to us. That's the trouble with traffic in this town; it's getting so out of hand now it's not even safe to cross the darned streets anymore.'

'I didn't say he was crossing a street.'

'No, you didn't.' Benson put down his cell phone and gave a cool smile. 'But my source in the White House did. They got a call the moment the police saw Conkley's ID.'

Teller and Cassler, seemingly unaware of any hidden messages passing between the two men, expressed shock and regret at Conkley's passing. But their comments lacked real depth; Conkley had never quite been one of them, and they soon moved on to other more pressing matters, such as discussing the current European and world market movements. In particular they talked about matters surrounding the potential energy supply problems via the Ukraine pipelines.

'We're getting closer,' Benson told them. 'It's slow progress but events over the past couple of days have helped to focus a few minds.'

'Such as?' asked Teller.

'Such as Travis being in jeopardy and CIA assets being arrested or killed while trying to help him. Moscow has finally started complaining about US interference and sending in a negotiator to talk to what they call "disparate groups", but that's their shorthand for pro-Russian rebels and how we should mind our own business because they're minding theirs.' He grunted. 'As you may recall, I suggested this might happen when the CIA took it upon themselves to send in a contractor to get him out.'

'Yes, and you were perfectly correct, Howard,' Chapin congratulated him. His tone carried a faint air of condescension. 'What's the situation there? You haven't said much about it.'

Benson shifted in his chair. Chapin was showing signs of becoming difficult, and he wondered if it was a result of his health issues. Not that he cared one way or another, as long as the old man stayed onside.

Privately he was still furious at finding that he'd been shut out of the loop at Langley, and questions from Chapin only served to remind him of his sudden inability to exert some pressure where it could count. The operations support room responsible for helping Watchman was now under red light rules, effectively prohibiting entry to all but immediate and senior personnel. He'd tried pushing Jason Sewell further on the issue, and even approached the director himself. But the answer had been the same: the facility was now closed to all non-essential staff, including himself. Not that he was about to tell these men, as he regarded it as a point of pride that he could go almost anywhere without let or hindrance.

'It's gone beyond any control I might have had,' he muttered vaguely. 'In any case, whatever happens now won't affect our plans for the future. President Putin has seen to that.'

'What's his latest word on the situation?'

'Not much. He's continuing to deny any Russian involvement and suggesting any "foreign" fighters assisting the rebels are "patriots".'

'Good.' Chapin stood up and looked at Teller and Cassler. 'Let's meet again when something develops. Keep checking the voicemail box for messages.'

As the men filed out of the room, Chapin touched Benson's sleeve. The senior lawyer waited for the others to move ahead along the corridor before saying softly, 'I think there have been enough accidents, Howard, don't you? I'm not sure how far you think you can take this, but I should hate for it to spread further.'

'Whatever do you mean?' Benson did his best to look innocent, but the glint of devilment lurking in his eyes was unconvincing. In spite of the momentary setback with his access to Langley, he was enjoying the secret power he was wielding elsewhere far too much, and exerting a terminal control over Conkley and Cready had been like a shot in the arm.

The senior lawyer was too experienced to have missed it. He had seen similar expressions in the eyes of other men over the years;

mostly people like Benson, who liked giving orders but rarely if ever had to carry out the deed. Over time he had come to the conclusion that for them it was a need, something primeval long hidden by circumstance and lifestyle, but which eventually found its way to the surface. He studied the senator's face for a few moments and wondered what they had created between them. Or whether it had always been there, waiting to surface. Had Benson been hiding another persona all these years, and their current situation was now allowing him an excuse to vent some secret desires?

If so, it was time to rein him in before he went too far and ruined them all.

His grip intensified on Benson's arm. Although he clearly wasn't well to those who knew him, the lawyer still had strong hands. 'I'm not a fool, Howard. I know what it's like to have the power to make life and death decisions. I had to use it more than once in my time. But I never got used to it, not like some. Not like you.'

Benson tried to shake him off, but failed. 'What are you saying, old man?'

Chapin leaned closer as an intern walked past and disappeared down the corridor. 'I'm saying, just in case you consider that any of us closer to home might become – what was it you called them once – "casualties of war"? – you might take note that I have a great deal of information that might prove . . . damaging, if I should meet with a fate similar to Conkley. Or Marcella Cready.'

Benson shook his head and jerked his arm free, his mouth dropping open. 'What the hell are you—'

'I just heard the news, Howard.' Chapin held up his smart phone. 'The wonders of modern technology and rolling reports, you see. Something we could have done with in my day, I have to say. I didn't want to air this in front of the others because I doubt they would have understood the significance. They're simple money men, not versed in the dark arts of intelligence work. But I might tell them yet, if the need arises. Cassler probably wouldn't give it a moment's thought; he's too wrapped up in his portfolios and making the next million. But Teller? He might care. A lot. He was once very close to Marcella Cready, did you know that?' The lawyer noted the flash of concern that appeared briefly in Benson's eyes. Then it was gone, to be replaced by an amused frown.

'I said before, Vernon, I have no idea what you're talking about. Truly. Are you sure your illness isn't having an adverse effect on your judgement? I'd hate to think you might consider talking outside this building. In any case, what's this "information" you say you have? Haven't you noticed how careful I've been in the past not to put anything in writing?'

Chapin smiled. 'Who said writing, Howard?' He raised a finger, making a circular movement which took in their opulent surroundings and the very fabric of the building. 'You should bear in mind that old wartime saying: walls have ears. Walls have ears.'

FIFTY-SEVEN

'**W**atchman, you have two miles to go before you reach a farm building marked as deserted. Just past it is a turning on your left. We're advised that this is an unmarked access road for forest workers and border patrols, although rarely used. Take this turning and you will be on a thousand-metre track to the border itself.'

'Copy that. Are there any active patrols in the area?' We were now so close I was ready to blow through anything that showed itself. But the proximity of freedom is a siren call to the unwary. Border patrols are usually connected by radio with regular checks by their control room to make sure all is well. And in a country where civil and military unrest was compounded by threats from across their borders, they would probably now be at a severe level of awareness. Running into a bunch of armed and touchy troopers under such conditions wasn't something that would end well.

'None visible and no marked obstacles that I can see. The track runs through a stretch of woodland to a simple fence. Beyond the fence is Moldovan territory. Your ride will be waiting for you there.'

'Good to hear. Is Callahan there?' I had to ask him about the leak; not that there was anything I could do about it right now, but the sense that we'd been betrayed had been digging away at me ever since Voloshyn's appearance at the Tipol, and I wanted him to know that I wasn't about to let it go. He could always refuse to discuss it, but I didn't think he would; he came across to me as a straight kind of guy with a bagful of experience and would go as far as he could to put things right.

Callahan came on. 'Go ahead, Watchman.'

'You've got a serious leak in the system. You know that?'

There was a long sigh. 'Yes, I know. I've initiated a background check of certain people. I'm sorry, Portman. My hands are tied. I can't say more.'

He sounded sick with anger, and I figured he knew or suspected who the likely leak had to be. It made me think the suspect must be someone of note, and not a staff member low down in the pecking order. But he wasn't about to tell me any names, and with good reason; although I was working for the CIA on this job, I wasn't part of their club, the inner circle of intelligence professionals. Like any organization with a pride in its own integrity, the CIA likes to clean house itself without involving outsiders.

'You know it's not Lindsay, though, right?' I had to make sure of that.

If he was surprised that I knew her name, he didn't say so. 'I know. She's in the clear, don't worry. I'm afraid it's a lot higher than that; somebody with top-level access to the facility. Be assured we will deal with it. Hold one moment.'

I heard him talking in the background. Then he came back. 'I have to go. Before I do there's something you should know about the man Voloshyn: he's almost certainly an FSB officer on second-ment. His employers, BJ Group, have security contracts with the Russian government, and in turn have connections with Russian organized crime.'

It provided answers to some questions about how Voloshyn might have been able to gain the knowledge that he had. It also ramped up the kind of opposition we were facing. It made me wonder which side of the fence Voloshyn was currently working on – or whether there was even a divide at all. 'Sounds to me like your mole must have the same connections.'

'Yes. Uh, Watchman, let me put you back to Lindsay. She'll help you with anything else you need. Stand by.'

It sounded like Callahan was having problems, and I wondered what was going on inside the bubble that was Langley. Work enough with people in the world of security and intelligence and you learn to pick up on their love of nuance and hidden meanings. It's almost as if it's a requirement of their job. But it's easy to get led into seeing things that aren't there, understanding things that aren't actually said. People talk in ways that imply without being clear, and after a while everything has a dual meaning, even when it shouldn't. However, I had a feeling that Callahan wasn't simply being elliptical; he'd found a way of sending me some kind of message.

Lindsay looked questioningly at Callahan as he moved away from the console. She had heard every word of the exchange between him and Watchman or, as she now knew from his slip of the tongue – if indeed it was a slip – the man named Portman.

'Sir?' she said quietly, her hand over the mouthpiece. She had a feeling she was about to step into unknown territory here and instinct told her she had to be very careful.

Callahan hesitated. He looked conflicted, and she wondered at the huge pressures being exerted on a man at his level. His reference just now to somebody with top-level access clearly referred to Benson; it had to. But she knew he was bound by his position as much as by the rules governing all staff of the CIA into secrecy at all times.

'I want you to conduct Watchman's debriefing. You think you can handle that?'

She was surprised, but nodded. 'Yes, sir. If you think so.' She knew that debriefings were usually handled by the Staff Ops Officer responsible, in this case Callahan. But if he decided to hand it over to her, how could she argue? In any case, it would be good experience for her.

'You'll do fine. Watchman's not one of ours, so we can't expect him to jump through post-operational hoops for us and write out a full report. But we need to know what went on over there. We'll have Travis's input, anyway.'

'Right, sir. Do I do it here?'

'No. I doubt he'll come here, anyway. Set up a meeting somewhere in town. Can you do that?'

'Yes, sir.' She hesitated, feeling a thrill running through her that she couldn't explain. Was this what it was like to be accepted? 'What do I tell him, sir?'

'He knows the background. Fill it in at your discretion. Tell him what went on in this room. You know what I mean.'

'Yes, sir. And afterwards?'

'Afterwards? Well, you come back and report to me. If you want it, there's a job waiting here for you. You've earned it.'

'Thank you, sir.' Lindsay sat for a moment as Callahan walked out, stunned by his words, by his confidence in her abilities. She turned to her desk and checked that Watchman was still on hold. She was surprised to find that she already knew what to say. She spoke into the headset, 'Watchman?'

'I hear you. What's up?'

'My apologies for keeping you. How well do you know the Washington area?'

FIFTY-EIGHT

The track led into a stretch of trees ahead of us, the tops curving inwards to form an arch, lending the area a soft atmosphere. I couldn't hear them but I was betting that birds were singing. At any other time and place it would have been scenic, serene, a place of tranquillity.

But not now.

A Mercedes four-wheel drive was standing in our way.

Two figures were next to it, one carrying a rifle. The other had a splash of white on one leg. They looked as if they'd known we were coming.

I pulled to a halt. We were less than a thousand yards from the border. From safety. Three hundred from the Mercedes.

I opened my door, motioning for Travis to do the same. 'When you get out, leave the door open.' If we needed to get back in it would have to be fast. I picked up the Grach.

'Watchman, we have you on screen. Why have you stopped?'

'We've got company and they're in the way.' The Mercedes looked like a G-Class 4WD, big and boxy and new. A big man's status symbol. A gangster ride.

A short silence, then: *'Copy that. Your lift is inbound on the other side, but they cannot cross. Will you be able to proceed?'*

'I'll let you know. Stand by.'

I checked the map in case there was an alternative route. There wasn't. A river formed part of the boundary between Ukraine and Moldova for about two miles, after which lay a small town, no doubt with official patrols and customs posts. If we didn't cross here, we'd be forced to go back, and that simply wasn't an option. What we needed now was another Su-27 fighter and a pilot with some attitude.

I used the binoculars and took a look at the man with the rifle. There was something familiar about the bulky figure and I think I'd known who it was from the first sighting.

Ivkanoy.

I swung left a fraction and checked out the person on the other side. Smaller, neater, leaning against the side of the Mercedes. The splash of white was a plaster cast on one ankle.

Olena Prokyeva. The woman sniper.

She was sporting two black eyes and the swelling across her nose must have made breathing difficult. But she was clearly mobile and still with Ivkanoy, although she didn't appear to be armed. Maybe he'd brought her along to show her how killing me should be done.

Ivkanoy shouted something towards us but his words were carried away on the breeze. I doubted it was a warm welcome. In fact he looked mad enough to spit and threw the rifle up to his shoulder.

'Out, now!' I said, and we both jumped out and moved to the rear of the Land Cruiser.

If the birds had been singing before, they'd now gone very quiet.

Ivkanoy's first shot went wide. The second ploughed into the ground thirty feet in front of the Land Cruiser. The third went over our heads by several feet. He followed them up with several more shots and a lot of animated yelling in between.

You really shouldn't try sharp-shooting when you're crazy mad with the target.

'What do we do now?' Travis asked. He was crouched behind the Land Cruiser, now wide awake and jittery, and I wasn't surprised. The threat of shooting is one thing; facing live incoming rounds is something else altogether.

'We fight back,' I said, and leaned into the rear of the car. I pulled out the OSV-96 and checked the scope for dust, then made sure the magazine was good to go. I didn't want to start a shooting war right here so close to the border, but Ivkanoy didn't look like he was giving up. In fact, he'd only just got started. There was a sudden burst of automatic fire and the snap-snap of rounds going by were too close for comfort.

When I looked round the side of the Land Cruiser I saw where the automatic fire had come from. Ivkanoy had been joined by another man. This one was holding what looked like an AK-47. He raised it and fired two short bursts, and the Land Cruiser jumped as it took several hits.

This guy knew what he was doing.

Fortunately, his boss was an idiot. He walked over and snatched the AK away and tried to hose us down gangland-style. But he'd only got a few rounds left and they disappeared into the trees around us.

He swore and shouted at his colleague, who handed him another magazine.

'Get down,' I warned Travis, and grabbed him by the arm, dragging him into dead ground at the side of the track. Even Ivkanoy couldn't miss every time with a thirty-round magazine. As we stopped rolling, the best part of the load came whipping by overhead and snapping into the foliage on the far side of the track.

This was getting silly. As lousy a shot as Ivkanoy was, he'd got us pinned down and unable to move. If we stayed right here he'd eventually come down the track to get us. If we tried to run past him, he'd have open season on us – him and his pal. Travis evidently thought so, too.

'Can't you shoot the crazy bastard?' he yelled. He looked almost guilty as the words came out, and looked away.

'You're the boss,' I said, and rolled out from cover and positioned myself alongside the Land Cruiser. I hugged the OSV into my shoulder and got comfortable. It was a heavy weapon but nicely balanced. I got Ivkanoy in the cross hairs. He was struggling with the AK's magazine, and I guessed it must have jammed through over-heating.

I swung left to check out the other man, focussing on his face. Well, damn me. Wheels within wheels. I didn't know Ukrainian criminal society was so small.

It was Voloshyn, the thug from the Tipol hotel. He was now holding a pistol and looked pissed, and I guessed it was because Ivkanoy had used all the ammunition for his rifle and had now screwed up the AK.

I swung further left and found Olena. She had hopped away from the car and was shaking her head. She knew I could see her and knew what I was holding. She didn't want anything to do with the damage I could inflict with it. Sensible woman.

I put my hand over my head and flicked a finger sideways, motioning for her to get into the side of the road. She caught on immediately and dived left. I wasn't being gallant; she was unarmed and I saw no reason to add a defenceless woman to my score sheet, even one whose trade was death.

I checked Ivkanoy again. He'd given up fighting with the AK and tossed it back to Voloshyn, who dropped the pistol and snatched the AK out of the air as if it were a twig. In a fluid movement he had the old magazine out and was snapping a fresh one in place and turning ready to fire.

My first shot sounded like a canon. The round whipped by his leg so close it must have burned. It hit the four-wheel drive, the impact blowing out the windshield and sending a shower of glass fragments, plastic and metal trim high in the air. The next one took out the front tyre, dropping the vehicle like a wounded buffalo. The third round drilled through the rear panel and whatever it hit caused the far side window to explode.

When I looked at Voloshyn through the scope, he was standing very still. Even from this distance I could see he looked sick. He turned his head and said something to Ivkanoy, whose voice came back sounding snappy.

They didn't look a happy crew.

Ivkanoy walked across and picked up Voloshyn's pistol. He said something and pointed down the track towards us. Voloshyn shook his head.

Ivkanoy repeated his instruction, louder and snappier. This time Voloshyn shook his head and walked away. He'd had enough. If Ivkanoy wanted to walk down here into the muzzle of a big gun, he could go ahead.

Ivkanoy lifted the gun and shot him in the back of the head.

Then he turned towards Olena, who was backing away with nowhere to go.

I put a round over his head as a warning. The crack must have made his ears buzz, but there was no reaction. He'd gone beyond reason, beyond instinct or sanity.

Olena stumbled and went down, and rolled on to her back, kicking with the heel of her good foot to get away. Ivkanoy walked over to her and pointed the gun at her head. It wasn't a threat; I knew by his stance that he was going to pull the trigger.

He wouldn't have heard my next shot; he was dead before he hit the ground.

I got back in the car and turned the key. In spite of the hits it had taken, the engine started first time. Some build. Go Toyota.

'Let's go home,' I told Travis, and we rolled forward down the track.

Olena stood up as we reached the four-wheel drive, hopping to keep her balance and holding her hands out to the sides to show they were empty. The mess of her face wasn't just because of the damage I'd done to it; she had splashes of blood and other stuff on her and looked about ready to throw up. Tough as she was, she avoided looking at the crumpled mess of her late boss. Some things I guess you never get used to close up.

She raised a hand in mute thanks. I didn't stop, but gave her a nod. Once I was sure she wasn't a threat I eased the safety back on the Grach and placed it on the floor. What she did now was up to her. If she had any sense, she'd get in what was left of the Mercedes and get the hell away from here and find a new profession.

As I drove round the other vehicle and on down the track, I saw in the distance ahead of us the dark silhouette of a helicopter curving towards us on the Moldova side of the border. It was black and carried no markings.

'Watchman, we have you on screen, you have clear access and your lift is waiting. Have a safe journey home.'

FIFTY-NINE

Lindsay Citera had chosen a good place to meet. It was a small lunchtime café with a few outside tables just off Wilson Boulevard in Arlington, Virginia. The buzz of downtown Washington was just across the Potomac to the north-east, which made this area just far enough out to make our conversation a private affair.

As long as she hadn't got some kind of tail on her, I didn't mind where we met.

I watched her take a seat and pick up a menu, order water from the waitress and tap her watch to demonstrate that she was waiting for someone. It was easy, casual and entirely relaxed, and I figured Brian Callahan had made a wise choice; she was a natural, whether she realized it or not.

Quite what she was feeling right now, though, was another matter. It was probably her first assignment outside of Langley, and she'd be inhuman if she wasn't feeling some kind of pressure. Covert work is not for the faint-hearted.

I gave it a couple of minutes, watching pedestrians and cars for signs of surveillance. But I was also watching Lindsay. She was using the menu to scope the men in the area, and I could almost sense her dismissing obvious types by age or appearance. Once or twice she tensed, but relaxed as they walked on by.

She didn't know what I looked like.

I breathed a sigh of relief and walked across the boulevard. I didn't need it, but seeing her reactions confirmed to me that it hadn't been her responsible for releasing my photograph to the people employing Greb Voloshyn. If she had she'd have been watching for me.

She saw me coming and something must have clicked – an instinct. Suddenly she smiled and stood up, and we shook hands, business acquaintances on a lunchtime meeting. Her grip was firm and I saw that I'd been partially correct in my image of her: young, confident, honey-brown hair cut short. And an engaging smile.

'You've come a long way,' she said, and sat down. It was quite an opener, seeing what she knew of my journey here.

'The directions were excellent,' I replied. 'And you've got a lifelong fan in Ed Travis. Not that he knows who you are.'

She nodded and flicked at her hair self-consciously. 'Thank you. I'm glad it turned out the way it did for both of you.'

We ordered a light lunch and I gave her a potted de-briefing. She didn't write anything down, so I figured she either had a great memory for detail or a recording device hidden inside her coat.

When I finished, she asked a couple of questions for clarification, the way good de-briefers should, then told me about Senator Howard Benson. She kept it short, sharp and matter-of-fact, and I admired her professionalism.

'But you're good and clear?' I asked. I knew Callahan had said it, but I wanted to make sure she knew it, too.

She hesitated. 'I am. I think.'

'Tell me.'

She took a deep breath. 'Yesterday I found some money in my bank account. A lot of money. And I don't know where it came from. I've reported it to Callahan but he hasn't got back to me yet. It could be a genuine banking error, I guess.' The look on her face told me she didn't believe that, and I knew she was going to do well in this business. She had good instincts and a high moral code, which was more than could be said for guys like Benson.

'Leave it to Callahan,' I suggested. 'You did the right thing.' It didn't take rocket science to see Benson having something to do with the money deposit; movers and shakers like him see opportunity way ahead of the need, whether attempting to suborn someone in Langley by making a deposit and counting on their silent acceptance of dumb luck, or by destroying their place in the organization out of sheer spite. It was the way they operated.

She relaxed, and I realized she'd been waiting to tell someone else about the money. Someone other than Callahan or anyone else inside the CIA bubble.

My phone rang and I hoped it wasn't another job. At least, not yet. I now had something important to take care of. I excused myself and answered the call.

'Mr Portman.' It was a man's voice but not one I recognized. Confident, relaxed. It wasn't a question. I didn't answer. Not that many people know my number and there was no caller ID to help me out.

He gave a brief chuckle. 'I guess that tells me how you've survived so long, Mr Portman. Or may I call you Marc?'

'What do you want?' I don't like guessing games, especially when I get a tingle on the back of my neck. I couldn't be absolutely certain I was being watched and in any case it was pointless looking; there must have been a thousand vantage points within a hundred yard radius of my position where he could be concealed. The thought that I'd been tracked wasn't comforting, a feeling he confirmed with his next words.

'Relax, Marc. I'm not a threat. I approve of your choice of lunch venue, by the way. Unexpected, open . . . careful. Attractive company, too.'

Damn. He was close. 'Glad to hear it. Who are you?'

Lindsay had picked up on something in my voice and was frowning. I signalled her to stay put and she nodded, although her knuckles were white around her coffee cup.

'Who I am doesn't matter. You don't know me; we've never met and never will. This is a friendly call, and the only time you'll ever hear from me. We're sort of in the same line of business, you and me. We both provide security, take care of problems. The only difference is it's time for me to close shop and take up another occupation. But I'd like to do you a service before I go.'

'That's very kind of you. Why?'

'Let's call it a courtesy, one professional to another. See, I know what you're planning; what you've been planning since coming back from Ukraine. Probably even more so now you've met Miss Citera. At least, if I know the kind of man you are, and I think I do, it's certainly on your list of to-do jobs.'

'I don't know what you mean.'

'It involves a certain senator who is, shall we say, less than a real asset to the American way.'

'What about him?' It's always safer to play dumb with cold calls. You never know who might be recording them.

I had already decided that if I was correct about Callahan's oblique method of sending me a message, he was hoping I might do something about Benson. I wasn't sure what that might be, but I couldn't afford to leave any footprints while I was in town, just in case. Meeting with Lindsay had been a risk, but worth it. At least I got to thank her for her help. She was a nice kid and I hoped she did well.

'You know what I'm talking about. Benson nearly got you killed, you and Travis. He tried to wreck an intelligence-led operation and he set the Russian dogs on you to discredit the CIA and make a profit into the bargain for himself and some pals called the Dupont Group. Incidentally, I've sent some damning information on those people to the FBI, so I think the Dupont Circle area of Washington will be seeing some dawn activity sometime soon. But Benson, he's something else, am I right? Pretty untouchable, I think you'll agree.'

'You tell me.'

He gave a dry chuckle. 'Cautious all the way. But I can't blame you. If I were in your shoes I know I'd be planning on doing something to even up things a little. Hell, what am I saying? I *am* planning it.'

'Doing what?'

'The senator has outlived his position. He's gotten dangerous and needs stopping. And I know, I *know*, there's not a person in this town who can touch him by legal means. I always figured everyone – and I mean everyone – was reachable in law. But not Benson; he's as good as Teflon-coated. Oh, he might lose a little gloss here and there when any of this comes out, but it won't stop him completely. Which leaves only one other way to do it. But that doesn't mean it has to be you.'

'Go on.'

'I'm saying this is my call. I have the means, the opportunity and most importantly the motive. I have some cleaning to do and he's right at the top of the list. Hell, he *is* the list.'

'You worked for him.' I was guessing but it didn't take much to know what his motivation was.

'Indirectly, yes. And you'd be right if you said my decision to intervene is out of self-interest. But that's the way it is.'

'You'll get caught.'

'No. After this, I'll be gone where nobody can find me – and I know they will come looking; it's how Benson plays things. He keeps evidence, leaves markers. I've taken care of most of them but I know I haven't found them all. But disappearing is what I'm really good at.'

'Well, good luck with that.'

'Thanks. You did fine work in Ukraine, Portman. You saved a good man. It would be a shame to spoil your future for no good reason. And they'll know it was you; it's the way their devious little minds work and you'll have no way of ducking it. Doesn't matter what you did for them in Ukraine, they'll still send the dogs after you. You know it.'

He was right. In with one hand, out with the other. 'So where do we go from here?'

'My advice to you is make sure you have your whereabouts for this afternoon set in stone, with some good witnesses. Miss Citera, for one. Then go home. This is Two-One, over and out.'

There was a click and the phone went dead. I knew if I tried to call back there would be no answer.

'Problem?' Lindsay asked.

I shook my head. 'No. But after we finish up here it might be wise to visit a public gallery or two.' Preferably, I decided, somewhere where our visit would be recorded.

'I thought men like you didn't do public.'

'This is one of those times when I do – as a precaution. Do you mind?'

She smiled, already ahead of me. 'Of course not. If I'm going to skip work I might as well get some culture along the way. And I know a couple of places with lots of cameras. Is that public enough for you?'

Like I said. A natural.

SIXTY

The afternoon was growing old when, just over sixty miles south-west of Washington DC, Senator Howard Benson strode up the gravel path to his weekend cottage in Lake of the Woods, Virginia. He was smiling, feeling good about himself and what he'd accomplished. He'd seen off the twin threat of Cready and Conkley, and not even the safe return of Travis and Portman had been enough to dent his self-confidence.

In fact, by some careful positioning, he'd been able to avoid being pulled into the aura of blame that was currently circulating in the corridors of the State Department and the CIA looking for a culprit. He'd also managed to ensure that his contact down the street, the one who went under the name of Gus Boranov, and who'd agreed to have Travis and Watchman taken care of, was keeping his head down with an eternal promise of silence about their recent exchange.

Even his colleagues in the Dupont Group had proved themselves satisfied by the results of their work – well, his work. Given a couple of weeks or so to let the dust settle, he was now confident of being able to deal with Chapin and his ill-considered threats. For now he was content to play along, being the friend and co-conspirator, the hand of influence inside the government machine. But all it would take was a phone call and whatever recordings the elderly lawyer might have made through his internal bugs in the library would be located and wiped clean. When that was done, his recent health scare would rear up into something real – and terminal.

Benson would make absolutely certain of that.

He used his key to open the door, breathing in the warm tang of newly varnished wood and the sharper scent of pine. He'd found the place by chance in a moment of idle on-line property hunting. Built as a small family weekend escape, it was ideal for a single man like himself who occasionally needed time away from the bear pit that was Washington DC. A single call and an above-market offer had been enough to secure it. Now he intended to enjoy it to the full. Maybe he needed some company to help warm the place up a little.

He walked into the main lounge. And stopped dead.

Somebody had been in here. He could feel it in the air. Not the workman who'd remodelled the decking in front of the glass picture windows overlooking the lake; they'd had no need to enter the house to do their work. And not the security team he'd been advised to bring in to sweep the place for bugs. But someone else; someone who had left the barest traces of their passing, like a silent footprint.

He dropped his car keys on a nearby coffee table and hurried up the flight of open redwood stairs to the first level, which held a shower room, dressing room and study. A further flight led to the bedrooms and a bathroom, and the veranda with a spectacular view across the water.

He felt his heart beginning to pound. Whoever had been here was now gone; he could tell that much. But they'd left more than mere traces of their passage. A sheet of paper lay on the floor outside the study. Other sheets lay scattered around inside the room. The oak desk had been plundered, the drawers ripped open and thrown aside, and a filing cabinet lay on its side, the file folders spilling out on to the floor.

He uttered a groan. It wasn't the furniture that concerned him. Whatever lay in them was of no consequence, the kind of paper records kept by every household across the land; bills, receipts, quotations and building and decorating plans. But nothing sensitive.

What took his breath away was the state of a panel in the wall behind the desk. What had been built to resemble a plain wall was actually a shallow filing recess, secured by an electronic key-card which slid into a concealed slot in the wood. It was where Benson placed his most treasured papers and flash drives, the things most valued that had kept him secure all these years from people who had imagined they could bring him down.

People like Vernon Chapin.

But instinct told him this wasn't Chapin's work.

The panel had been smashed and ripped off, exposing the shelves and trays built into the wall. More papers lay about the floor, and he felt as if his heart was going to explode as he saw what else was there.

Photos. Dozens of photos. Obscene and horrible in their vile depictions, the kind of things no normal society would ever condone or understand. He groaned again and kicked them aside in revulsion.

There were CDs, too, and flash drives he didn't recognize but could guess at their contents. This was the kind of destruction of a man's character that would never go away, false as it was.

He turned to the computer on the desk. It was switched on, humming quietly, and he knew the worst was yet to come. Pictures, flash drives and CDs could be destroyed. But not websites or downloads buried deep in the guts of the system for investigators to find, placed there by an expert.

He felt the final nail of destruction go in when he saw the screen come alive. It was his contacts list, private as well as public, linked to his email and other sites.

This was going to destroy him.

Benson found he was crying. The tears of anger and frustration coursing down his cheeks at the realization that somebody had visited upon him the worst kind of retribution, punishment of a kind that could never be imagined by anyone in his position. No matter what he said, the stigma would stick forever. He'd be finished.

He kicked his way out of the room and stumbled downstairs, hardly able to breath. He veered towards the phone, then stopped. What was he going to do? Call the police? Announce a press conference to protest his innocence? It wouldn't work; there were too many people ready to line up against him.

But what he could do was take as many down with him. Politicians, senior government staffers, members of the general intelligence community and the military who had opposed him . . . he had something on them all. He went to a cupboard next to the fire in the main room. Pulled back a sliding door and reached inside for a catch to release a concealed safe built into the wall. Inside he had enough evidence to keep the media and the Washington legal profession busy for years to come.

His cell phone rang.

He debated ignoring it. What was the point? But arrogance quickly took over.

'Yes?'

'Don't bother checking your hidey-hole, Senator. There's nothing there.'

It was Two-One.

Benson nearly threw up with the shock of hearing the man's voice. He turned to the cupboard and found the safe door already open, the empty shelves taunting him. Nothing. Not a scrap of paper or an electronic storage item left.

'What – why are you doing this?' He felt cheated, his voice rising in a shriek of bitter resentment at this betrayal. 'Who paid you to do this?'

'We both know why, Senator. One: you would have betrayed me eventually, sold me out. It's what men in your position do. As for who paid me . . . there's nobody. This one is for free. On me.' Two-One chuckled softly. 'Goodbye, Senator. Oh, and you might like to take a look out the window. There's a surprise out there for you.'

'Wha—?' Benson swung round towards the picture window, with its magnificent view over the lake, to the blue sky and the multitude of greens among the trees on the far shore. A flicker of colour came from a sail boat curving gently across the water, and close to, not far from the shoreline in front of the house, a low, sleek shape that he guessed was one of the open water canoeists who roamed the area in all weathers.

It was idyllic. Serene. The kind of scene he had paid for but had never seen enough times to fully appreciate.

It was the last time he was to lay eyes on it.

He frowned, wondering why the canoeist was holding his paddle into his shoulder.

Then he heard a *ping* and saw a star appear in the centre of the glass. At the same time he felt a shocking blow to his chest, as if he'd been punched. He staggered a little and looked down, the phone dropping from nerveless fingers. A bright red flower had blossomed out of nowhere on his shirt front, horribly vivid, yet somehow unreal. He stared down, uncomprehending. Then the pain began, coursing through his body as his system responded to the invasive shock and trauma, making his legs go numb and his bladder give way in a heated rush that at any other time would have been horribly embarrassing.

Instead he felt sick.

He heard a second *ping*, but only vaguely, and another flower appeared alongside the first.

Reason told him it should have hurt, just like the first one.

But it didn't.